JUDY BREEDON

RESCUE FLIGHT

To Denise
Hope you enjoy!
Judy Breedon

Published by Zaccmedia
www.zaccmedia.com
info@zaccmedia.com

Published December 2013

ISBN: 978-1-909824-07-2

British Library Cataloguing-in-Publication Data
A catalogue record for this book is available from the British Library

You may contact the author at judyauthor534@talktalk.net

— CHAPTER 1 —

Pamela Crichton critically surveyed her reflection in the mirror. She wasn't sure if she liked what she saw – nose too short, mouth too wide and an ugly scar running across her cheek from her eye to her nose. As she applied the special make-up to hide the scar, making her look permanently sun tanned, she knew that she would never be called beautiful. Her best feature was her long dark hair which was always clean and shining, and she preferred to wear it long and loose, hiding behind it from prying eyes.

She had worked hard at school and passed all the exams needed to enter medical school, and thoroughly enjoyed the following years. After her finals she didn't feel ready to settle down and felt the need to travel. More than anything she wanted to help in a third world country. She knew that if she did go straight into General Practice, then there would be little possibility for ever fulfilling that ambition.

She spent a few weeks in Rumania, and the experience left her feeling helpless and upset. Even less did she feel the need to settle down, and when she heard of a doctor getting a team together to go out to Sarajevo when another cease-fire had been agreed in the war that had completely split the former Yugoslavia, she jumped at the opportunity. For the past few months Pam had been there, tending the sick and turning a deaf ear to the growing rumours of a continuation of hostilities.

The team had flown from the UK to Ancona in Italy before boarding a military plane to Bosnia where they'd had to don flack jackets and helmets before being driven into town and taken to their lodgings. They'd had a military escort all the way, but even then some of their medical supplies had been lost.

The town of Sarajevo was situated in a basin surrounded by hills, which gave cover and protection to the attacking armies, and the UN troops had a difficult time trying to keep the peace, and not inflame the explosive situation. Soldiers could be seen everywhere, wearing their familiar blue helmets or berets, but even if they hadn't been there, the damage and devastation in all parts of the town proclaimed a city under siege. There were few buildings that had not been damaged in some way, yet the church stood tall in the midst, each window intact, and with very little sign of destruction.

The tramcars were running as normal, the main form of transport for the majority of the people. The tracks threaded their way through the private sector, one or two storey houses with their familiar red roofs, and down through the town, past the empty buildings with no glass in the windows, and alongside buildings that were hanging together with reinforced concrete blocks and metal netting twisted into grotesque skeletons.

Pam and the rest of the team were always aware that they were in Sarajevo, a city on the edge of war, and they got used to seeing the United Nations peacekeeping forces everywhere they went. They worked at the State Hospital, mainly treating patients injured in the recent fighting. There was a lot of plastic surgery needed to give them the chance of leading any kind of normal life. It was heart breaking to see young children with limbs missing. The team did all they could to stop infections and give relief from pain, and after a few weeks Pam was surprised how she came to accept these injuries.

They worked long hours, and made many good friends with the local hospital staff. They had to work closely with them, not wanting to usurp their position, and thinking always of the welfare of the patient. Pam had been agreeably surprised at the standard of care, and hadn't realized what a modern hospital it had been before the war. The operating theatres were well equipped, but the electricity supply was unreliable. Their main problem was lack of drugs and a shortage of other vital medicines, and, more importantly, a complete lack of plastic or reconstruction surgeons. Those who had worked in the State Hospital had either been killed or had left Sarajevo to work in hospitals nearer their families.

The visiting team found the work rewarding as they watched the patients getting stronger as the supply of painkillers they had brought with them took effect. The most frustrating part was not being able to communicate, particularly with the children. A lot of the adults had some knowledge of English, but the children could do no more than cry and point to their injuries. Still, TLC – tender loving care – is the same in any language, and many hugs and smiles made up for the lack of understanding.

The citizens of Sarajevo were virtually prisoners in their own town, cut off from the outside world and suffering from a shortage of food, electricity, gas and water. Even during the official cease-fire, there was the constant threat of sniper fire from the surrounding hills and ruined buildings. The sound of firing as grenades and shrapnel peppered the State Hospital, and the knowledge that a high velocity rifle could inflict the most devastating tissue damage, sending a wave of destruction through body and limb, was a constant threat that, amazingly, they had learned to live with.

Everyone Pam spoke to had lost relatives and friends, many women and young girls were raped, and she heard harrowing stories of people losing their whole families in one day.

During their free time, Pam and her colleagues would stay close to their lodgings, and they never went out alone. When the sun shone and it became unbearably hot indoors, it was so inviting to walk on the grass under the dappled shade of the trees. A timely reminder that this was not to be was the sight of their flack jackets, helmets and torches, constantly to hand for use in an emergency.

The majority of their work was done at the State Hospital, but they also held regular clinics at other hospitals throughout the area, the farthest away being at Srebrenica, about 80 miles away as the crow flies. It was Pam's turn to run the clinic, and she was preparing to leave early for the long journey north.

"Doctor, your car is ready to take you to Srebrenica," Kajic, her driver and interpreter, called from the hallway outside her room.

"I'll be about 20 minutes," she replied, forcing herself to concentrate on the work at the clinic, rather than looking back.

"Want any help Pam?" her colleague asked as she opened the door.

"No, I'm just slow this morning," she replied. "I don't seem to be able to get my mind into gear. For some reason I feel lethargic, and if I could get out of this clinic, I would."

"We all feel like that at times, but if you really can't cope I could ask someone else to go."

"Oh no, please don't. I'm just being silly. I really enjoyed my last clinic there, and don't know why I feel so reluctant today."

"All the best, then. I'll get a bottle of wine in for when you get back."

"Something to look forward to! OK Kajic, I'm on my way."

During the long journey, Pam found herself once more looking back on her life in Sarajevo.

It was on that routine visit to Srebrenica that the troubles undertook a subtle change, and Pam realized the horror and significance of those dreadful words "Ethnic Cleansing". That night the Moslem Enclave was attacked by the Serbs across the border. In vain did she tell herself that she was in a UN Safe Area, and that the troops were there to protect her, but they were such a small number in comparison with the rebel forces.

Whole families were turned out of their homes in a few short hours, not even having time to pack what they needed to take with them. Their houses were looted and often burned, and it was all done with military efficiency.

Those who were lucky had managed to grab photographs of their loved ones. Photographs were all that remained for most of them now. They could no longer tend the graves of their dead, and feared that there was no chance of them ever returning to live in their own homes.

Pam was frightened, and immersed herself in her work to take her mind off what was happening. The hospital staff was wonderful, working all hours and moving from one patient to another as if everything was normal. The hospital continued to function as best as it could under the circumstances, and the way they coped with the extra casualties was an inspiration. The patients remained stable, and a number of babies were born, quite oblivious of the troubles around them – life must go on after all!

The main services in the town were disrupted, and with no sanitation there was the potential for an epidemic to the general population. Some food and water was distributed, but this was totally inadequate for the number of people. The majority of women and children started to leave the town, walking with what they could carry, and leaving their men folk behind. Boys over 16 were detained with the men of military age, only the old and infirm being allowed to leave with the women and children.

Most of the refugees headed towards Sarajevo, waiting for help from the World Relief Agencies, whilst the major powers argued amongst themselves as to what was the best thing to do. There was talk of the UN ground troops being withdrawn, and if that happened there was no chance for anyone left in the town.

As the situation worsened, it was decided to evacuate the hospital. All those patients who had any chance of surviving such a move were to be medi-vaced out of Srebrenica, and as Sarajevo was now over crowded with refugees, it was decided to take them to Zepa, where they could be looked after at the local hospital.

The situation had deteriorated rapidly, and life was becoming unbearable. There was nothing more Pam could do, until she decided to rescue some of the children. If she could manage to get them away, they would be safe in England until such time as they could return home to live a normal, peaceful life. She contacted the British Embassy but their response was disappointing. They wouldn't commit themselves to allowing any refugees into the UK, yet the more she considered the situation, the more Pam was determined to save the children. So many had been abandoned or separated from their families, and someone had to take responsibility for them.

It was a traumatic evacuation, not knowing how long the journey would take, or even where they would find food or water once their supplies had run out. The weather was particularly hot and the slow climb over the mountains and through the airless valleys was too much for some of the weaker patients, and their bodies had to be hastily covered with stones and left at the roadside. Some of the vehicles over-heated in the unusually hot weather, slowing down the whole convoy, and making the journey take twice as long as it should.

When they arrived in Zepa the UN troops helped them to stretcher the patients into the hospital, which they found to be over-crowded and under-staffed. There weren't enough beds for everyone, but they were able to make the patients relatively comfortable on the floor of the wards and in the corridors. Medical supplies were short, but they made the best of what was available.

Following on their success at Srebrenica, the attacking armies turned their sights on Zepa, and once again Pam found herself in a town at war, and the feeling of frustration and fear threatened to overwhelm her. The UN could do little to protect them, and Pam was advised to leave as soon as she could organise some transport.

She wanted an escort back to the State Hospital and her friends at Sarajevo, but no one would take responsibility for a female doctor and her driver and she was advised not to travel alone with just her driver for protection. Pam was advised to leave Zepa and to make her way to Tuzla, where there was a United Nations Air Base, and where arrangements could be made to have her flown home to England. She felt it was a bit like running away, but common sense told her she had done her best, and that it was only prudent for her to return home now.

She left Zepa early next morning with Kajic, the young boy who acted as her driver. Her grand ideas of helping the orphans of the war were abandoned. The children in the hospital were too ill to be moved, and all she could do was look out for herself. It became increasingly obvious with each passing hour that she would have to go quickly, and the fact that she was separated from the other doctors made her situation even more desperate.

Since the Bosnian-Serb army had taken the town of Zepa, the highway was crowded with refugees making for Tuzla. They had no option but to join with them, and moved slowly along the dusty road, stifled by the unrelenting heat, and getting more and more irritable at the lack of speed. A journey that should have taken hours turned into one that took days.

They were so used to seeing people with minor injuries that they no longer stopped and offered their help. They just continued their long slow journey, and maybe Pam would not have stopped when she saw a girl crying at the side of the road, but Kajic had an instinct for finding people in need, and he stopped the car and pointed. The girl was rocking too and fro, and holding what looked like a bundle of rags. Pam got down from the car and knelt beside her. The bundle turned out to be a newborn baby, not more than an hour old. The mother was in poor shape, still retaining the after-birth, and the baby in need of a bath.

Pam did all she could, delivering the after-birth, administering stitches, and sponging the baby down. She had a soft silk scarf in the car, in which she wrapped the tiny boy. Mother and baby were then put into the vehicle, and they continued on their way.

The mother said her name was Dina, and she was just 15 years old. She told them of some of her friends who'd had to abandon their babies as soon as they were born. It wasn't unusual to find newborn babies on rubbish tips, or hidden under rocks at the roadside. It wasn't that these mothers were criminal, but that they were desperate. These babies were mainly the result of rape, and consequently were unacceptable. Their own families and friends often shunned the mothers, and those who were already mothers couldn't cope with an extra mouth to feed. It took all their strength to feed and shelter their existing children, and it was a very hard decision to leave their babies. This young mother had been on the point of abandoning her son when Pam had stopped to help.

A few miles further on Kajic turned the car into a side road, the wheels creating clouds of dust on the unmade road. He had a sister who worked in an orphanage a mile up the road, and he wanted to make sure she was safe. They left the car outside the main building and walked round the deserted compound, which had obviously been evacuated in a hurry.

There were signs of bloodshed in the main building, and the bodies of some of the victims lay where they had fallen. The stench of death was nauseating, and the place buzzed with flies.

Standing alone in the Matrons office, Pam heard the most blood-curdling noise she had ever heard – a long wail that rose and fell in a frenzied passion. She stood perfectly still as her blood turned cold and her arms came out in goose pimples. It took a second or two to realize that the sound was, in fact, human and coming from the other side of the compound. She ran into the kitchen to find Kajic cradling the body of his little sister. She had been shot through the head. The sound of his grief issued from his parted lips, and his eyes were glazed with shock.

At last Pam was able to get him to put his sister down. Together they dug a grave and buried her inside the compound. In the heat of the day they had neither the energy nor the time to bury the rest of the bodies.

They searched the buildings, and found two children, silent and scared, but still alive. They also found the supply truck, and siphoning the fuel out of their car, they managed to fill the tank. After a quick search, Kajic found where the supply of diesel was kept, and they loaded the containers into the back of the truck. They also took what blankets they could find, and every scrap of food from the kitchen. Water was also essential, and they filled as many containers as they could find.

Thus armed, Pam put Dina and her baby, together with the two children, into the back of the truck. They had blankets to sit on, offering small comfort as they bounced over the unmade road. Kajic moved the vehicle slowly out of the compound, the gears crunching until he got used to the action of the clutch, and they soon re-joined the other refugees on the highway. Pam didn't know what to do to console Kajic, so they drove along in silence, each with their own thoughts. When the children demanded her attention, Pam was relieved to have something to do.

Sometimes she walked alongside the truck for a change, and tried to get news from those who were leaving Tuzla and trying to rejoin their families back in Zepa. She heard of other children who had been left to fend for themselves, either deliberately or having got separated from their families and another three were added to their number by the time they reached the outskirts of Tuzla.

What they saw filled them with dread. A makeshift camp had been set up outside the air base, and there were literally thousands of people, all expecting help from the troops. Tents had been erected in lines, with water pipes at the end of each row. There were some blankets provided with each tent, and food was distributed from vehicles at various points around the camp. There were people everywhere and the constant noise of their talking and the children's cries filled the air. Gangs of young children roamed unchecked – they had nothing else to do but make mischief.

Pam and Kajic were fortunate enough to be allocated an empty tent. Kajic went off in search of food and water, and Pam in search of some means of communication. Kajic was silent in his grief, refusing to talk unless absolutely necessary, and performing his tasks in an automatic way.

Her new resolve to leave Bosnia alone had been rejected once she became responsible for Dina and her son, and when the other children joined them she knew for certain that it was what she had to do. There was no way she could leave them in that terrible place. She had to take them home until such time as they were able to return to find their families, if, in fact, they were still alive.

Pam had thought she would be able to fly out of Tuzla to Ancona, and from there to England. But she was told that only military planes were flying from Tuzla, and they had orders not to take any civilians, although they would be able to take Pam home if she would go with some of the wounded troops, but there was no way they would take civilians.

They explained that if they took one person, then all the thousands of others would expect to be airlifted out, and they just did not have the resources. She would have to make alternative arrangements for the children, but they couldn't make any suggestions. If she insisted on taking them with her, then she would have to find her own way home.

Amy Renfrew was woken by the sound of birds singing in the cherry tree outside her bedroom window, heralding the start of another long boring day. What was she going to do with her life? What would she be doing in 10 years time? Or even in 5 years? What was she actually going to do today? These questions floated through her mind. She had no idea how to answer any of them, and felt she had let her life drift for too long. She couldn't see any escape and longed for some purpose to her life.

David and Amy's mother Annie Renfrew, and Pam and Matthew's mother Rosie, were twins. They had lived all their lives in the country and been content to marry and settle down within a mile of each other. They had lead a happy life, the two families so close that the children were more like brothers and sisters rather than cousins.

After the death of their parents in a horrific car crash, Pam, Matthew, David and Amy had gone to live on their grandparents' farm. It had been a wonderful place to visit, but living there all the time was different. There was nothing exciting to do, and the village, a short walk from the farm, had little to offer in the way of entertainment.

The highlight of their social life was the monthly Young Farmers disco held in the Village Hall.

Granny had spent all her working life on the farm, and she didn't understand the needs of the modern generation, though she would always listen to them but it wasn't the same. Grandpa was wiser, but as he grew older, the farm work left him feeling tired and he spent most evenings asleep in his chair.

Amy was the only one left now; Pam was in Bosnia, David in the military and Matthew at Manchester University (UMIST). Amy still didn't know what she wanted to do for a living. It had been easy for Pam, as she had known ever since the accident that she wanted to be a doctor. David had been army mad from an early age, and always intended joining the military as soon as he was old enough. Matthew had only made up his mind to go to Manchester after his friend had offered to share his house with him and had been fortunate enough to get accepted on his chosen course.

Amy longed for a bit of excitement in her life, but the future looked bleak and she was overcome by a feeling of depression. Making a strong effort, she promised herself she would walk into the village and hoped to meet up with some of her friends.

There was a lad in the village that Amy was keen on. Jack Palmer lived in a converted barn on his parents' farm. He was older than Amy, very handsome and chased by all the girls in the neighbourhood. Not least of his attractions was a BMW sports car, which he had won in a competition.

Much to her disappointment, he didn't seem to notice Amy particularly. It was only recently that he seemed to become aware of her presence. He was friendly and had even bought her a drink at the last Young Farmers disco but she didn't think he was really interested. She was hoping he would ask her out, not just for the pleasure of his company, but it would upset Holly Branson, who had made no secret of the fact that she wanted to go out with him, and it would go a long way towards settling an old score!

Her thoughts rambled on until the smell of bacon frying told her that Granny was already hard at work. She always had a full breakfast waiting for Grandpa when he had finished milking, then as soon as breakfast was over, she would bake the bread that had been set to rise earlier. It was Amy's job to collect the eggs and feed the chickens, ducks and geese. Later she would be expected to help in the dairy. They made their own cheese, and had a small farm shop selling poultry, cheese and a variety of seasonal vegetables.

It was impossible to be unhappy for long on such a beautiful day. Amy had enjoyed doing her chores, accompanied most of the time by her pet dog, Bess. Grandpa had always said that nothing lived on the farm that didn't work, but he had given in to her pleas when she told him she would feel safer wandering about the country lanes with a dog to protect her.

The village was bustling, as it always was on Market Day. The little café was busy and Amy was disappointed to see that none of her friends was there. She was lucky to get a table by the window. She ordered a coke and sat alone, wondering if she would see Jack. She felt a hand on her shoulder, and turned in anticipation, but it was only Joe, the lad who helped Grandpa on the farm.

"Mind if I join you?" he asked and sat down without waiting for a reply. "Not meeting anyone, are you?"

"Not that I know of," she replied, moving her leg away from his. She hated the way he was always trying to touch her.

"Can I take you to the disco on Friday?" he asked. "I can borrow my Dad's car and take you there in style."

There was no way she would go with him, and certainly wouldn't let him drive her home afterwards. He always had too much to drink, and it was hard work trying to stop him from pawing her.

"Thanks, but no thanks," she said. "I'm not sure yet if I can go."

"Then make it up to me now, and come for a walk along the river and we can go skinny dipping by the old bridge. I'm sure Bess will enjoy that then we can go back to the farm together for evening milking."

"You're not serious?" she asked, disgusted at his suggestion.

"There's no way I'll walk along the river with you, let alone go skinny dipping. Why don't you take Holly Branson, I'm sure she'll oblige if you ask her."

"I'm sure she will, but she's away at the moment and, besides, it's you I want. Why don't you like me, Amy?"

"I just don't. Let's leave it at that," she hadn't the heart to tell him that the thought of him touching her made her flesh creep. "I have to go now. I've got some shopping to do."

She finished her drink and collected Bess from outside and was returning to the market when she saw Jack getting out of his car.

Always a favourite with Bess, she nearly pulled Amy off her feet in her excitement to get to him.

"No, Bess. What a fuss. Amy, can't you keep her under control?" he asked between laughter and annoyance. "Do get down Bess, you know I can't stand having my face licked!" He forced Bess to sit before turning to Amy. "Your Gran told me you were in the village. Have you got time to come for a drink?"

"I've just had one, but I'll sit with you," she replied, wondering why he had spoken to Granny. They returned to the café, and Joe waved to them to join him.

"If you're hoping to take her to the disco on Friday, Jack, let me tell you that she's not sure if she can go. I've already asked her."

"Then we'll both be disappointed," Jack replied, smiling at Amy in a way she found irresistible.

"What did you want to speak to me about?" she asked, trying to change the subject, but wondering if Jack really had wanted to ask her to the disco. It was typical of Joe to spoil it for her.

"I was wondering if you'd heard from Pam recently," he said, dashing Amy's hopes for Friday evening. "According to the news, it's getting pretty rough out there, and they're advising all British civilians to leave."

"She told me before she left that the medical team would be well looked after as they're desperately needed and hinted in her last letter that she might stay on longer than she had agreed, as there's still plenty of work to do."

"She must be mad going out there," Joe said. "I don't know why she can't spend her time and energy working for the National Health Service instead of looking after foreigners. There's so much work needed in this country that it seems wrong for people to go abroad, particularly when this country has trained them and we, as taxpayers, have paid for their training. She should stay here and give us our money's worth. Don't look at me like that, Amy, it's just my opinion after all."

"Don't you think it's time you went back for evening milking?" she asked, hoping he would go and leave them alone.

"Alright, Miss Prissy, I'll see you later."

"Are you really worried about Pam?" she asked, turning her attention back to Jack.

"Things are getting pretty bad out there, according to the news. Did you see the article in the paper this morning? It sounded pretty awful, and seems to be getting worse by the day. Sarajevo is not one of my top ten places to visit at the moment!"

"But what can we do? She's in the best place to know what it's like, and I'm sure she'd come home if she were in danger. I'll try and get in touch with her, but you can't always get through on the phone and the post can take days. Calls are expensive and we can't stay talking for long. If she's working, she can't take the call, and if not, she's catching up on much needed sleep, so we keep phone calls for emergencies only."

"Well, if you do hear anything, let me know."

Jack left as soon as he had finished his drink, but their conversation had disturbed Amy.

Pam was allowed onto the air base at Tuzla when she had been identified as both English and a doctor, and allowed to put a call through to England. She had no difficulty in phoning home, but was beginning to despair that there was no-one in when she heard David's young sister Amy pick up the phone.

"Hello," she said, "Who's calling?"

"Hi, Amy, it's me, Pam. I can't stop on long, so can I speak to David, and he can fill you in later."

"He's not here. How are you? I've been worried about you now that the situation is getting worse."

"I'm OK, but I need to get in touch with David urgently. I'll try and ring home at about this time tomorrow if you can ask him to wait for my call."

"He's on holiday, and wouldn't say where he was going, or who with."

Pam swore under her breath, then laughed bitterly. "On one of his dirty weekends, no doubt, just when he's needed at home."

"I don't know about that," Amy replied, "but he didn't say how long he'll be away. If it's that important, I can try and find out where he is."

"Yes it is important. I need help getting out of here with some children in my care. If we have any chance of leaving we must be prepared to go at short notice. I want David to make it easy for us to enter the UK and find somewhere for us to stay until it's safe for the children to return home. If the situation continues to deteriorate I want to be prepared to leave at a moment's notice and anything he can do in the UK will make it that much easier for us."

"I'll see what I can do, but can't promise anything," Amy replied.

"Thanks Amy. Do your best and I'll ring again tomorrow if I can. Bye now."

Amy sat looking at the phone for a long time, asking herself who would know where David was. The person who might know was his friend Liam O'Grady. Liam had left the military some months ago, but they still kept in touch and regularly went out together.

Pam wrote a long letter stating her fears, how utterly hopeless she felt, and her desire to help the refugees. She explained that she could no longer be contacted at Sarajevo and was not sure where she would be in a few days time. If David had managed to smooth the way for them to return to England that would be good, but it was amazing how quickly events had moved on, and her main concern now was to leave Bosnia quickly. She was sorry to have to involve him, but she knew she wouldn't be able to manage on her own. She wanted him to think of a way to get them all safely out of the country. She was still at liberty to travel, and would be prepared to meet him anywhere he wanted. Perhaps they could meet at one of the border towns and he could help them get home from there. She had no fixed ideas, and would rely on his expertise in finding the right rendezvous. She begged him to hurry to her rescue. One of the medics, due to fly home that afternoon, offered to post the letter as soon as he landed in England.

It was not until later that Pam realised the danger she was putting her cousin in. Was it fair to ask him to risk his life for a bunch of people he had never met? Of course not. She couldn't ask it of him. And yet, hadn't he joined the army for just such an emergency? She knew him well enough to know that the excitement would outweigh any danger he might find himself in. It was just the sort of thing he would enjoy doing, and she knew he would jump at the chance. It gave her a warm feeling to know that he would be willing to risk everything to come to her rescue.

But would Pam be able to live with herself if anything awful happened to him? What if he were killed? No, she couldn't live with that, so she decided that she'd tell him she would make her own way home.

She asked Kajec for his advice, and he suggested going by road, taking the highway to Zagreb in the north, then following the River Sava to the border and through into northern Italy. Alternatively, they could make their way to the coast, and follow the coast road north to Trieste and cross into Italy at the same border.

Kajic said he was willing to go with her if it was what the doctor wanted. He was non-committal as to whether or not they would have trouble driving north, but was inclined to think they would be able to get through without too much difficulty. A couple of hours later they heard a report that the Italian border was being closed to refugees, and people were being turned away.

Their second choice was to get out through Switzerland or Hungary, and if that proved to be impossible, at least they would be a long way away from the fighting.

Always on the look out for any information that could be of use to them, Kajic learnt of a family who were preparing to leave Tuzla and if the doctor was determined to leave the country, he would see if they could go together. They had friends in Split who were willing to help them sail across the Adriatic to Italy. It was a long boat ride, but they had a sea-worthy vessel strong enough to do the journey. If Kajic approached them he felt sure they would be willing to take the doctor along with them. She could ensure their physical well being in exchange for a free passage. He would ask them if they would be willing to take the children and Dina as well. This positive thinking made Pam feel better, and she was able to face the rest of the day with determination. She wouldn't run away on her own but try her best to relieve the suffering of the few people in her care.

The medical staff from the base was overworked in the refugee camp and Pam's offer of help was gratefully received. She was advised to leave Tuzla as soon as possible, and her new colleagues thought her mad not to take advantage of the offered flight and leave immediately. They said there were so many refugees she couldn't possibly help them all, and the few she could help was like a drop in the ocean. It was then that she remembered Mother Teresa's words – that the ocean was made up of drops!

They were too busy and too tired to argue with a stubborn woman who was determined not to listen, so they got on with their work and left her to her own devices. She spent the rest of the day in the medical tent and fell into an exhausted sleep in the early hours.

Sometime during the night, the young mother kissed her son and wrapped him in a blanket before creeping out of the tent. Kajic watched what Dina was doing, and felt genuinely sorry for the girl. He did not have the energy or the inclination to stop her from going, and silently wished her luck. He knew the baby would have more chance of a normal life if the doctor would look after him.

With the daylight came the uncertainties and realities of her situation, and what had seemed possible in the dark of the night, seemed insurmountable amongst the noise and squalor of the refugee camp. Everyone present was trying to get away, either to their relations or to a safe place where they could start to re-build their lives.

Why should she succeed where they had failed? What made her so special that she could achieve what they couldn't? Then she thought of David, knowing he would come to her rescue. He would know what arrangements were needed to get them away, and she could rely on him to work out a route for them to follow, and once at the border, he would be waiting to help them across. All she had to do was remain at the camp until they had made their plans.

The heat and the noise in the camp gave Pam a headache, and she was impatient to get away from the crowds. Kajic had come back with the news that the family going to Split had already left. Their way home did not lie in that direction. Pam was impatient to get going, but she had to remain until she could contact Amy again and prayed that Amy would have the answer she was waiting for.

Pam kept herself busy helping in the medical tent, looking after the children, and trying to comfort Kajic. She walked round the camp, and was shocked to see whole families living in tents, and taking it in turns to lie down. They spent hours queuing for food, and water was desperately short.

Military personnel distributed food, but the meagre rations were barely enough to keep them going throughout the day. Rumour was rife that supplies were running out, and in a few days there would be no food available. The large military planes flying into Tuzla carried supplies necessary to keep an active force mobilized and as the number of UN personnel on the ground was growing day by day, their needs had to be met first.

The lack of water and sanitation was becoming desperate. Fever was breaking out, and everyone was affected. Death was an everyday occurrence, and they had got to the stage of having mass graves. No one seemed to know how many people were in the camp, or even how many had died.

Long before the appointed time, Pam had gained admittance to the base, and her request for another call to England was granted. She waited impatiently for the call to be put through, and cried with relief at the sound of Amy's voice.

— CHAPTER 2 —

Amy was alone in the farmhouse when the postman called. There was only one letter with her name written on the envelope in Pam's distinctive writing. As she tore the envelope, she was relieved to see an English postmark, delighted that Pam was already back in England as she eagerly read the short note, asking her to contact David as a matter of urgency and to give him the enclosed letter. She explained that a friend had posted the letter on his return to the UK, and that her situation had not changed.

Knowing she couldn't get in touch with her brother, Amy had no scruples about reading his letter. She had to sit down as she learned that Pam was still out there and in danger, and was still as determined to leave Bosnia with as many refugees as she could.

Pam gave more details about what she wanted David to do, and drew a graphic picture of what life was like. She feared that if she didn't return home within a few days, she probably wouldn't get out at all. She had been told that the route home through Italy had been closed to all but military traffic, and she begged David to help. She stressed that she couldn't cope on her own, and would need to rely on someone she could trust. She wanted him to make arrangements to meet up with her, possibly close to one of the borders. He would need suitable transport, and the means of getting them into the UK with as little fuss as possible.

Pam said she would phone home when she could to find out if Amy had managed to contact him, and what arrangements, if any, he had been able to make.

When Amy spoke to the Duty Officer at the Barracks where David was stationed, she was disappointed to learn that he hadn't said where he was going, and was assumed to be at home. He was due back with his unit in ten days' time.

It wasn't like him to be secretive, so she asked his friend, Liam O'Grady if he knew where David was. All Liam could say was that he had gone with a friend on a last-minute holiday to the States. He had seen it advertised, and had left the next morning. Liam said he could probably find where David was staying if it was an emergency, and would let Amy know as soon as he had any news. If that failed, then she would have to wait until he returned to the UK, which shouldn't be longer than a week.

She felt excited at having something to do even though she had no idea how to set about it, but Jack had told her of his concern for Pam, so it seemed only natural that she should take the letter round for him to read. She would enjoy spending more time with him and was glad of the excuse to call at his home.

"What do you mean to do Amy?" he asked handing the letter back to her.

"Help her if I can. Do you know how I could set about it?"

"No."

"I am frightened, but determined to help. I haven't a clue how to set about it, but if we can talk it over, we may come up with something. Firstly, we should try and find out how best to clear the way for them to enter England safely."

"Well, we could ask someone on the parish council. If they can't help, they may know someone who can. The chairman's a friend of my Dad's and I wouldn't mind asking for his advice."

Jack rang his Dad's friend, and the most useful information they heard was that there was a Surgery that evening at the local municipal buildings, at which the local Member of Parliament would preside, and be available to answer questions from her constituents. Amy asked Jack to go with her, and he said he would pick her up in the early evening.

"I'm not sure what to say to our MP," Amy continued, "because Pam can't say how many people will be with her. All I've managed to do so far is to leave a message for David at the barracks and with Liam. He seems to know more than he's prepared to tell me, but if he can't find him within the next few hours, then there's only me left to help Pam bring the children safely home and nothing you could say will stop me from trying."

"Alright then, Amy," Jack said, "sit down and think it through properly. You've got to ask yourself how on earth do you get a woman and an unknown number of people out of a country where they are not wanted, and which is on the brink of civil war, and bring them back into a country that doesn't really want them, and will do its best to keep them out?"

She was naïve enough to assume that it would be easy to get on a plane and fly into Bosnia. She expected to bring them home again without too much trouble, but requests for a plane ticket anywhere in the former Yugoslavia were turned down as no commercial flights were operating in that part of the world for the time being.

"If it was that easy," Jack explained, "Pam would be able to fly home with no problems. There might be a problem with passports for the children, but I'm sure she must have thought of that. You know, Amy, the more I think about it, the less I like it. Is there anything I can do or say to dissuade you?"

"You make it sound impossible," she replied with a sigh. "But I've got to try. You do understand that, don't you Jack? I've got to know that I've done all I can, even if I fail. Unless Liam can find out where David is then it's my responsibility."

"Do you think Pam would expect that of you? She told you to ask David, not to go out there yourself. I'm convinced she wouldn't expect it of you."

"I know she'd do the same for me. It doesn't matter what you say, you can't make me change my mind."

"Then let's try and find a way that won't involve too much risk, and will keep us away from the fighting."

Amy hadn't liked to deceive Granny, but knew she wouldn't understand their reasons for going to the Surgery at the municipal buildings. If she thought Amy was getting involved in Pam's affairs, she would try to stop her as it was far too dangerous a situation for a young girl to be involved in, so she arranged to meet Jack at the end of the road.

Granny didn't like that young man, didn't trust him, but she was careful not to let Amy know her true feelings, as her head-strong granddaughter would be more than likely to go against her advice. She was sorry that Amy had taken a dislike of Joe, a hard working lad, who would make a good farmer one of these days.

Jack thought it best they put their question early in the debate, so as not to get sidetracked on other issues. All questions had to be submitted on arrival and Jack was lined up to put the second question to the speaker.

Amy stood up and asked what the Government, and their MP in particular, was doing about the worsening situation in Bosnia, which had dominated the headlines in that morning's papers.

"There are women and children being persecuted and killed," she continued. "As a caring country, isn't it our duty to help the refugees?"

"It's not a question of not wanting to help," the MP replied. "We need time to research the whole situation and come to a democratic solution in stages, rather than go off in one direction when it may be prudent to deal with it from another direction."

"But these refugees need help today, not tomorrow." Amy was

determined to keep the topic going, and not let the chairman move on to the next question.

"Are you saying then," Jack said, "that you cannot help these people without a lot of time being wasted on discussions. If my son falls and hurts his knee, he wants me to comfort him straight away, not in a weeks' time."

"No self-respecting person would refuse to help a child in need," Amy responded. "We want someone in power who will help!"

A murmuring of agreement spread through the room, until the chairman tried to bring the meeting to order.

"Well, of course we would like to help the children," she said. "I don't want you to think that we are unfeeling in this matter."

"Are you saying then, Mrs. Speaker," Jack said, "that if, by some means, a group of these women and children do arrive in this country, you'll extend the hand of friendship and allow them to stay?"

"We would, of course, extend the hand of friendship, and render appropriate assistance. Allowing them to stay would depend upon their circumstances and would require careful consideration."

"Does that mean No?" someone asked.

"It means precisely what I have said," she replied.

"Mrs. Speaker," Amy called until the room was relatively silent. "Mrs. Speaker, do you mean that if a group of these poor unwanted and homeless children did arrive in this country, you would send them back to face the horrors of war?"

"No, I don't think in all conscience we would do that, but the chances of that happening are very slight. I can say that we would, under such circumstances, do everything in our power to find the best solution at the time. We've got legislation in place to deal with refugees and asylum seekers, and they'll have to fall in line within the guidelines of current legislation. The best I can do is speak to my colleagues in the House, and let you know our conclusion."

"Pam will be disappointed," Jack said as they drove home after the meeting. "I don't know what she has in mind, or how she intends to bring anyone out, but if she does succeed, then she'll have to take the attitude that they are here, and what is the government going to do about it. If they did refuse to allow them entry into the UK, the press would have something to say about it, I would make sure of that! There's little enough we can do to help, but that is something positive we can do!"

The first glimmer of hope came as they watched the evening news. They had been trying to assess the situation, when the news of the hijack of a Japanese plane, owned and run by a company operating out of Tokyo, was reported.

This news in itself wouldn't have caught their attention, but the reporter was speaking to one of Jack's old school friends. Malcolm Wainwright had been spotted at Heathrow Airport waiting for his return flight to the United States. Malcolm's father was the Chairman and part owner of one of the leading airlines in the world, Wright Flights International, and Malcolm was in charge of the catering side of the business. He worked closely with his father and the board of WFI, and as such was asked his opinion on how a plane could be hijacked with such apparent ease.

Malcolm Wainwright was adamant in blaming the Japanese airline for lack of security, and loud in his praise for the pilots, crew, security and, in fact, all the employees of Wright Flights International, stating that they were the safest airline in the world to travel with.

"So you put the blame for the hijacking in Tokyo entirely on the airline, do you?" the interviewer persisted.

"Well they can't be blameless now can they?"Malcolm continued. "If they'd taken the most basic security measures, this should never have happened. I can state quite categorically that no one can board one of our planes with any kind of weapon, and neither can the ground staff leave anything on the plane that could be used in a hijack. Our security is second to none, and it is virtually impossible to take anything onto any of our aircraft without the knowledge of at least one of our employees."

"What if someone in your employ was bribed? Surely you cannot be 100% certain of everyone?" the interviewer persisted.

"We sure can," Malcolm replied. "We run a tight ship, and pay well for good service and loyalty. If anyone is ever found to be dishonest, untrustworthy or disloyal for any reason whatsoever, they are dismissed on the spot, and the chances of them getting employment with another airline is nil."

"So you claim that WFI are the worlds' safest airline?"

"I sure do. I might even go so far as the say that if any terrorist groups have any ideas about hijacking any of our planes, then think again. It ain't possible."

"Are you prepared to put your money where your mouth is and offer some sort of compensation in the event that you are proved wrong?"

"Don't be so bloody stupid!"

"Oh come on, Mr. Wainwright, you can't make such a sweeping statement without backing it up."

"There really is no possibility of that happening and this conversation is crap." Malcolm was starting to get irritated with the way the interviewer was trying to manipulate him.

"So, if someone, anyone succeeds in hijacking one of your aircraft within, say, the next two weeks, would you be willing to pay a substantial amount to a charity of your choice?"

"Of course not, that's asking for trouble. I'm not going to issue an invitation to every thug in the world to try and board one of our planes. That'd be completely irresponsible and put our passengers in danger," he replied. "But if anyone does try, as a result of what you've just said, then I'll hold you personally responsible and sue you for everything you've got!"

"That's hardly fair, Mr. Wainwright. You're the one who said WFI is the safest airline in the world, and the responsibility is yours alone. I suggest that you put aside, say, $50,000, to be paid to a charity of your choice, without any strings attached, in the event of a mishap. Surely that's not asking too much?"

"You're out of your mind. Wright Flights International will not, under any circumstances, submit to such a demand, and this interview is at an end."

“What is it Jack? You look like the cat that’s got the cream. Have you thought of a way I can do it?”

“I certainly have. We’ll take Malcolm’s advice and hijack a plane! We’ll get WFI to fly us to Bosnia!”

“Do be sensible! This is serious, you know. It’s not to be made fun of.”

“I am being serious. Can you think of any other way we can get there quickly with enough room to bring them all back?”

“Do you know the first thing about hijacking? How could we get on to a plane and persuade them to take us to Bosnia? Haven’t you seen the security precautions at the airports? And what about the passengers? Would you want to take them as well? And if the plane was full, there wouldn’t be room for Pam, let alone the children.”

“If we go about it the right way, there must be some way we can get round the problems as they arise.”

“We might, but it doesn’t seem likely!”

“Can you think of anything better?”

“You know I can’t.”

“Then the least we can do is look into it! We do know someone connected to an airline.”

“You mean the chap on the television?”

“Yes, Malcolm Wainwright. Maybe I can persuade him to help us. Perhaps he will be charitable enough to lend us a plane!”

“Do you really think he’ll do that?”

“He might, but if he refuses, I’ll get him to help us hijack one of his own planes.”

“Do you honestly expect me to hijack a plane? You must be mad!”

“Can you think of any other way we can get there quickly and have enough room to bring back Pam and as many people as she wants? It couldn’t be simpler.”

“When you put it like that, it does sound ideal, but do you honestly think this friend of yours will lend us a plane?”

"The least we can do is ask, but I'm sure I can get something out of him, one way or the other."

"But how? What makes you so certain he'll help?"

"Oh, he'll help right enough. I know I can get him to do what I want, but the question is, which option? It will be easier if he lends us a plane, but it will be more exciting to hijack one, but either way, we'll be able to get Pam and the children home."

"Do be sensible Jack. If he won't lend us one, then we're no better off. It's a waste of time to think about a hijack. As I said before, how could we possibly get a plane etc. and persuade them to take us to Bosnia? And what about the passengers? Would you want to take them as well? And if the plane was full, there wouldn't be room for Pam, let alone the children."

"If we go about it the right way and can get Malcolm to come in with us, we might just pull it off."

"We might, but it doesn't seem likely."

"Alright then, you come up with something better!"

"I've already told you I can't."

"Then stop finding fault and saying we can't. If it's properly organised, there isn't anything we can't do."

"Alright then," Amy sighed, "tell me how you propose that I set about it?"

"The first thing to do, is go to the States and talk to Malcolm Wainwright. I'm pretty certain I can persuade him that he owes me one for something that happened at school. It could work and we owe it to Pam to try. Always remember that our main concern is to get her home without any delay."

"You keep saying 'we'. Does this mean that you're intending to help?"

"Don't take this the wrong way, Amy, but I don't think you could manage on your own. I know Malcolm and think I can get him to co-operate, so, yes, I am coming with you."

"I can't ask that of you Jack. She's more like a sister to me than a cousin and I'd do anything for her, and if it doesn't work out, then at least we'll be together, like our mums and dads were when they had that accident. I've got nothing to lose, but it's different for you. You could lose everything."

"Not if we lay our plans properly. If we work it out to the last detail, we should be able to pull it off."

"Well, if you think we have a chance, I really would appreciate your help."

"I know it's hard, Amy, but this isn't going to be a picnic, and we've no idea what it's like in Bosnia. If Pam can't stand it, how can we? She has an interpreter and knows a lot of people. She has a job and friends to help her. We'll be completely alone, unable to communicate, in a foreign land we neither of us know nor have visited before. And there is a real possibility that we'll not return. It is very noble of you to want to be with your cousin if the worst happens, but I want to do all I can to help you both through this. I couldn't sit at home worrying about what you are doing, where you are, and if you're in danger. If I'm there with you, at least I'll know that I've done everything I can to help and protect you and Pam, because it doesn't bear thinking of what they'd do to you if you were captured."

Amy felt an overwhelming sense of relief.

"Do you really mean that, Jack?" she asked.

"Of course, silly. Don't you know that I've been crazy about you for months now, but every time I try to get close to you, you seem to back off. Is it because of Joe? I know he's been chasing you. He makes no secret of the fact that he's always asking you to go somewhere with him and I wasn't sure if you preferred him to me."

"No, of course not, but I didn't think you cared for me, and I can't stand Joe. I don't care if I never see him again. I told him I wouldn't go to the disco with him on Friday in the hope that I could go with you."

"That's a date for next month then, if we're back safely!"

"Don't joke about it. I'm not even going to think that it might go wrong. We've got to believe in ourselves and assuming that we do succeed in getting a plane, then what do we do."

"One step at a time" Jack replied. "We can't rush things, Amy. We've got to be thorough and work out our every move. Firstly we must assess Pam's circumstances and we need to know as much as possible about her situation, just where she is, how many people she has with her, and where we're going to meet her. Tell me everything you know, and all that you've learnt from the news."

"She's at a place called Tuzla. I saw in one of the papers that there's a refugee camp there with thousands of people. Tuzla is a military base, with an airport, but they say they can't guarantee her safe passage to England. Even if they could get her away, she couldn't take anyone else with her."

"Is she prepared to come out alone?"

"Not unless it's absolutely impossible for her to bring the children. I believe there are some adults with her as well, and she'd like to bring them all out. She is free to leave the refugee camp, but thinks there will be travel restrictions at the border, and is relying on David to meet her there."

"Then that's what we'll do!"

"What should I tell her if, when, she phones?"

"Don't tell her that you haven't contacted David. That will only upset her, and she's got enough on her plate. I'll get an atlas so we can find out exactly where we can meet her."

They studied the map of Bosnia, and, on the understanding that nothing went wrong, and they did manage to get hold of a plane, they would tell Pam to meet them at a place called Osijek. There was an airfield there, and it was far enough away from the fighting to be still open.

Jack pulled Amy into his arms and kissed her.

"When Pam rings I have to let her know where we'll meet her, and what we want her to do," Amy said, sitting down on the window seat. "There could be some reason why Osijek doesn't suit her, so we may have to find another rendezvous. What does concern me is the number of people we're going to need. I'm not convinced that you and I can do it on our own. We really do need David. I don't think we'll manage without him."

"What about asking Matthew? He is her brother after all and should be closer to her than David. Do you think he'll help?"

"I've thought briefly about asking him for his advice, but am not sure if he will want to know. He's more interested in his own career, and can talk of little other than his prospects and his new girl friend. Even after we'd all gone to live on the farm, Matthew hadn't fitted in with the rest of us. It seems quite natural for Pam to turn to us rather than her own brother, and I feel it will be a waste of time to contact him. I'm certain he wouldn't put himself out for anyone."

"Then we'll have to put our thinking caps on," Jack replied. "If we do manage to hijack a plane we'll also get a pilot to fly it, as well as a navigator and crew. They'll have to help get Pam and the children on board, and we'll also need someone to stand guard whilst this is going on. The crew will be able to look after the children during the flight as they will be scared and possibly travel sick."

"Don't worry about their welfare," Amy responded. "Pam will see to that side of it."

"OK, and I do agree that we need David. What will we do if his mate can't get in touch with him, or if he won't be willing to come along?"

"I'm absolutely certain he'll come if he knows what we're planning. If Liam O'Grady can't find out just where he is, then I feel inclined to tell him what we want David for, and ask his help."

"What do you know about him? Do you think we can trust him, because the fewer people who know about this, the better."

"I know he'd help David if he knew he was in a fix. They've been friends for a long time. It's only recently that Liam left the army to work in the family firm."

"Well, if David trusts him that much, I don't see why we can't. We'll do our best, with or without him. We have to get into a virtual war zone, which will be difficult, and then we have to get out again, which could be even more difficult! But whatever happens we'll see it through together. We'll do it, Amy, one way or the other. Just be positive and go on from there. I can't see anyone stopping us, as no-one would be expecting us to do such a daft thing!"

"You think it's a daft idea?"

"Let's say 'unexpected'. Go for it, but we'll have to do as much preparation as we can."

“I’ll feel happier once we’ve started, but I’m scared at the prospect of having to hijack a plane. It seems such a desperate thing to do.”

“Then try and think of it in a different light. Something positive that will make you feel better about it.”

“I know,” Amy said after a short pause. “How about we think of it as a rescue flight?”

“Well, that’s exactly what it is, a flight to rescue your cousin and the refugees!”

— CHAPTER 3 —

Liam O'Grady had been born in Northern Ireland and spent his childhood in Belfast, accepting as normal the soldiers patrolling the city streets and the no-go areas. He became a member of the IRA whilst in his teens, and had been actively involved with them ever since. On leaving school he was persuaded to join the military, as the IRA wanted him to keep them informed on troop movement in Northern Ireland. It was easier than he had expected, as there was always someone willing to talk about friends either in Belfast or due to go there. As he trained and grew close to his comrades his conscience troubled him a little, but he knew this was war, and which side he was on.

His heart quickened when informed that his regiment was to be sent to Northern Ireland, and he enjoyed his double role, his loyalty firmly fixed with the Irish paramilitary, his only concession being his determination not to endanger the lives of his particular comrades.

He fell deeply in love and married a young widow with three small children. Bridie Finnigan came from a large Irish family who owned their own business. She wanted Liam to leave the military and work for her brothers, but he loved the camaraderie and the opportunity to serve overseas. She had to be content to remain by his side, bringing up their family and mixing with the other soldiers' wives.

He knew Bridie would be pleased with his decision to start working for her brothers, who operated a fleet of civil aviation transport planes working out of Shannon in Southern Ireland. It seemed strange to him that they had chosen somewhere as remote as Shannon, but their business was doing well, and Ireland proved to be a good mid-point for transporting goods around the world. They were now a well-established and respected company, and had offices in various capital towns throughout Europe and the Americas. Liam was put in charge of the London office, and his one regret was that he was stationed in England.

He found the work mundane and longed for a bit of excitement. When he had gone into partnership with his brothers-in-law, he had expected to travel, visiting clients all over the globe and negotiating the freighting of a variety of goods from one place to another. As it was, he spent most of his time behind a desk, shuffling papers and checking weigh bills. One of his chief responsibilities was the transportation of hazardous cargoes, and all the paper work involved. Customs forms had to be filled in, checked and double-checked, and although he was kept busy, he was still in England and away from his beloved Ireland.

If it had been anyone other than Bridie's family, he would have left months ago, and looked for a more suitable job where his survival skills and love of the outdoors could be put to use. But after being away from his family for months on end, he had promised Bridie he would settle down, get a nine to five job, and spend more time at home. This last statement, to spend more time at home, was only correct in so far as he didn't spend weeks away at a time, but he was so busy that nine to five soon turned into eight to seven or even later. Bridie didn't seem to notice that he was irked by these restrictions or maybe she turned a blind eye, comforted by the fact that he would return to her every evening. She needed a husband, and their children needed a father.

He hated his job, and started looking about for some lucrative way of changing his life; some way of getting his hands on enough money to maintain the sort of life he wanted to lead. He accepted that he would have to live abroad if he was to get out of his commitments to the IRA. He was no longer used by them for paramilitary activities, his main job being the supervision of fund-raising, particularly in the States where a lot of sympathizers were to be found. He was tempted by the money he handled, but unless he could find a foolproof way of stealing it without their knowledge he dare not touch it. He knew perfectly well that if he was only suspected of stealing from them, he would be killed.

Nevertheless, he was always alert to the possibilities offered, and was convinced that if he waited long enough, the ideal opportunity would come his way.

Amy decided to tell Liam briefly what they intended to do after he said he had reason to believe that David was in the States with a friend. He had narrowed his search down to two possible hotels and had left messages at both, with an urgent request for him to get in touch with either himself or with Amy.

He was quiet at first, the quickening of his pulse was the only sign he showed of the excitement he was feeling. The IRA was expecting a large amount of money to be shipped from the USA, and he had already arranged for it to be taken on board Wright Flights International flight WF254 out of Chicago. And now here were these two young people wanting him to get them to Chicago so that they could persuade Malcolm Wainwright to help them hijack one of WFI's planes. If he could get them on board WF254 he felt certain he could convince the IRA that the hijackers had stolen the money, and with careful planning he saw no reason why they should suspect him of being involved.

Liam said he would help them to get to the USA and knew David would expect him to do all he could to stop his sister from virtually committing suicide. His only regret was that it was David's family, but there was no way they could carry out their plan without his help, so he considered it as payment for helping to bring Pam Crichton home.

By the time Amy spoke to Pam, they had decided what to tell her, without causing her any more worry. Without actually saying so, they indicated that David would soon be on his way to Bosnia, and Amy asked her to make her way to Osijek airport, north of Tuzla, where he would be waiting for her. Pam thought it would take her a few days to get there, and from what she had heard at the camp, felt confident that she would be able to make it without being stopped. If David wasn't there for any reason, she would continue to the border and cross into Hungary. She insisted that if she didn't make it for any reason whatsoever, David was to return home without her.

Osijek was far enough away from the scene of conflict that they hoped it would be an easy place for them all to get to. Amy arranged to meet Pam on the following Monday.

Amy packed what few belongings she needed in her rucksack, and left a letter for Granny saying that she had gone to spend a few days with an old friend in Yorkshire. She hoped Granny wouldn't be worried, as it wasn't the first time she had been to Jenny's at short notice.

They arranged to meet at Liam's office and he told them to bring as much money as they could, explaining that their expenses would be phenomenally high.

"Liam says we should get as much money as we can as our expenses could be phenomenally high," Amy told Jack. "I know it's a lot to ask, but if you are determined to come with me, do you think you could sell your car? That's the only way I can think of to raise as much as we may need."

The look on his face told her all she needed to know!

"There is no way I am going to sell my BMW. Even though I won it in a competition I wouldn't part with it, even if it were my own sister who was in trouble! I have a reasonable limit on my credit card, which could be used for withdrawing cash before we leave England, as we don't want to be traced through credit card transactions overseas."

They drove straight to London, and when Jack found out what sort of business Liam was in, asked if he could provide a plane. Liam went to great lengths to explain why it was not possible. Freight planes were not equipped to carry passengers, had no heating in the main compartment, no seating and no facilities for providing refreshments for more than the cockpit crew. Toilet facilities were limited, and there were no facilities at all for dealing with young children. He could see all the advantages of using a commercial plane and asked how they intended to go about it.

Jack explained his connection with WFI through the Chairman's son.

"You know Malcolm Wainwright?" Liam asked, and started to laugh. "And you intend to hijack one of their planes flying out of Chicago?"

"Well, why not?" Jack asked pettishly. "I don't see what there is to laugh at. Can you share the joke with us?"

"No, no. There's no joke. It's just that I've met the old man a couple of times, and wouldn't like to cross him. He's not the easiest of people to deal with."

"You don't think Mr. Wainwright would go against his son, do you?" Amy asked. "It's Malcolm we want to help us, not his father."

"You never know. They're not a very close family from what I hear, but if you can get Malcolm to co-operate, the best of luck to you."

"Jack feels certain Malcolm will do all we want."

They explained to Liam how they had found a way of smuggling a weapon on board, and he was impressed with their proposal. As he thought it through he started to laugh again, but refused to say why. He thought the idea would work and said to leave it up to him to get everything they would need.

"If my memory serves me right, there's a regular WFI flight from Chicago to Manchester. I'll find out the flight number in a minute."

"Can we get to Chicago on time for the next one?" Jack wanted to know.

"I don't see why not. Yes, here it is. Flight WF254. I think we've got to make that our target plane. We'll have to get going today, but there are certain arrangements I have to make before we leave."

Amy showed them Grandpa's shotgun, which she had borrowed for the occasion and placed in the back of Jack's car when he wasn't looking. Both men agreed they would need some sort of weapon, but were determined to leave Grandpa's shotgun behind, and after some persuasion Amy let it be put in Liam's office safe, together with their passports. They didn't want anything that could trace them to the USA, or implicate them in any way.

Liam said they could use the facilities at Shannon to get them to the USA. The Freight Terminal was large and open, and there were hangers filled with incoming and outgoing freight. It was easy for Liam to get access to the freightliners, and he didn't see any undue problem in getting them all on board. They could be fixed up with overalls and given a clipboard. It was unlikely they would be stopped, but if they were, all they had to do was say they were inspecting the cargo.

Liam was looking forward to being active again. He had been behind a desk for too long, and longed to be back in the hub of things. He telephoned Bridie, and told her he'd been called to head office for an urgent meeting and would be away for a few nights. He kept a change of clothes ready for when he had to go to Shannon at short notice.

Even more important was the fact that a flight was bound for St. Louis, Missouri that same evening and with any luck, they would be on it!

The next job was to go down to the local Post Office to have new passport photographs taken. Liam told his secretary he was taking his visitors out for half an hour, and when they returned she was to let them wait for him in his office. He would be away for a couple of hours longer, as he had some business to transact in Soho.

"Now what can we do whilst we're waiting?" Jack asked, taking hold of Amy and moving towards a big leather-topped desk. He took her in his arms before lifting her on to the desk. He expertly removed her clothing, parted her legs and entered her in a frenzy of passion. His mouth pressed hard against hers stopped her from screaming as she felt her body being stretched and torn. The more she tried to push him away, the harder he kissed her and held her in a vice-like grip. It was not until he was completely satisfied that he pulled away. He adjusted his own clothing and went to look out of the office window, leaving Amy on the verge of tears.

Liam knocked on the door of a quiet looking shop in a small back street. The shop looked innocent enough, selling anything that could turn a profit and attract customers. A sign in the window stated that the proprietor would be back in five minutes.

Ten minutes later, Liam tried again. A sleepy voice called out in response to his third knock, wanting to know who was there, and what was wrong. Liam stepped back from the shop entrance onto the pavement, and looked up at the bow window on the first floor. As soon as he saw Liam, the man swore. He closed the window and a few minutes later Liam heard the scrape of the locks on the shop door.

The man stepped aside to let him in. The shopkeeper was wearing a pair of old trousers, a grubby string vest, and had a cigarette hanging from the corner of his mouth.

"Come in, my friend, but why so insistent?" he wheezed. "Can't a man get a few minutes sleep without you waking him up? Come on in, don't keep me standing in the doorway."

He held out his hand for Liam to shake. "As you see, Old Josh is still with us. A little worse for wear, but still breathing!"

"Judging by that cough, that won't be for much longer," Liam answered.

"Ah, you always were a shrewd one, my friend. But Old Josh is no fool. When I get old, I will stop all this smoking." He laughed till the tears ran down his cheeks. Old Josh must have been well into his eighties!

Although he had lived in London for over half a century, he still had an accent, which was hard to define. No one seemed to know where he came from, and he wasn't the sort of person who would take kindly to personal questions.

He offered Liam a cup of tea and they went through to the back of the premises. He asked what he could do for him and Liam told him he needed two handguns and a rifle, together with the appropriate ammunition. He would also need five passports, a pair of wire cutters and a rope ladder.

"Impossible, my friend. Quite impossible. You could not afford such items, even if Old Josh could supply them."

"Maybe we could come to some arrangement that would suit us both," Liam said. He knew Old Josh's way of doing business, and this was no more than he had expected.

"Let's see. What would you be wanting with these items? You thinking of stealing the Crown Jewels?" Again he had to wipe his eyes as his laughter changed into a fit of coughing.

"The Bank of England, more like!" Liam replied.

"Ah, my friend, you always were the funny one. OK then, to business. How soon would you want the merchandise, if I could supply it?"

"I need to have it by four o'clock today."

"Impossible my friend. Impossible. Do you think I have it on my person? Do you think I keep the rifle down my trouser leg, eh." Another fit of coughing was followed by his deep humorous chuckle.

"What I do know," said Liam "is that if there is anyone in England who can get hold of these things for me, and on time, it's you. That's why I've come specially, just to see you."

"You did that? Ah my friend, you speak the truth. There is no-one in the whole of England who could do this thing for you," he waved his expressive hands to indicate the whole of the country, then shook his head. "Maybe not even Old Josh!"

"Then perhaps I will have to go elsewhere," Liam replied. "Is that house in the square still functioning?"

Old Josh's face went so red that Liam thought he was going to burst a blood vessel, but he could see the anger in his eyes, and knew he had made the right move.

"Ah my friend, you really know how to hurt a body. That was not a nice thing to do, to remind me of my terrible brother. I would die rather than let you do business with him. You see what a good friend I am to you? I will get your merchandise by this evening. Do not go to that fool. All you will get from him is rubbish. He is no better than the dirt under my feet. I am tired of talking about him, we will not discuss him any more."

Old Josh and his brother had rowed many years ago, and even though they lived in the same district, they had not spoken to each other for over 40 years. It was sad that they had never settled their differences, as they were both lonely in their old age.

"Come back tonight at 6, and I will have everything ready for you," he said. "Is that all, my friend?"

"Thanks, Josh. I'll come back at four."

"Are you deaf, my friend? Didn't you hear me? I said six o'clock."

"That's too late. The Bank of England closes before that!"

"The Bank of England indeed!" Again his deep chuckle. "Alright, I'll have them by four o'clock, but why you should try and kill Old Josh with over-work, I don't understand, I thought we were friends."

"I wouldn't have come to you if we weren't! I know I can rely on you. Make sure they all fire straight, and I want the rifle to dismantle quickly and easily. I'll test them before I take delivery."

"Of course, of course. Don't I always supply the best? You would not have come all the way, special, if you didn't know that Old Josh always supplies the best," he shook Liam's hand again, before succumbing to another fit of coughing. "Come back at 4, and we will spend a pleasant half hour in the cellar. I always enjoy shooting with you, and we'll have a little wager on the best shot. And don't forget to bring the money. Cash, mind you. I don't want anything that can be traced."

"How much?" Liam asked.

Old Josh pulled a scrap of paper from his pocket, and took the pencil from behind his ear. He wrote down a phenomenally large amount.

Liam took the pencil and wrote a new figure, half the amount of the first. This went on until a price was agreed. It was quite extortionate, but Liam knew the merchandise would be reliable, and he meant it when he said that few people would be able to supply his needs the same day. One has to pay for the convenience, after all!

Back in the shop, he opened his wallet, and took out five photographs, one for each of the passports. Old Josh put them in his pocket without even looking at them.

"All Irish?" he asked.

"No, three English, one Irish and one American," he said. "I've marked the details on the back, so there can be no mistake."

The old man nodded, and turned in the direction of the kitchen. Liam opened the shop door and stepped out into the sunshine, joining the throng of people intent on enjoying the delights of London on such a hot sunny day.

He then went into the West End and bought two identical briefcases. On the first, he set the tumble locks to read David's date of birth on both the left and right hand locks, and made a small scratch on the leather close to the handle. For the second briefcase, he used the birth date of the American named on the fifth passport.

Liam was interested to learn that Jack had been hunting since he was old enough to handle a gun, and wanted to know how accurate he was, so when he went to collect the merchandise from Old Josh, he took Jack with him, but they weren't well received!

"You should have come alone, my friend," Old Josh had insisted. "He may be a friend of yours, but Old Josh doesn't like to meet new friends. How do I know I can trust him?"

"I give you me word," Liam said. "Besides he's coming with me when I hold up the Bank of England, and if I can trust him with that, then surely you can too."

"Well, Old Josh is not as young as he used to be, and is very suspicious of strangers. You know that, and it is not nice of you to bring him here. But here he is, so Old Josh will trust him for your sake, my friend. But do not bring anyone here again, you understand?"

"Of course," Liam said, nodding his head in agreement.

They went down to the cellar where the merchandise was laid out on a table. Targets were set up and they spent the next half hour shooting and adjusting the sights until they all aimed true. Liam had always considered himself a good shot, but Jack had a sharper eye and steadier hand, and could center the target every time.

"Well, my friend, Old Josh did not like you bringing strangers here, but it is a pleasure to see our young friend shoot so well. It makes me almost glad that you brought him. Old Josh has not seen such shooting in a long time. It makes his old heart glad to meet someone who, with a bit more practice, could be as good as Old Josh himself in his younger days. Ah, but there was no one to rival Old Josh. No one could come anywhere near him in his hey day. He was the best shot in the whole of the world. I do not boast, my friends, but what Old Josh says is the truth. Ask anyone who knew him when he was in his prime. There never was anyone as straight or as true as Old Josh."

He shook his head, and lost himself in memories of the past, as old people are apt to do.

Old Josh had been able to supply exactly what they needed. The rifle dismantled to fit inside the briefcase, together with the wire cutters and the rope ladder. The handguns nestled snugly in the palm of the hand and they all fired accurately. The passports would pass the closest scrutiny, and he couldn't have been more pleased.

Feeling relieved that things were moving at last; Jack and Liam made their way back to the office, where Amy was waiting impatiently for them. There was a note on his secretary's desk from David Renfrew, giving the name and number of his hotel, and stating that he would be leaving New York the following day. He would wait for Liam to get in touch before he travelled north.

They showed Amy all the things Josh had supplied and a shiver of excitement coursed through her veins. They were well and truly committed now, and there was no turning back!

"Memorise all the details," Liam explained whilst handing out the new passports. "If anyone makes a mistake at customs, the whole thing will come to nothing, and we'll all be arrested."

Amy's hands were shaking as she tried to remember all the details on the passport, going over every detail every few minites.

It was a mad journey to the ferry terminus, Liam speeding wherever he could, and keeping alert for any sign of traffic cops. They got there with only a few minutes to spare and were fortunate enough to get tickets.

As they went into one of the lounges Amy heard someone describing the sea as being "as calm as a mill-pond". Which millpond he meant, she'd no idea, but as soon as they left the shelter of the harbour, the gentle motion of the waves made her stomach churn, and she had to lie down.

On reaching the Emerald Isle they drove straight to Shannon where they were met by Liam's brother-in-law. Jack suspected their business had been used illegally on more than one occasion, and wondered how often Liam had used the services of Old Josh. It was obvious they had done business before, and Jack decided to try and find out what illegal activities Liam was involved in.

They entered the airport through the freight office, in time to board the freightliner bound for St. Louis. This was not the ideal destination but at least they would be Stateside. Dressed in overalls and carrying clipboards, they boarded the plane without attracting any attention or going through any form of control. The freightliner was packed with crates carrying a variety of goods, and they managed to find a space were they were able to stretch out and settle down to an uncomfortable and boring journey.

Liam wanted to know why Jack expected Malcolm to help them, and it was on that cramped flight that Jack told them how he intended to put pressure on his old school-friend.

"It was during his last term. I caught him with his pants down, as the saying goes! We all knew he and Martin Ingram-Brown were lovers, and when Malcolm sneaked out of the dorm one night, I followed to see what he was up to. Sure enough, he met up with Martin in the old attic room. I sat on the landing for about an hour, and was just about to return to bed, when I heard someone coming up the stairs. It was the history teacher, Mr. Askew. I wanted to leave but there was nowhere to go except into the old store cupboard. I got inside, and had to pull the door too and hold it to stop it opening again. I watched Mr. Askew through the crack, and saw him open the attic door and shout at the boys. There was some commotion, and they ran out of the room. I could see the panic on their faces. They both knew that if they were reported, they would be expelled.

"Martin is the son of a member of the aristocracy, and his disgrace would reflect badly on his father, so he'd do anything to stop it getting out. He was determined to do all he could to stop Mr. Askew from reporting them. He started to plead with the teacher, but Mr. Askew was adamant in his decision to report the pair to the Headmaster."

"Go on," Amy urged as he paused to remember exactly what happened.

"Martin was a big lad, and he started to push Mr. Askew towards the stairs. As he reached out to grab the banister, Malcolm deliberately put his foot out and Mr. Askew tripped over it and fell down the stairs."

"Was he hurt," Amy asked.

"He died of a broken neck."

"Are you telling me that they murdered him?" Liam asked.

"Yes. They weren't to know that he'd break his neck, of course, but they quite deliberately pushed him down the stairs. I've no doubt that's what they intended to do. They pretended they were as shocked as everyone else next day when we were told that one of the masters had died in a terrible accident!"

"We know where Malcolm is now, but what happened to Martin?" Amy asked.

"I don't know. I haven't heard of him since the end of that term, when he and Malcolm both left."

"Have you ever told anyone about this before?" Liam wanted to know.

"No. I couldn't face the scandal at first, and the longer I remained silent, the harder it was to speak out."

"It all sounds a bit dodgy to me," Liam said. "If Malcolm's got away with it so far, why should he feel threatened now? Surely if you were going to say anything, you'd have done it straight away. After all, it is only your word against his. He might not feel it a big enough threat to make him help in the present situation."

"But I didn't tell you about the tape recording," Jack continued triumphantly. "I'd taken my recorder with me, in the hope of getting some evidence that would get them expelled. They were such an obnoxious pair, that they were a disgrace to the school!"

"You've actually got a recording of what went on that night?" Liam asked.

"Sure do. It's here, in my rucksack."

"Surely there must have been an inquiry, and the recording would have been all the evidence needed to convict the boys. Why didn't you speak out then, and why haven't you said anything until now?" Liam wanted to know.

"I don't know why I didn't say anything at the time, except that I didn't want to get involved. It didn't look good for me to be seen as someone who would take recordings of other peoples' activities. Anyway, whatever the reason, I didn't say anything at the time."

When Jack went to the toilet, Liam asked Amy what she knew about him, how long she had known him and why she had involved him now. What he had just told them didn't make sense. He said he had taken the recording with the specific purpose of getting the boys expelled, so why hadn't he used it to do just that? It didn't ring true that he wouldn't speak out because of his own reputation. If he was worried about that, he wouldn't have been there in the first place.

Amy said she'd known Jack ever since she had gone to live on the farm. They hadn't seen a lot of each other until fairly recently, when they'd both started going to the monthly disco. She had been surprised, and pleased, when he said he would help, and Liam wanted to know if that was before or after they'd seen Malcolm Wainwright on the television.

"It was after the broadcast," she replied. "I'd been surprised, and pleased, that he wanted to come, and I definitely got the impression that he wanted to meet up with his old school friend again. Is there anything wrong in that?"

"Not necessarily. I'm just not sure where he comes into all this, but you know him best, and I hope we can trust him. I don't know what it is, but there's something odd about his attitude. Maybe it's his youth, and the fact that he's been spoilt. Look at his car, there aren't many people of his age can afford one of those."

"He didn't buy it. He won it!" Amy said, laughing. "His parents, like most farmers, have their good years and their bad years, but I don't think they could have afforded to buy it for him. His brother and sister certainly don't have anything like that."

"Well, well" he remarked as Jack returned. "Let's try and get some shut-eye before we land."

When they arrived in St. Louis, the plane taxied to the depot where they joined the team of workers preparing to unload the freight. One of them gave Liam three identity cards, and stick-on labels, which were fastened to the back of their overalls. They were directed along a utilities corridor, which took them into the Baggage Claim area, where they removed their overalls in the toilets.

Their luggage had been put on carrousel three, and they mingled with passengers from a flight from Amsterdam. Their fake passports were glanced at, but not questioned, and they were able to walk unchecked into the busy concourse.

— CHAPTER 4 —

David was waiting for them at O'Hare International. He had driven a hire car from New York and booked rooms at a motel close by. He was eager to know what the fuss was all about, and was asking questions before they left the concourse.

They told him everything they had planned and what they'd achieved so far. He was relieved they'd left Grandpa's shotgun behind!

He was impressed with Amy's idea, his only regret being that she was involved, and he had not been there from the start. He said he and Liam would take over now, and tried unsuccessfully to persuade Amy and Jack to return to England. As Jack pointed out, only he could influence Malcolm, and so much depended on his co-operation.

"Why didn't you let us know where you were going on holiday, and what is all this secrecy about," Amy wanted to know.

He tried to make some excuse, but she insisted on the truth. He told her he had seen a bargain break advertised, and had taken Holly Branson to New York for a few pleasurable days.

"Holly Branson! But I thought she was going out with Joe," Amy exclaimed in disgust.

"She'll go out with anyone who can give her a good time!" he laughed. "It's just a few days fun with no strings attached. We both know where we stand and are happy with the arrangement. There's no harm in that!"

"I see why you didn't say anything. Can you imagine Granny's face if she saw you two together? She'd be really upset."

"She would indeed, and equally so if she knew what you are intending to do and she'd expect me to put a stop to it. Once Jack's seen Malcolm, will you leave it to Liam and I, and return home before you get into trouble. I don't want to be responsible for anything happening to you if we don't succeed."

"Try and make me!"

"Alright I will. I'll send you to stay with Holly in New York, and she can keep you with her until I get back, then we can go home together."

"I'd run away."

"No you wouldn't, because you'd have nowhere to go and it would be too late. By the time you get to Holly, we'll be airborne and, because you love us, you won't say or do anything to stop us."

"But that's blackmail!"

"Call it what you like, girl, it's what I'll do if I have to, and if you make trouble I'll tell everyone you're a runaway and I'm sending you back to your parents. No-one will believe you then, no matter what story you tell."

"Listen, David," she pleaded, "it was me Pam turned to for help, and so far I've not done too badly. Now you come in, want to take over and send me home. Well, if you must know, it does frighten me; what seemed like a plausible thing to do is turning into something I hardly dare think about, but I'm determined to see it through to the end. There's nothing you can say to stop me. And on top of all that I'm learning that my brother is a hard, calculating bastard with no feelings for anyone else!"

"I don't mean to be unfeeling, but someone has to take responsibility and it comes naturally to me. I'm sorry if you think I'm treading on your toes, but you don't have the experience or knowledge to pull it off. I've been in the army all my adult life and I've been trained to cope with all the shitty jobs thrown at me. I've got to be cold and calculating. I've got lives depending on the way I organise things and the decisions I make, and if I make a mistake on this occasion, it'll be your life as well as my own that's at risk. I want to make sure we all return safely, and if it means being a hard bastard, then that's what I'll be!"

"You can't boss me around and expect me to do as I'm told all the time. I'm not a child."

"Then stop behaving like one!" he snapped. "Think, girl. It won't be a picnic. It's dangerous out there. We're going into a country that's at war! We've got to know what we're doing, and we have to be prepared. We only have two handguns and a rifle between us. Will that be enough to protect us all? I doubt it! Don't you understand that we've got to be sensible and not take anyone who isn't needed. They won't think twice before shooting us, and we've got to be prepared to defend ourselves against whatever they decide to throw at us."

"It doesn't matter what you say, I'm going, and that's final." Amy stamped her foot in defiance.

"You can't try to push people around and not get hurt yourself and I don't want to be responsible for involving you," David put his hands on her shoulders and looked into her eyes. "We're doing this for Pam, and I ask myself if she really wants to involve you. I know she asked you to get me to help, but I'm sure she didn't intend for you to get involved."

"Maybe not, and when you put it like that, I do understand," she said, "but just remember that I'm as involved as you, and I don't like to be treated as if I don't know anything!"

"I know, but you've not got the experience Liam and I have."

"And what experience do you have in helping Pam once we've got her on the plane? Will you be any help with the children? Will you be prepared to feed them, wash them, and change the babies' nappies? Will you be able to comfort a scared child who has never left its mother before? Need I go on?"

"She does have a point." Amy was surprised at Liam's support.

She could see David struggling within himself, not wanting to take her with him, yet acknowledging that she would be useful on the return flight.

"If you're absolutely certain this is what you want," he said looking deep into her eyes, "then I won't try and stop you."

Liam turned away so that the others could not see the look on his face.

Jack went to the imposing waterfront building where Wright Flights International had their offices and was told that Malcolm Wainwright was out, and not expected back until the following morning and suggested he make an appointment.

He spent some considerable time talking to the receptionist, trying to persuade her to let him have Malcolm's home address. He ended up taking her out for a drink, time which he could ill afford, but she seemed to enjoy herself and he flattered and teased her until she told him where Malcolm lived. He made some excuse about finding the little boys' room, left the building and went straight to Malcolm's apartment. He never did find out how long the girl waited, or what her reaction was when she realised he had deserted her, and she was left to pay the bill!

The concierge wouldn't let him go beyond the foyer, insisting Mr. Wainwright wasn't at home, but as he was expected back in the office the following morning, Jack had to gamble on his returning home later that night.

His patience paid off when he saw Malcolm get out of a cab. Jack ran up to him and slapped him on the back.

"Hi there," he said. "How nice to see you again. The doorman told me you were away, and I thought I was going to miss you. I'm only over from England for a couple of days, and particularly wanted to speak to you."

Malcolm had turned white, and stammered something incomprehensible.

Jack took his arm and led him through the foyer to the lift. When

Malcolm tried to speak, Jack squeezed his arm, and he remained silent. He unlocked his apartment door, and Jack pushed him in so hard that he tripped and fell.

"You!" Malcolm said with loathing. "What're you doing here? You promised never to see me again."

"Oh come on, man!" Jack said. "What did you expect? You honestly didn't think I'd let you alone for ever, did you?"

"Yes I did. And why not! You gave me the tape in exchange for a very expensive car. You promised that was the end of it, and you wouldn't ever come near me again! So what do you want, and why have you come?"

Malcolm's father had never really approved of him, and no matter how hard he tried, Malcolm never felt he could live up to his expectations.

Richard Wainwright came from an old Irish-American family. His ancestors had left Ireland to make a new home for themselves in the United States of America. His great-great-grandmother had died on the crossing, leaving her husband to raise their 11 children on his own. It had been hard, but most of them had survived, and each progressive generation did better than the last.

It was Malcolm's grandfather, Malcolm Wainwright the 1st, who had been interested in air travel, and he'd been delighted to find the same enthusiasm in his second son. From an early age Richard had pestered his father into taking him along when he piloted a crop-duster for a local firm. The war gave Malcolm senior all the flying experience he could wish for, and he was determined not to give it up. Once the war was over he approached everyone he knew who might be able to give him a job, but there was a glut of good pilots, so he started thinking about working for himself. From the lucky chance of being in the right place at the right time, he had bought his first plane and acquired a licence to carry passengers as well as freight.

Thus Wright Flights International had been born.

Richard had only made one genuine mistake in his life, and that was to fall in love with Claireena, a beautiful young girl from Chicago. They were hardly apart during that summer, and when she found she was pregnant they'd run away to Las Vegas to be married.

By the time Malcolm was born, Richard had realised all the disadvantages of a hasty marriage. Their first passionate longings had died down and they had little else in common.

The boy looked like a miniature of his mother with fine, girlish features and dark hair. When Claireena let his hair grow long, people used to mistake him for a girl, until Richard insisted his son's hair be cut short, and he should always be dressed in blue.

Claireena didn't have any more children, and she saw her husband and son growing further and further away from her under the influence of her mother-in-law. She was never accepted into their social group, and discouraged from being seen in their company. Richard spent most of his time at the office, and she suspected him of having a number of affairs.

By the time Malcolm was five years old, she had left her workaholic husband for another man, leaving Malcolm to be brought up by his grandmother, who found it more difficult than she had imagined raising a lively 5 year old. She employed a succession of paid helpers, not one of them reaching the high standard she set.

Richard gave his son everything that money could buy, but all Malcolm wanted was to spend time with his father, and to win his respect and praise, both of which were never forthcoming. Richard was hurt and angry when Claireena had left him for someone else, and each time he looked at his son and saw the delicate features and effeminate face, he felt a deep hurt inside, which he was determined to hide at all costs. That he was greatly to blame for her leaving, he never even considered.

Malcolm had a lonely childhood, not mixing with the other children in his neighbourhood, as their parents had not approved of his mother. His grandparents rejoiced when Claireena left, but Malcolm was devastated. His mother was his only playmate. He seldom saw his father or grandfather, and when he started to get attached to one of the women employed to look after him, his grandmother sacked her.

When Malcolm was old enough he was sent to England to be educated. The boy found it hard to be parted from all he knew and dumped in a totally unknown environment. He was pleased to be leaving his grandmother, but he didn't want to be away from his father for months at a time. Yet being sent away proved to be a mixed blessing.

During the course of his work, Richard spent a lot of time in England, and when he could he would go and see Malcolm. He would call at the school and take his son out for a meal and occasionally they would spend a whole weekend together. These times were precious to both of them, each getting to know the other, and for the first time they spent time together without the influence of other people.

Malcolm survived his first term at school by bribing various people to be his friends. He was a very tactile person, and at first he wanted to hold hands with his contemporaries for the sake of friendship, but as the years passed, for an entirely different reason. He found himself attracted to various boys at school, and he was totally unable to form any sort of relationship with girls.

During the holidays Malcolm worked for WFI as a junior clerk, and would have remained in that position but for his family connections. On leaving school he was transferred to a more senior position, which he found beyond his capabilities. He wasn't a clever person and found the added responsibility irksome.

It was quite by chance that he discovered in himself a love of cooking, and he started to experiment. Soon he was demonstrating his skill to the board of Wright Flights International, with a choice of in-flight menus. He was given the opportunity of working alongside the Catering Director, and found he actually enjoyed dealing with the suppliers, bartering and insisting on the best produce available. As his recipes were introduced into the bill of fare, WFI was getting the reputation of serving gourmet meals on all its long haul flights. This new role made Malcolm feel at ease because he was contributing in his own right, and not as the son of the chairman.

Now here he was, back in trouble again. He hated Jack. And he hated Martin. All this mess was their fault. They had betrayed him. They had let him down at a time when he most needed them.

"Get up off the floor, you look ridiculous," Jack said getting hold of his hand and pulling him to his feet. Malcolm sat on the chesterfield, his head in his hands.

"What are you doing here?" he asked, trying to think positively and not let Jack know just how scared he was feeling.

"I want your help."

"I might have known you wanted something, but I don't see how I can help you," Malcolm looked up and for the first time showed some interest.

"Of course I want something, there's no way I'd come to see you if I didn't have to!" Jack replied cruelly. "I want you to help me get a friend out of Bosnia."

"That sounds like a good idea. To get them out, I mean. But I don't think I can help. I don't know anyone in that part of the world, and I've never been there. It isn't exactly the best tourist spot at the moment, either." He laughed at his own joke.

"I've worked out a way of doing it," Jack continued, "but I need your co-operation."

"You won't get it. I wouldn't help even if I'd the inclination, which I don't. It's not my friend, so why should I bother?"

"No, she's not," Jack sneered in Malcolms' face. "You don't go in for beautiful girls, do you? Now if I'd asked you to help rescue a beautiful young man, would your answer have been different, I wonder?"

"Hey man, that's not fair!"

"Life is not fair, Mister Wainwright. Life was not fair when you and Martin became, er, what they call today, 'an item'. And it was less fair when you were caught by one of the masters in the old attic. And it was even less fair when you panicked and he was deliberately pushed down the stairs and broke his neck. No, Mister Wainwright, life is not fair!"

Malcolm turned a sort of greenish white. He looked as though he was going to be physically sick, and it was some time before he was able to speak. What he did manage to say didn't make much sense, a sort of incoherent muttering that ended in the words "you promised never to say what happened!"

"That was then, this is now," Jack told him.

He looked at Jack, rubbing his hands together, licking his lips and trying to read what was in his mind.

"We didn't deliberately trip him up. He slipped! It was a tragic accident when he fell down the stairs. Everyone agreed on that."

"Yes, but some of us know better, don't we, Malcolm? And some of us have proof!"

"No." He shot the word out. "You gave me the tape in exchange for the car."

After a pause, he continued. "You never did tell me how you got hold of the tape in the first place. I've often wondered what made you take a recording that night. And why come to me. Surely Martin is just as involved. Have you spoken to him about it?"

"Who do you think it was made the tape? He left his recorder running every time you were together. He was more interested in watching his own back, than what you thought or felt. If ever you decided to turn against him, he'd have enough evidence to keep you quiet."

"No, I don't believe you! He loved me! He wouldn't do that."

"But he did. It was Martin who gave me the tape."

"He must hate me, the bitch! But it doesn't make sense that he'd give it to you."

"Maybe he thought he could trust me. He'd always taken an interest in me, even though I didn't return it, and I'd been with him occasionally. 'Don't knock it until you've tried it' is my motto, and I wanted to know what you got out of it. It did nothing for me, but Martin seemed to be satisfied, so when everyone was trying to find out what happened to Mr. Askew, he said I was the only person he could trust, and asked me to hide his tape-recorder. He'd wrapped it up and tied it with string, but when I opened it, I discovered that he'd left the tape in it and, of course, I listened to it, and took several copies. I thought they'd come in useful, and one already has."

"I didn't know he even liked you. He never told me."

"There's a lot Martin didn't tell you."

"I thought he was faithful, as I was to him. Have you taken the tape to him? He's in a much better position to help you than me. What's he given you in return?"

"Nothing, as yet. I've neither seen nor heard from Martin since school, neither have I any desire to meet him again until he's more in the public eye. It was not my wish to meet up with you again, but in this instance, you can help me, and I mean to make it quite clear there's nothing you can do to stop me from going to Bosnia. Nothing. Do you understand that Malcolm? If I have to sacrifice you, I will, with pleasure."

"I don't want to stop you! Why should I? What concerns me is that you've kept a copy of the tape all this time, and never said a word," he muttered. "I should've known I couldn't trust you. You promised that if I gave you the car, you wouldn't see me again. What a fool I was to believe you!"

"Exactly. I'm glad you know me so well. I haven't bothered you before, because you've never been in a position to help me, but now you can, and to make sure you do I'm prepared to use this information to get your complete co-operation."

"What is it you want?"

"That's quite simple. I want to borrow a plane."

"You're mad! I couldn't lend you a plane even if I wanted to, which I don't!"

"Why not?"

"Because we don't keep a spare! All our craft are in use, or being serviced. We can't afford to have a plane standing idle. Whilst it is on the ground, it's not making money. It's as simple as that!"

"Then if you refuse my request, there is only one answer. You are going to help me hijack one of your planes," Jack said, as if it was the most natural thing in the world.

"Ha. Ha, ha. You know what I thought you said? You want me to help you hijack one of our planes!"

"I did."

"You must be out of your mind! You don't know my father. He'd cut me off without a penny, and my life wouldn't be worth living. No way."

"Alright then, I'll go to the police and tell them everything."

"No, no, no," he pleaded. "Just listen a minute, Jack. We're old friends, damn it. We went to school together! We must stick by each other. You can say it was an accident. Martin will confirm that. There's no need to do anything rash. It can all be cleared up now, and then perhaps I can get on with my life without always thinking about it. Perhaps it's better to get it in the open now."

"That's up to you Malcolm! I'm quite happy to tell your father exactly what happened. As for school friends sticking together, when did you ever consider anyone else but yourself? If I remember rightly, you were the worst sneak in the school!"

"It wasn't my fault. I couldn't help it. I hated school, and no one even liked me. So I tried to get the teachers to like me. I thought if I helped them, they'd respect me, and then you lot would start to like me. I only wanted to be friends!"

"No-one wanted your kind of friendship!" Jack sneered. "We'd enough problems of our own without adding you to them. Surely you know you can't buy friendship. It has to be earned."

"That's all very well for you. You excelled in team games, and everyone wanted you on their side, but I never could abide sport. Getting all hot and sweaty, and running round after a stupid ball. I thought you all mad."

"Not as mad as you're going to be if you don't listen to what I have to say. I've urgent need of two things. First, a plane. Second, a large amount of money. You gave me the idea of how to get a plane, and I've come to you for the money."

"I can't give you any money, and how could I have given you the idea. I haven't spoken to you for years."

"It was through the television. You talked about hijacking a plane. Surely you remember that?"

"But I said I wouldn't encourage anyone to hijack one of our planes. It would be crazy to suggest such a thing. It wasn't meant as a challenge. I thought I'd made that perfectly clear. If anyone was to blame, it was the interviewer. Go speak to him."

"But I am speaking to you, and asking nicely for your co-operation."

"You're mad even to think about it. It's impossible. We've put on extra security throughout the world to prove that WFI is the safest airline today. It's not possible for you to get hold of one of them."

"On my own, I agree. But I could if you were prepared to help."

"Well I won't! You must be stupid to think I'd even consider it."

"Is that your final answer?" Jack asked, his face just a few inches away from Malcolms.

"Yes it is. Get out of here. How dare you come in here making such wild demands? Get out. I don't want to see you ever again."

Jack stood up, walked over to the telephone, picked it up and asked the operator to connect him with Richard Wainwright.

"What are you doing?" Malcolm tried to get up out of his chair, but was prevented by Jacks' hand on his shoulder.

"Just letting Daddy know what a bad boy you've been," he sneered.

"He won't believe you."

"Oh, won't he? Are you so certain? I can give him a graphic account of everything that happened that night as well as the recording. I'm sure he'll believe me by the time I've given him all the sordid details."

Malcolm sat biting his fingernails and his eyes filled with tears.

"I don't understand any of this. Why do you want me to help you, and what is it you want me to do? And what are you going to tell my father?"

"Nothing, if you're prepared to help. Hello, is that Mr. Wainwright? Just hold the line please."

"What are you going to say to him?"

"Nothing, if you do as I say. Speak to him now, and tell him you'll be delayed and won't be going to work for a few days because you have to go back to England."

"But what will I say when he asks why?"

"Oh, for heavens sake, can't you think of anything for yourself? Tell him you've personal business to attend to, if you can't think of anything better."

Malcolm's hands were shaking when he put the phone down. He glanced towards the door, but knew it was futile to try and run away.

"Come on then, tell me the worst!" He sat down on the edge of his seat, twisting his fingers together and looking decidedly uncomfortable.

"We need a plane to fly into Bosnia to collect a friend and the people she's caring for. And we need the money to finance such an undertaking. That's all."

"That's all! Don't you know it's impossible? There's no way you could get within 100 yards of one of our planes without a valid boarding pass, and even if you had one, you couldn't take anything with you to make the crew do as you demand. Our security is too sophisticated to allow any sort of weapon to get through. And if you think I'll be able to smuggle anything on board before departure, you're mistaken again. I just can't help you guys."

"Well now, I beg to differ. As I see it, you're the one person who can get away with it. We've worked it all out between us, and know it will succeed."

"Who else is involved? I'm sure you're not doing it on your own."

"No, there are others involved, but there is no need for you to know anything about them. The less you know, the better for you!"

"Oh, thank you for being so considerate!" Malcolm sneered.

"It's a pleasure," Jack responded. "I'm glad you appreciate my consideration! Now, where do we start? I think the first thing is to get hold of some money to grease the wheels, as it were."

"How do you mean to set about that?" Malcolm asked innocently.

"That's simple. You will give me all the money you can lay your hands on."

"You really are mad! I'm not paying for your crazy ideas."

"Why not? We'll have a lot of expenses, and have already spent a considerable amount. We can't afford it, but you can."

"What makes you think I keep any money here? It's all in the bank, and I can't get my hands on a large amount just like that. You know that sort of thing takes time."

"Knowing you of old, Malcolm, I'd be amazed if you hadn't a tidy sum hidden away. You never felt comfortable without some money available at short notice. Unless you've changed, which I doubt, I would bet that it is no trifling amount. So tell me, just how much is there here?"

"Nothing!"

"I don't believe you. You always had plenty of money at school, too much for your own good! You couldn't have changed that much."

"That doesn't mean I've gotten some here."

"There must be a safe. Tell me where it is or I'll trash the flat, and you as well."

"Don't hurt me again. So there is a safe, but I don't keep a fortune in it."

"How much?

"Only a few dollars."

"How much?" Jack raised his hand as if to hit Malcolm.

"All right, all right! A few thousand, that's all."

"That'll do to start with," Jack smiled, pleased at the way things were going.

"You can't have thought this through properly or you wouldn't even be thinking of hijacking a plane. Don't you know how dangerous it is? You couldn't possibly get away with it, and one day you'll thank me for not helping you."

"Thank you? For what? Trying to stop us from helping a friend to get away from a place of terror, where she could be killed at any moment? Is that what you mean? So far as I'm concerned, nothing is more important than getting her home safely. She is my priority now, and no one is going to stop me."

"I'm not stopping you from doing that. You can still go and get her if you want, but you don't have to hijack a plane to do that. Go on a regular flight."

"Do you honestly think I'd bother with you if it was as simple as that? You must have a higher opinion of yourself than I have."

"There's no need to be nasty."

The expression on his face made Jack furious, and he grabbed him by the throat and started to shake him. Malcolm went red in the face, and his fingers clawed at Jack's hands. His eyes started to bulge, and his legs gave way, until Jack was holding him up by the throat. He was on the point of losing consciousness when Jack let go. Malcolm fell to the ground and choked for breath, his hands rubbing his neck, and loosening his tie.

Jack was ruthless in his handling of Malcolm and there was a look of excitement in his eyes – he was enjoying what he was doing! Not so Malcolm, who cringed on the floor and started to sob. Life had been so unfair, and just when he had started to feel things were getting better, this had to happen!

Jack walked over to the bar, and poured a brandy, which he made Malcolm drink even though the strong spirit burned his throat.

"You bastard," he said, coughing until there were spots of blood in his mouth. "You bloody bastard, look what you've done. You almost killed me."

He was screaming, and Jack had to shut him up before anyone heard him. He got hold of Malcolm's collar, and threatened to finish the job off properly. Malcolm started to whine in a high-pitched voice, and Jack shook him until he was silent and on the verge of collapse.

It was pathetic to see him cringe, but he made a strong effort to calm down and said he would do exactly as he was told if Jack promised not to hit him again.

He wanted to go to the bathroom to be sick, and Jack made him keep the door open. He wasn't going to let Malcolm be on his own until they were safely on the plane. He plied him with strong black coffee until he had calmed down, and was beginning to look more like his normal self.

Jack rang the motel and told David everything had gone to plan.

Flight WF254 was due to leave on schedule, and there was no reason why they should not be on it.

Their plan was for Amy and Jack to travel second class, and Liam first class. David and Malcolm were to make their own travel arrangements. That meant David would have to stay overnight with Malcolm, so when he heard that Malcolm was willing to co-operate, he got Liam to drive him to the waterfront apartment.

This suited Liam as he said he wanted to attend to some business, and it was the ideal opportunity to sort out a freight problem with one of his clients.

Liam drove David to Malcolm's apartment, taking the briefcases and returning to the motel with Jack and all Malcolm's available cash.

To let her brother know he couldn't manage without her, Amy went to the nearest Travel Agent and got one first class and two tourist class tickets for flight WF254 paying for them with the money they had just received from Malcolm.

David wanted everything to appear normal, and asked Malcolm to follow his usual routine and arrange for two first class seats on the chosen flight.

Malcolm said his chauffeur always drove him to the airport when he was leaving the country. He was usually dropped off at the VIP entrance, but occasionally he would use the main entrance and enter the terminal with the general public. His chauffeur usually carried his luggage, and handed it over when he got to the security check.

The unmarked briefcase was packed with the minimum of clothes needed for a few nights stay in the UK, together with an assortment of letters, business cards, calculators etc, so that it looked like any normal business trip. Amy had been busy whilst Liam and Jack were in Soho, typing a number of letters on different letterheads, calling for a meeting to be held in London, giving the impression of an American company setting up a business deal in England.

Other personal items were added, and they were able to build up a scenario of someone from the southern States. The handgun was placed in the folds of a pair of striped pyjamas, and the fifth passport supplied by Old Josh was laid on top, made out in the name of an American businessman. In this way they managed to give the owner an identity.

It was decided that David and Malcolm would risk using the main entrance to the airport, instead of the VIP lounge, as there would be a lot more people about, and if they had to abandon the briefcase, they could deny any knowledge of it, insisting they had all they needed in the one briefcase in their possession. They would be astonished at the coincidence of the second one being the same make as theirs, and understand how easily anyone could have made the mistake of thinking it belonged to them.

After a quick search of the apartment David found a ball of string. He tied it firmly round Malcolm's wrists, and tied his hands together behind his back. He then fastened the other end of the string to his own wrist. That way, he knew every time Malcolm moved as they settled down for a few hours sleep.

Liam said he was going out for a breath of fresh air, and left Amy and Jack alone in the motel. It was a lovely night, crisp and cool and Jack said he had been sitting around for too long. He wanted to go for a walk, and insisted Amy stay behind in case the others tried to get in touch.

He ran in the same direction Liam had taken, and was rewarded by the sight of Liam across the street. Curious to know what he was doing, Jack watched as a car stopped and the driver, a tall familiar figure, got out and shook Liam's hand. They stood talking for a short time before the car drove off.

Jack could hardly believe his eyes, yet he had met Richard Wainwright before and there was no doubt in his mind that he was the man Liam was talking to. What was he up to and how long had he known Richard Wainwright? He had told them that he had met him before, but not explained how or where. He must have known him well enough to contact him, and arrange a meeting. Would he endanger their lives for his own ends? After all, Amy didn't know much about him, although David was confident of his loyalty, but it hadn't sounded right when Liam said he wanted to meet a client.

There was no way he would let anyone know he was in the States, otherwise why bother with a false passport?

Jack had found out that Wright Flights International ran regular flights to Manchester, so why had Liam chosen this particular flight when they would have been more certain of getting to Osijek faster by using an earlier flight?

Something was not right, but there was nothing Jack could do for the present. He would keep a sharp eye on Liam.

Amy lay in bed, hoping Jack would join her and at the same time dreading a repeat of the pain she was still suffering. From the time he had said he would go with her, she'd hoped they would find the opportunity to spend the night together. She wanted to know the thrill of lying in his arms before falling asleep and waking up together in the morning. What she hadn't realised was the pain their love-making had caused, but she had been reassured when Jack told her it would be easier next time. These conflicting thoughts were uppermost in her mind when jet lag and the excitement of the day soon had the better of her and she fell into a deep but troubled sleep.

Jack looked at Amy as she lay asleep in the large double bed. She looked so young and he shrugged away a twinge of conscience. She had made it quite clear that she was willing to sleep with him, and he had every intention of taking advantage of the situation. But not just yet, he had more important things on his mind, and wouldn't go to Amy until after Liam had returned to the motel.

When he eventually walked through the door, Jack asked Liam if he'd had a successful business meeting. He told Jack he'd had a good evening, but wanted his bed. He wasn't prepared to say any more about his activities.

Jack climbed into the big bed next to Amy. She stirred and snuggled into the folds of his arms, her exclamation cut short by a kiss. It was late by the time they got up next morning and Liam had already gone out.

Liam couldn't figure Jack at all. Why was he helping Amy? Was he doing it to get her into bed? If so, he'd succeeded, but it was a desperate way of going about it. From what he'd seen, he thought Amy would be a willing partner whether Jack gave her his support or not. So was he doing it for Pam? But she seemed to be more of an acquaintance than a true friend, so why had he decided to risk so much with no apparent explanation? Liam would make it his business to find out.

— CHAPTER 5 —

Richard Wainwright was a hard man. He had scrimped and saved in his early days at Wright Flights International, and many a deal had been made that could be interpreted as shady, if not exactly illegal. Many people hated his guts after being pushed aside to further his own career. He was quite capable of taking others' ideas and passing them off as his own, and had the reputation of doing anything to stop a prospective rival. He knew whom to contact to make someone disappear quietly, and the fact he had no hand in the affair was enough to ease his conscience. He wasn't troubled by moral issues and scorned those who held to their principles. There was only one way to go and that was up. No matter how much he made, how successful he became, there was always more wealth to be accumulated, more power to be gained.

Yet, strangely, he had his own ethics. If someone proved themselves to be ambitious and worked hard for the company, he would encourage them and they were rewarded with a good salary. On the other hand, if they didn't pull their weight, they were sacked on the spot.

He was also a passionate man – both physically and emotionally. If he saw a woman he fancied, he knew his powerful position worked like an aphrodisiac and he would be generous until he tired of her, then end their relationship without a second thought.

His one regret was his own marriage – what a foolish mistake even for one so young! He should never have married Claireena and regretted the fact that he had fallen in love with a beautiful face.

He was also disappointed in his son, and wished Malcolm would change into someone more like himself, but that would never happen. They were entirely different people with different standards. He blamed his ex for mollycoddling their son and turning him against his father. Yet he had felt a twinge of pride when Malcolm had taken over the catering side of the business and made a success of it. Not that cooking was a fitting job for a man, but it seemed to be the only thing he was interested in. He had made a mess of everything else he had tried to do, and been an embarrassment to his father.

The fact he didn't like girls added to Richards dislike. He found it repugnant. That he could have fathered such a being was beyond his imagination and he was sometimes convinced Malcolm wasn't his own son – yet for all her faults, he knew his wife hadn't been unfaithful in the first few years of their marriage.

Second only to WFI was his passion for his homeland. After generations of living in the States, he still considered Ireland his home. He couldn't forgive the English for making his forefathers leave their home and cross the Atlantic to start a new life in an alien country. He had traced his ancestry back as far as he could, and his hatred for the English had increased with each act of violence against his own people. He thought nothing of what the Irish had done to the English and felt they deserved everything that was thrown at them.

Here, indeed, was his only reason for tolerating Peter Callahan – the fact that he was of Irish descent, and also working for the IRA. Callahan was a distant cousin, and had started to make a nuisance of himself, but Richard had his own way of making Callahan toe the line, and was aware of just about everything he was involved in. He knew he was chasing Mary McDowell, one of WFI's employees. She seemed harmless enough and a search into her past revealed nothing of significance. He believed the relationship was purely sexual.

On his return home after a particularly busy and exhausting day, Richard poured himself a strong drink and relaxed in his favourite chair in front of the large plate-glass window with a panoramic view of Chicago and Lake Michigan. He was starting to doze when the phone rang. The familiar Irish brogue gave him a thrill, and the tiredness of the day was forgotten. How he loved to hear the soft gentle lilt of his homeland! There was something pure and sweet that was lacking in the Irish voices of those who had lived in the States for a long time – some indefinable quality that only the true Irishman possessed.

The IRA's request for funds had never been turned down, but on this occasion they were desperate to receive the money urgently. He said he would contact whoever he thought would be able to help, and hoped they had the money to hand.

His next few calls were to IRA fund-raisers, only known to each other by their contact numbers. If anyone guessed the identity of their fellow sympathisers, they never let on, and it was an unwritten law they would never reveal anything that could lead to anyone's identity being discovered.

Much to Richard's surprise, all the money was promised and arrangements put in hand to have it shipped to Ireland via Manchester, England. He decided to use flight WF254.

Richard was instructed to arrange for Peter Callahan to make the pick-up. Not for the first time he asked himself if he could be trusted, but he had come through before, and there was no reason why he shouldn't this time.

They were both descendants of the same Irish immigrants, but Peter's side of the family had never done particularly well, and there had been a certain envy when Malcolm Wainwright 1st had started the airline.

On leaving school, Peter had approached Richard, and on the strength of their relationship, asked for a job. He had been employed in a menial position, and soon started to embezzle from the firm. He had been caught and sent to prison for a short time, and from then on Peter was determined to get even with the Wainwright's. He wanted to ruin Richard and make a fortune for himself at the same time, so waited patiently for the right opportunity.

He had worked hard for the IRA and knew of others on the same level as himself, but the bigwigs were always anonymous and mostly people no one would suspect. Many a time he had tried to find out who was behind the jobs he had been given, but his enquiries always came to a dead end.

His contact told Peter just what to do, and his suspicions were roused when told they would be using a WFI flight again. Surely this wasn't a coincidence when other airlines flew regularly to the UK out of O'Hare International? Intrigued by this co-incidence he drew up a short list of anyone with Irish connections and the influence needed for such a position, and came to the conclusion that it had to be one of the Wainwright men. He quickly dismissed Malcolm as not being clever enough, so it had to be his father.

For the first time he was certain he had something against Richard Wainwright and he intended to use it in full measure! Peter had always been regarded as the black sheep of the family, and now he was learning that the paragon was as bad as himself.

The irony of the situation just suited his sense of humour.

He phoned Richard at home and, using his own password, pretended to be ringing from Ireland. He was surprised when Richard recognised his voice, and told him to meet him later that evening.

At first Peter tried to blackmail him, but, as Richard pointed out, his word would be accepted more readily than Peters' and a word in the right place would put Peter behind bars again. He also pointed out that it was not his choice to use Callahan. He also had to follow instructions, and if it was left to him, Callahan would never be used by the IRA again. If anything went wrong with this particular job, Richard threatened to make him disappear.

Peter was to collect the money and take it to Zac Powalski who would transfer it to his own luggage after making sure it was all there. That would be the end of Peter's involvement.

This time it was such a tight schedule that, with a bit of ingenuity, Peter realised he could arrange for the money to be taken direct to the airport, handed over to Zac in the employee's car park and taken straight onto the plane. That way Powalski wouldn't have time to check the contents.

It was too much to expect Peter to handle such a large amount and not want it for himself! He had waited a long time for this opportunity and his patience had paid off. Whatever Wainwright intended to do, he wouldn't be able to have Peter arrested for a crime Richard was not supposed to know anything about and if he harmed Peter, he would incriminate himself at the same time.

It was too easy to take most of the cash and replace it with bundles of newsprint to the same weight, only leaving a few notes on the top of each bundle. By arranging to give Powalski the money at the airport, he wouldn't have the opportunity to do more than look inside the case and would take Peter's word for it that everything was as it should be. After all, he had always followed instructions faithfully, and never let them down before.

So simple yet so effective!

Zac Powalski was scheduled to fly as second officer on flight WF254 and had acted as courier for the IRA before. He enjoyed the excitement and delighted in deceiving the crew, who were under the impression that he was a serious and rather pompous individual. He also enjoyed the ease with which he could trick customs. He generally carried a large suitcase on trans-Atlantic flights, whether he was smuggling or not, and the rest of the crew had learned to accept his eccentricity of taking so much luggage even on the shortest of stopovers.

When he was in his early teens, Zac had visited Ireland and been caught up in the aftermath of a bloody battle. He had been whisked out of danger before he'd had time to find out what was really happening, but the adrenaline rush was still as vivid now as it had been then. How he longed to be able to fight for what he believed in and keep one step ahead of the enemy. He had planned to become a GI as soon as he was old enough, but his application had been turned down on medical grounds.

His next love was flying, and, by falsifying his application, had got his pilots licence, and started work with WFI. He had started to smuggle on a small scale at first, and enjoyed the game of duping the authorities. This soon became a habit that was hard to break until Richard Wainwright discovered the false application form. He knew he had enough evidence to have Zac grounded for life and, always on the lookout for the main chance, Richard had Zac investigated by his own people and discovered his smuggling activities. He decided on a course of blackmail to make Zac do his bidding.

That he would come to like the man never even crossed Richard's mind, but a friendship blossomed between them, and for a long time they had enjoyed an easy and relaxed relationship, each helping the other and feeling confident in their dealings. They had regularly got drunk together and knew more about each other than most people. In fact, Zac was Richard's only close friend, yet there was no one in WFI who knew of their friendship. They didn't even acknowledge one another if they met on the concourse or in one of the restaurants.

There had been times when Zac had risked his career for Richard. He had smuggled items in and out of the USA, risking imprisonment and the loss of his reputation with the probability he would never work again. He loved the excitement of knowing he had an illegal package on board, and the ease with which he took it through customs and handed it over to whoever was waiting for it.

He had been surprised when Richard told him a member of the IRA would be on board WF254, and given him a brief description of Liam. He didn't like the sound of that, didn't like anything that couldn't be explained. He wanted to know why the shipment was being guarded and if they were expecting trouble. Richard was unable to answer his questions, but Zac felt uneasy about the whole situation.

Friendship only went so far, and if the need arose, Powalski would betray Richard to save his own skin. He knew Richard had enough evidence to have him convicted times over, but it also worked the other way around, and though he had not yet resorted to blackmail, it wasn't for lack of opportunity, but things weren't so desperate. When the time was right, he wouldn't hesitate to use Richard for his own ends.

There was little that went on in the world that the IRA was not aware of. They had some of the best brains in the country working for them and one of their main tasks was to raise money to fund their activities. With this in mind, they had set up an elaborate scheme for laundering whatever currency they were able to get hold of. There were a number of "safe houses" where their operatives could stay until the heat was off after so-called crimes had been committed, and these would also be used as collecting houses on a random basis. 90% of the merchandise intended for the IRA was transported through one or other of these addresses.

The premises were fronted by legitimate businesses, and Zac Powalski was aware of three in current use. One was a Shipping business, another a Barbers Shop and the third a Gym and Massage Parlour. They were all places where anyone could come and go as they pleased, and were run on a strictly legal basis.

Zac was told to take the money from flight WF254 to the Gym and Massage parlour.

Charlie Monroe swore as the persistent ringing of the alarm clock dragged him up from a deep sleep. He sat up and looked at his partner, stretched over three-quarters of the bed and snoring gently.

There was a time when he had admired her broad hips and full breasts, but of late she had been completely unable to rouse him, and he was beginning to tire of her. They'd had some good times together, but she had started to talk about marriage, and he had fled like a startled rabbit. The more she persisted in her efforts to make a permanent home for them both, the more he turned away, and he had started looking round for someone else. He now had his eye on a pretty young girl who had recently joined Wright Flights International, and they both worked at O'Hare International Airport, Chicago.

His partner moved in her sleep, revealing the firm strong breasts and dark rounded nipples that had first attracted him to her. Yes, it was a pity, but she would have to go!

When he finished shaving, he looked at himself critically in the mirror. His clear brown eyes were quick to laugh and he tried to ignore the laugh lines that were just starting to show, and the slight softening of his cheek muscles. His teeth had all been crowned and gleamed white against his tanned skin. No one would guess he had reached his half-century, and he was proud of his 50 years.

Yes, he was a good-looking guy, and knew how to turn on the charm. No one could be more attentive and caring, and he had a vast amount of experience in making girls fall in love with him. He certainly loved the thrill of the chase, and was sometimes disappointed when it was over.

An hour later Charlie was clocking in with the other ground staff at O'Hare International. He was due to work a double shift, standing in for one of his colleagues, and the prospect of 24 hours on duty didn't bother him. He had done it before. There had been a lot of talk in the press recently about long hours making people less vigilant, but he didn't agree with that. He was proud of his stamina. Lack of sleep didn't impede his judgment, and he prided himself on doing a good job.

As a senior member of the security team, his work took him into all sections of the airport, but he spent most of his time working in Terminal C. There were the usual number of passengers about, and he knew it would get quieter in the early hours of the morning, when he would be able to catch up on his paper work, and chat with his fellow workers.

He was always trying to think of different ways people could smuggle things aboard 'his' aircraft. In this way he was constantly on the lookout for anything unusual, or anything even slightly out of the ordinary. He had a gut feeling that had to be listened to, as it nearly always proved to be right.

He walked round the terminal, chatting to the cleaners and the catering staff, inspecting the washrooms and all the areas open to the general public. Everything seemed to be normal, yet for some reason he felt uneasy.

He thought about his domestic arrangements, and started to get excited at the prospect of yet another affair. He had been into the Personnel Office and found that the young girl, Mary McDowell, was working that evening and he would make it his business to speak to her. That had been the sole reason for taking on the extra shift, so he could make contact with her and invite her out. He had been cautious so far in his dealings with Mary, but he had read the signs, and felt she was ripe for his plucking.

Along with the rest of the security staff, he was irritated with Wright Flights International, and their insistence security had to be double-checked since that stupid interview on British television. The fact that they had never been involved in letting any hijackers or undesirables through security didn't make any difference. The chairman had spoken to them personally, and Charlie couldn't help laughing at the way the old man had tried to ignore the damage that could have resulted from the way the interviewer had tried to manipulate his son, but the seeds had been sewn, and he was concerned someone might target WFI to prove young Wainwright wrong. There was no mention of a bonus for anyone who prevented an attempt and that rankled with the ground staff, particularly those who had been instructed to double their vigilance.

Charlie had come across Wainwright junior on more than one occasion, and he had found him to be ineffectual and irritating. He had always been sure young Wainwright owed his present position to nepotism, until he'd had the opportunity of flying with WFI. He had been surprised at the quality and style of the food provided, and been told that since young Wainwright had taken over the catering arrangements, the quality and variety of meals had improved ten-fold.

As part of his training, Charlie needed to take a routine flight with each of the airlines operating out of Chicago, and he had flown to various parts of the United States until it was time to fly with WFI. He had been promised a first class stand-by seat on a flight to Paris, France, and he had looked forward to this trip more than he cared to admit. On the day of departure he was first at the check-in desk to monitor all that was going on. He was just getting ready to board, when a telephone call came to inform them his stand-by seat was needed by the chairman's son, and young Wainwright had arrived shortly afterwards, being escorted through the VIP lounge and onto the aircraft.

Maybe that was one of the reasons why he didn't like the man. Or maybe it was his effeminate manner, which contrasted strongly with Charlie's own masculine personality. Charlie worked out at the gym at least three times every week, tanned regularly on the sun-beds and was proud of his physique. Malcolm always looked thin and undernourished, and was seldom seen laughing and enjoying himself.

On one occasion when Charlie was on duty, a piece of luggage had been left unattended in the VIP lounge, and he had been sent to investigate. Malcolm, his father and his fathers' girlfriend were already in the lounge, together with a number of other people awaiting their various flights. They were asked to leave whilst the luggage was examined, and the look of panic on Malcolms' face made Charlie want to laugh, but when he heard the comments made by Mr. Wainwright and his girl, young enough to be Malcolms girl-friend, not his fathers', he realised for the first time how difficult it was to be the chairman's son, and Charlie gave thanks for the careless attention he had received from his own parents. At least they hadn't tried to mould him into something he was not!

———◂o▸———

For the fifth time that shift, unaccompanied luggage was removed to a safe area, where it had to be examined, and, if there was any suspicion of a threat to the airport it would be blown up.

The routine kept Charlie busy as he waited for Mary McDowell to clock on. She would be wearing her uniform, and looking particularly attractive. He loved to see a girl in uniform!

When she arrived, he 'just happened' to be walking back to Terminal C from the employees car park, and it was natural they should walk together. She showed her usual friendly disposition, and giggled when he asked her to go for a drink after work on the next occasion they were both on early shifts. She looked surprised, and her giggles turned into laughter. She gave her refusal without even considering the proposition.

Charlie wasn't used to being turned down. Generally women were delighted to receive an invitation from him, and he had never been laughed at before. He wondered for the first time if he had misinterpreted her friendliness, but on consideration dismissed this as being maidenly modesty. They talked in generalities until they reached the check-in desk where Mary worked, and parted on a happy note. Charlie decided to return later to renew his invitation.

The long shift wore on, and the terminal was particularly busy with flights departing and arriving every few minutes. Charlie was kept busy, and called yet again to the main concourse, where some more luggage had been left unattended. He ran into Terminal C, his walkie-talkie in his hand, only to be told the luggage had been claimed. He was starting to get annoyed at these false alarms, when he spotted Mary walking purposefully towards the security checkpoint. He was surprised to see her, as she should have been busy with flight WF254, due to leave at any minute. He asked her if everything was OK, and she nodded and said she was waiting to escort someone.

Frank Proctor had been flying planes for the past 30 years, and he loved every minute of his job. Although people said one airport was much like another, he had managed to visit many places of interest, and met many interesting people.

If asked what his hobby was, he would say people. Talking to them, dining with them, or just being with them. That was one reason why he enjoyed his job so much. Whilst in the cockpit, he had a co-pilot to keep him company, and the aircrew to see to his every need. When at the airport, there was the ground staff, and his colleagues from the various airlines that operated out of the particular airport he was in. That was one reason why he didn't like living alone. He got too lonely.

He was due to fly a routine flight from Chicago to Manchester. He had flown flight WF254 on a number of occasions, but he was particularly looking forward to this trip because of the cabin crew. Or, more particularly, one member. Frank had been married for nearly 20 years when his wife died of cancer. That was 4 years ago. He hadn't been interested in any other woman since that time, but recently he had started to take notice of Chrissie Faversham.

They lived in the same suburb of Chicago, and even though they both worked for WFI, they had not met socially until they were both invited to the house of a mutual friend.

Frank had been invited to share their Thanksgiving meal, and he rather resented the fact that Chrissie had been invited specifically to meet him. He didn't like to be manipulated. It wouldn't have been so bad if a few other people were there as well, but it seemed too obvious as they were the only guests. As a consequence he had been quite cold, almost rude, to her. Towards the end of the evening she had taken him to one side, and asked if she had offended him in any way. He told her it was nothing she had done, and to prove it he had offered to take her home.

A wagon had shed its load across the highway, and they'd had to spend a couple of hours waiting for the highway patrol to clear the area. It was during that enforced time of waiting that they started to get to know each other, and when they eventually reached her home, they made arrangements to meet again.

They had been going out together for almost eight months now, and the thought of seeing her again sent a tingle down his spine. They had a lot in common. They both loved the theatre and were keen on classical music. They liked nothing better than to go to an evening outdoor recital, and recently the weather had been exceptionally dry, and they had managed to attend a number of outdoor events which had not been spoilt with the rain.

Chrissie, too, had lost her partner to cancer, so they both knew the heartbreak of watching a loved one die, and the round of sleepless nights followed by weeks of anxiety. She had been determined she wouldn't get involved with anyone again, as she didn't feel she could cope with any more heartache if things didn't work out. Yet Frank was such fun. They did the things together that it was impossible for a woman to do on her own, and soon she found that friendship was turning into something stronger. She couldn't think of the future without including him in her plans.

She had married when she was at university, and within three years was the mother of two young daughters. The elder, Fiona, was herself at university in England, and the younger girl, Jane, was still at Fairfield Boarding School. It had been a hard decision to leave them at the school when her husband died. Life would be lonely enough without the extra heartache of not seeing her children during term time. Yet it had been their decision to remain at school, and not to interrupt their education.

Chrissie visited Jane when she could, and maybe the fact that they didn't see too much of each other made them even closer. Jane was delighted her mother had met Frank, and she hoped they would get married. She knew Chrissie was lonely, and found it difficult to meet people because of her shift work. Therefore, it was wonderful that Frank also worked unsociable hours, and they were able to arrange for them both to be on the same schedule a lot of the time.

Frank and Chrissie had just returned from a few days vacation, when they had packed their bags and taken off to tour around in Franks' Porsche. They had visited the Grand Canyon, and had an exciting day white water rafting on the Colorado River, but Chrissie was firm in her refusal to go Bungee Jumping and determined not to let Frank go either. They walked a lot and took an interest in the natural history of the places they visited as one day merged into another. It was on that trip that they first slept together.

Neither of them had realised just how much they had missed their partners. Their lovemaking was long and sweet and their relationship took on a subtle change. They now truly belonged to one another, and

Frank asked Chrissie to marry him. She knew in her heart that was what she wanted, but felt it only right to consult with her daughters before giving her answer.

Jane received the news with delight, and wished them both every happiness. She had already written to Fiona, and told her how suited they were, and knew she would love Frank. It was wonderful to see their mother so happy.

When Chrissie learned she was to fly on flight WF254, she had made arrangements to meet Fiona in Manchester. It would be good to see her again. Chrissie had been disappointed when Fiona had got herself a summer job in England, and did not intend to return home until the following Christmas.

Chrissie loved it when she flew with Frank, and was looking forward to the flight. Fiona would be waiting at the airport to meet them and they would be able to spend most of the 24-hour stopover together. She was sure they would all get on, and if so, she would tell Frank she would marry him. She knew that if Fiona didn't like him, then she would follow her heart and marry Frank in any case, but it would be good to have the blessing of both her children. After all, Frank would be their stepfather.

She was a little relieved that Frank didn't have any children, as she didn't feel confident at becoming a stepmother. She had seen too many second marriages fail because the wife did not get on with her new husband's children. When she married for a second time, she had to be certain it would last, and that she was getting married for love and not for companionship in her old age. It was the first time Chrissie was purser in charge of the cabin crew, and it was a good feeling to know she was flying with Frank. She knew him to be a good pilot, one of the best, and she felt relaxed and confident. It was years since she had felt so happy and self-assured. Everything seemed to be going right for her at last, and she could see nothing on the horizon that would spoil her happiness.

She arrived at the airport in plenty of time to prepare for the flight, and met up with the rest of the crew. Dave Branson was to be the First Class Steward and five stewardesses, Belinda Page, Sue Howser,

Hannah Weston, Effie Constantine and Paula Smith were there to look after the rest of the passengers. It was Paula's first transatlantic flight, but the rest of the crew were experienced and would need very little supervision.

Dave Branson had been upset when he was told Chrissie Faversham was to be the purser. He felt the job should have been his, but he had worked with her before and knew her to be a hard-worker, dedicated to her job and very capable. Perhaps his turn would come when Chrissie left WFI. He had been watching her recently, and knew she was in love with Frank. Company policy did not allow husband and wife to work together, and in all probability Chrissie would give up her job with Wright Flights International.

He was pleased with the rest of the crew. The only one he hadn't flown with before was Paula Smith. She had just started on the long-haul flights, and he was pleased to be working alongside her. He liked her delicate beauty and her short dark hair gave her an elfin look, which he found particularly attractive. Given the opportunity, he would try and take her out to dinner during their stopover in Manchester.

Belinda Page and Effie Constantine shared an apartment in down town Chicago. They hardly ever worked on the same flight and were both looking forward it. They had flown with Frank Proctor before, but were both in agreement in their dislike of the first officer, Zac Powalski.

Sue Howser had been a friend of Chrissies for many years, even before they both went to work for WFI, and she had known Dave Faversham, Chrissies husband, very well. She had, in fact, helped to nurse him through his last weeks of cancer, and she was delighted that Chrissie and Frank had got together, and seemed to be on the verge of marriage.

Hannah Weston had flown with Dave Branson once before, but didn't know any of the others. She had recently joined WFI after many years' experience with a rival airline. She knew each organisation worked in a different way, and was anxious not to do anything wrong. She was quite happy to be supervised by Chrissie, and was willing to learn the ways of WFI.

First officer Zac Powalski and Frank Proctor worked well together, although they weren't particular friends. Zac knew Frank was seeing Chrissie, and it didn't please him. He did not like the crew to be anything other than professional, and if there was a personal interest, it could make for a wrong decision if an emergency did arise. He had always made a point of taking a polite interest in his fellow workers, but never attended any social events for the aircrew. The only time he spent with them away from the aircraft was at the hotel during a stopover, and even then he kept himself to himself.

Once the briefing was completed, the flight crew boarded the plane and carried out all the usual checks. They had everything ready by the time the passengers were ready to board.

It was Chrissie's job to stand by the door and welcome them whilst her colleagues showed them to their seats. Frank stood by the open cockpit door immediately behind her, and placed his hand on her waist. She turned and smiled at him, and knew that they were going to have a good flight.

Zac Powalski was not happy about the way he had received the IRA money in the employee's car park. Anyone could have seen what was going on and he didn't like it. He had made certain the security camera was pointing the other way when he had taken the case from Callahan, but he hadn't had enough time to do more than open the case and look at the contents. Neither had he had time to phone Richard to get his acknowledgement of the new arrangements. Although he had never been let down by the IRA's organisation before, he still felt uneasy about the whole business. He was risking more than anyone else, and felt he should have been informed of any change.

He wasn't convinced by Callahan's reasons for being so late. He should have delivered the case to a pre-arranged place hours before Powalski was due at the airport. Instead, Callahan said he had been delayed by an accident, and only just made it to O'Hare in time to meet Powalski in the employees car park minutes before Powalski had to report for duty. He only had time to glance in the case, but everything looked normal, and he had to accept Callahan's word.

The first class passengers were boarded first. There was a man with an Irish accent, six FTF's – first time fliers – and four American businessmen. Two couples had been up-graded from economy, and were delighted at their fortune. The final two seats were reserved for a member of the staff of Wright Flights International and his guest. These last two passengers were late, and when the rest of the plane was fully boarded, they still hadn't arrived.

Zac Powalski listened to Frank talking to the Tower, and automatically went through the procedure prior to take off. It looked like being a routine flight, with no foreseeable problems.

The flight was likely to be delayed, and he didn't agree with inconveniencing the whole flight for the sake of two VIP's. If the passengers couldn't make the flight on time, they should wait for the next. Nothing was so important that hundreds of people should be put out for just two latecomers. Not only would the passengers and crew be thrown off their schedule, but also all the people waiting to meet them would have to hang around the airport, and business meetings could be missed or delayed. No, it wasn't a good thing to wait, but the decision wasn't his to make, and he would have to put up with whatever Frank decided to do.

They couldn't afford to wait too long, nor could they afford to leave behind such important passengers. Frank spoke to the WFI desk and was told the two remaining passengers were in the terminal, and would soon be ready to board. He made some derogatory comment about the privileges of being the chairman's son, and instructed the crew to prepare for take-off as soon as the passengers were boarded and the door closed.

When the chauffeur arrived at Malcolm's apartment David did all he could to delay their departure. Consequently they arrived at O'Hare International exactly 8 minutes before their departure time.

The chauffeur stopped the limousine outside the terminal building and Malcolm handed him the marked briefcase as David put the second briefcase on the pavement. He placed it in such a way that the chauffeur could not fail to see it when he got back into the limo. They made their way through to Terminal C.

A member of the ground staff was waiting to escort them to the departure gate. Mary McDowell was worried they wouldn't get there on time, and used her experience to cleave a way through the throng of anxious passengers.

At the ticket desk, they explained they only had hand luggage, and were waved on towards the security check. Malcolm thanked the chauffeur and put his briefcase on the conveyer belt. They watched it go safely through the machine, and David picked it up and started walking towards the gate.

The two men were busy talking about last night's boxing match, and apparently unaware they had left one of the briefcases behind, when they heard a shout. The chauffeur was panting along the corridor, the briefcase in his hand. He was known to most of the staff connected with WFI, and his concern seemed genuine enough. He tried to by-pass the security area and run down the corridor towards his employer. A security woman called him back, and told the chauffeur to join the queue of Japanese tourists who had just arrived in Terminal C. She stressed that all hand luggage had to pass through the x-ray machines.

"Mr. Wainwright. Mr. Wainwright sir," he kept shouting.

Malcolm turned and asked if it was someone wanting him. They saw the red-faced driver waving his arm in the air, and indicating the briefcase in his other hand.

"Oh, my briefcase!" Malcolm shouted remembering everything he had been told to say. "Bring it here quick man, or we'll miss the flight. We can't go to the meeting without it. Hurry man! The plane is about to leave, and for every minute of delay, it costs. We've no time to spare!"

The chauffeur wasn't sure what to do, and started to hesitate. What would happen if he tried to by-pass security? If he went to the back of the queue, then it would be certain that the two men would miss their flight, with the consequent problems and expense for WFI.

Charlie Monroe knew it wasn't right for the briefcase to miss the security checks, and he was just about to confirm his colleagues decision, when Mary asked them to hurry, and gave him such a dazzling smile, that it confirmed his first opinion of her reaction to his advances. He was tired enough to be willing to take the risk and ignore the possible consequences of such a request, so he grabbed the briefcase from the chauffeur. He didn't carry it through the security arch, as he knew his own weapon would set the alarm bells ringing, and it was company policy not to draw attention to the fact that the security staff was armed.

He ran down the corridor and handed the briefcase to its owner. He was rewarded by yet another dazzling smile from Mary.

"I hope you catch your flight, sir," he said as he gave the briefcase to Malcolm. "After all, you are hardly likely to hijack one of your own planes, particularly when you'll be flying on it!"

They all laughed.

"Have a nice day," he called after them.

"We will," David shouted back.

They ran to the gate where the ground staff waved them through, and boarded the plane. They were shown to their seats in the first class section, where Liam was already sitting.

As soon as they had fastened their seat belts the plane taxied from the gate, and joined the queue of other planes lining up for take-off.

Soon they were settling down for the long journey across the Atlantic, the briefcase safely on board.

— CHAPTER 6 —

The flight deck of the Boeing 767 was built for a 2-man crew, with one observer/navigator seat. The cockpit was spacious compared to some airliners, and was designed to the latest comfort and efficiency standards, using the most advanced ideas in information displays and digital technology. Both the captain and his first officer had many hours flying time on that particular aircraft, and they found it easy to fly. The plane was larger than David would have liked, given the choice, but quite capable of doing the job in hand.

Malcolm and David were shown to their seats as "Welcome to Wright Flights International" appeared on the overhead screens, to be followed by the usual safety instructions regarding emergency exits, life jackets etc. to be followed by a short WFI commercial stating how wonderful the airline was, and giving details of its various destinations.

The pilot introduced himself as Frank Procter and his first officer Zac Powalski. The cabin crew was under the leadership of the purser, Chrissie Faversham. He hoped everyone would have a comfortable flight, and assured the passengers that the crew was there to help them enjoy the journey.

David glanced round the cabin. The six FTF's were over excited and enthusiastic for their proposed holiday in the UK. They wanted to tell everyone that this was their first flight, and how they had planned and saved to go on the holiday of a lifetime, back to the UK to see where their ancestors had come from. The excitement and anxiety made their voices extra loud and they all seemed to be talking at once. David felt certain they would dine out for months on the story of how their plane had been hijacked!

Two men seated immediately in front of Malcolm and David looked like typical businessmen, resigned to spending hours travelling in order to get to their next meeting. They appeared to be with the two men occupying the seats immediately in front of them. He hoped they wouldn't get any trouble from that direction.

Liam sat behind and to his left and had an empty seat next to him. They didn't even look at each other; to all intents and purposes they were just people who happened to be travelling on the same flight. Two English couples occupied the last four seats, and they, too, appeared to be travelling together.

Malcolm kept looking at the empty seat next to Liam. If he was thinking of changing places David knew Liam would object. He had already spread his belongings out and was settling down for a long flight.

Dave Branson, the first class steward, was very attentive, being kept busy by the FTF's, who wanted to know everything that was going on and asked a lot of questions.

Chrissie and her colleagues were quick to assess the passengers. From experience they recognised those who were potential troublemakers. On this flight, there was the usual mixed bag, young children and babies, who always took more looking after than adult passengers. Bottles needed to be heated, and they needed constant attention if they were to be quiet and not disturb the rest of the passengers. Slightly older children could be a nuisance in the aisles as it wasn't reasonable to expect them to sit still for hours on end!

A party of old people would also have to be kept under close observation. The cabin pressure remained constant, but the older traveller was noted for registering even the slightest temperature change, and this sometimes caused problems. Also, they were loud in their disapproval of the youngsters running in the aisles and a diplomatic word here and there was needed to keep everyone calm.

A snack was served shortly after take-off, which gave the cabin crew the chance to speak to everyone. The majority were quite content to while away the journey, and had brought their own entertainment with them, and the constant chatter of voices could be heard from those who were travelling with friends.

Amy sat across the aisle from Jack, and was disappointed at the number of young families on board. She guessed how difficult it was keeping the children entertained on a long journey, but one advantage was that they had toys and games, and she hoped the refugees could make use of them.

Back in first class, Malcolm was nervous, and couldn't settle to anything. He sat by the window so that he would have to push past David if he left his seat. He said he felt like a prisoner, but David pointed out that most people wanted a window seat and he should stop grumbling. He tried reading for a few minutes, but his mind wandered and he abandoned his book. He tried listening to the taped music, but couldn't find anything that took his fancy. He couldn't settle to sleep, even though he must have been tired. He constantly picked at his fingers, and David started to get irritated by him.

He tried to talk to Malcolm to calm his nerves, but he refused to answer. He was behaving like a spoilt child rather than the responsible adult he was supposed to be. After a number of futile attempts at conversation, David felt the best thing to do was to ignore him, and so he settled down to sleep. He must have slept deeply, for when he awoke he felt refreshed and eager to get on with the job.

Liam also slept, but David knew from past experience that he was only catnapping, and would be fully awake the moment he was needed.

Chrissie Faversham was worried about Mr. Wainwright. She had never flown with him before, and was surprised how nervous he was.

He hardly spoke to the man he was travelling with, and deliberately turned his back on him. He was obviously irritated by one of the FTF's – a woman with a high-pitched voice that never stopped. The constant irritating titter was enough to drive anyone crazy, and even the little Irishman made some comment as he passed her on his way to the toilet.

At one stage, the captain left the cockpit and walked down the plane, talking to the passengers, and checking that everything was well. He stood by the galley and spent some time chatting to the purser.

The only time Malcolm showed any interest was when the main meal was served. He was careful in his choice of menu and enjoyed what he ate. He took particular note of how it was served, and even went so far as to walk down the main cabin to see if the other passengers were enjoying their meals. The little Irishman decided to stretch his legs at precisely the same time.

Jack watched with interest as Liam followed Malcolm through the main cabin. The look on Malcolm's face was comical when he saw Jack.

"I didn't expect to see you here," he said in a loud whisper.

"I never intended to spend the rest of my life in the US," Jack replied. "Of course I'm here. I've got to make sure everything goes to plan. You obviously haven't thought it through."

"You can't make me do anything I don't want to, and I hope I never see you again."

"You've said that before and look where it got you. Now be a good boy and return to your seat. You're disturbing the passengers."

Jack was afraid their conversation was being overheard.

Malcolm was about to say something more but thought better of it and returned to first class in something rather like a tantrum.

When the film came on, he settled down to watch. The comedy took his mind off his present predicament, and he even laughed aloud. He fell into an uneasy sleep before it ended.

As Malcolm slept, David took the briefcase out of the overhead locker, and went to the toilet. He put the handgun in his pocket and when he returned to his seat, Liam knew he was armed.

It was long after the plane had departed when Charlie Monroe felt the familiar gut feeling that something was wrong. Why was young Wainwright so late and why had he come from the main entrance and not used the VIP lounge? On a good day, when the terminal was empty, it might have been quicker but when it was busy there was no advantage. It didn't seem right. Something was wrong.

Charlie was on the point of going to see his boss, when he realised his part in allowing the briefcase to miss all the security checks. He kept telling himself it was only one piece of luggage, and a piece belonging to the man who would lose most if there were a hijack. He had already confirmed that the plane had left on time, with young Wainwright on board. Nevertheless, he would be happier once it had returned to Chicago.

He rang the chauffeur and was told that he had arrived at young Wainwright's apartment in plenty of time, but they had been delayed by a number of trivial things. He said he honestly could not remember how the briefcase came to be left on the pavement, and felt that Mr. Wainwright's associate must have left it there, assuming that the chauffeur would carry it for him. He had watched his passengers enter the terminal building before returning to the limo, and it was then that he had found the offending piece of luggage. All he could do was run after them, and hope he could catch up with them before they reached the departure gate.

Flight WF254 had been the last flight on Mary McDowell's shift, and as soon as the necessary paper work had been completed, she would be ready to go home. She was disappointed to find Charlie waiting to walk her back to her car and didn't know what to make of him.

She was in a bad mood hurrying back to the employees' car park, and not wanting to talk to anyone. She seemed nervous and Charlie wanted to know if he had upset her. When she said it wasn't that, he asked her out again. This time she was adamant in her refusal. She said her boyfriend would object, but again Charlie took it as an excuse, not believing she had a boyfriend and determined to let her get to know him better. He tried to kiss her hands, but got his face slapped instead. He was so shocked he staggered back and watched her get in her car and drive away. He rubbed his cheek with a thoughtful expression on his face. From his experience, young girls liked an older man because they had more money, more experience, and really knew how to give a girl a good time. He liked a girl with spirit, and decided to leave her alone for a few days, before trying his luck with her again.

Mary had only been working at the airport for a few months when she had suspected Charlie of looking out for her. He had sat next to her in the canteen too many times for it to be a coincidence. At first she had been pleased that someone was taking an interest in her, as she didn't know many people in Chicago. She had lived all her life in a small town in Ohio, and the move to a large city had been both exciting and lonely. She had found it more difficult than she expected to make friends and had been grateful for his attention.

Someone told her he was divorced, and known to have a succession of girl friends. She was told to be on her guard against someone who had a short temper and the reputation of being a ladies' man but Mary hadn't taken any notice of the advice, as it came from a girl whom she suspected of wanting to attract Charlie herself, and thought it a case of petty jealousy.

As the weeks progressed, though, his attentions became more marked. She did everything she could to let him know she didn't want to be anything more than a friend. But the more she tried to put him off, the more he seemed to be attracted to her. She got on well with the other people who worked at O'Hare International, and enjoyed the social events organised on a regular basis. It was one way of getting to know more people, and she was always sorry if her shift prevented her from going. It was at one of these gatherings she had first met Charlie, and he had gone out of his way to introduce her to lots of people, and she had been grateful. It gave her a nice feeling to recognise someone as she walked through the airport, and she was always pleased to stop and talk to him for a few minutes, but she never thought of him as anything other than a friend.

She found shift work difficult, being on duty when most people were out socialising, and sleeping when they were at work. It might not have been quite so bad if she worked the same shift all the time, but shifts were worked on a rota basis, so it was difficult finding time to fit in any activity on a regular basis. As a result, she found herself going about with people from the airport, people who also worked shifts, rather than friends made outside work. At least there was always someone on the same shift, and they could fit in shopping or a trip to the movies together.

The only person she knew well who didn't work at the airport was Carol Comyn, her flat mate. Mary had replied to an advertisement in the local paper, and she and Carol had become good friends. It didn't bother either of them that they didn't see each other every day, and they each respected the others' need to sleep at different times.

Mary was genuinely surprised when Charlie first asked her out. She didn't think he believed her when she spoke of her boyfriend, but there was no way she would go out with anyone of his age, and she remembered the warnings she had been given.

Carol laughed with her when they talked about Charlie, and Mary wished Carol could see him. He kept his hair really short, and looked more like a thug than an airport employee. Everyone on the staff knew he was armed, and Mary could guess what power it gave him. She felt sorry for the man, but that didn't give him the right to pester her. She was determined the next time he tried to walk her back to her car, or sit with her in the canteen, she would tell him straight she wasn't interested, and would he leave her alone.

Yet she had deliberately used him to hurry up the VIP passengers through security, being aware it was her responsibility to get them boarded quickly, and she had not hesitated to use his infatuation to speed them along. She had learnt that a dazzling smile could bring the strongest man to his knees, and she was young enough to enjoy the power such a smile could evoke.

Mary was very close to her sister, Sonia, and she missed her more than any other member of her family. She wrote long letters to her every week, and told her all about life at the airport, the remarks made by harassed passengers, and the comical things people did when they thought they might miss their flight. She also told Sonia about various people she had met, some of them quite well known, and others, like Charlie, that Sonia was unlikely to meet. Mary had a great sense of humour, and was very willing to share her thoughts about Charlie Monroe with her sister, and he was often mentioned in her letters. She made him sound like a character in a comic strip, and Sonia always enjoyed reading about him.

Mary was strongly attracted to Peter Callahan. She had seen him at O'Hare on two or three occasions before he approached her and asked her out. They had got on well from the start, and spent some part of every day together.

It was good to know someone cared for her, and she enjoyed the feeling of knowing there was always someone available to talk to and laugh with. She was proud of his dark hair and blue eyes, and enjoyed being seen with him.

Peter told her he worked for a firm of couriers, specialising in the transportation of valuables, but she wasn't sure exactly who or where, but he seemed to have plenty of money and the time to see her, whatever shift she was on.

When he asked her about the security at the airport, she was willing enough to talk about it, and told him everything she knew. She wasn't suspicious, even when he asked if she was willing to go away with him if he could lay his hands on a large amount of money. She joked about doing anything to make her rich, and he was encouraged to tell her a little of his plans. He begged her to listen and reserve judgment.

With some outside help, he intended to hijack a plane and hold the passengers to ransom. They always had a lot of money on them when they travelled, and he intended to rob them and get away with their cash and jewellery. He couldn't see how his plan could fail once they were airborne, and that was where Mary could help. He wanted her to get him on board a Wright Flights International plane and promised to share the spoils with her.

If he got himself into the Departure Lounge at Terminal C, and Mary could get him on a flight, it should be plain sailing from then on. They would have to choose a trans-Atlantic flight, where they would expect the passengers to be taking more cash than on a domestic flight. He would make the plane divert to Ireland, where he had friends who would help him get away. He told her that being of Irish descent, he had been useful to the IRA, and was involved with the American Irish in supporting his relatives back home and had no doubt they would look after him for as long as he needed.

Mary would have to leave Chicago once the flight had left, in case she was interrogated and her nerves got the better of her. They would meet up at a pre-arranged place as soon as it was safe for him to leave Ireland.

He asked her to consider his proposal, and let him know soon, as he was fed up with his life and wanted nothing more than to spend time with Mary, living the life of the rich and idle somewhere in the sun.

He assured her there wouldn't be any danger if she followed his instructions to the letter, and it would be easy for her to disappear. It all sounded so simple that Mary was tempted, and started to get excited at the prospect of having a lot of money.

They worked out just what they each had to do to get Peter onto an overseas flight, and exactly what they would do before and after its departure. They chose flight WF254, and once they were satisfied they had worked out every detail of their activities, Mary began to feel scared. She said she thought it would work in principle, but still was not convinced that she wanted anything to do with it. Peter told her she had a couple of days to think about it, but that he would go ahead with or without her. It was up to her to make it easy for him, and if she wanted a share in the money she knew what to do.

Whilst Mary was trying to make up her mind, another and better opportunity came Peter's way in the form of the IRA money he had been asked to collect for shipment on flight WF254. He couldn't believe his luck in using the same flight he and Mary had chosen.

Previously, he'd had plenty of time to deliver the money, but on this occasion he had been instructed to get it to Powalski immediately, making sure it was delivered in time for a flight that same day. He was to take it to the airport himself. That left him with the opportunity to delay as long as he could, and hand it over at the last minute. He arranged to meet Powalski in one of the employees' car parks just before he had to report for duty so that he would not be able to check the contents of the case. That way no one would know if some of the money was missing from the shipment when it was handed over.

Consequently, all thoughts of his previous plan were dismissed as he revelled in his new fortune. Things were going right for him after all, and, once the heat was off, he would be able to start a new life with Mary.

He felt it prudent not to tell her of this change of plan. He loved her, and the least she knew about the IRA the better for both of them.

She had spent many sleepless nights deliberating what to do about Peter's plan. She wanted the money, but she asked herself if it was worth the risk. She was a trusted employee, and if things didn't go according to plan, she could end up in prison. With a record, she knew she wouldn't be able to work for an airline again, and she loved her work.

Reluctantly she decided to tell Peter she was not prepared to help just yet, but needed more time to think about it. He had said he would go ahead without her if she refused to help, but if he was prepared to put it off for a week or two, she would be willing to do her part as long as she was told precisely what to do and when. She had to be clear in her mind that she wouldn't make a mull of it.

Mary didn't know why she was so nervous dealing with WF254. Peter had promised not to go ahead with their plan just yet, and she believed him, but it didn't stop her from thinking about what might have been if they had decided to proceed.

At first, everything was routine, and she told herself not to be stupid but when she was asked to hurry two late passengers to the departure gate, she was suspicious at this change from routine. Normally, if someone was late, they had to wait for the next flight as it cost too much to keep a full aircraft waiting on the ground. For one panic filled minute she thought it was Peter, trying to get on board in spite of her refusal to help, but when she was told she had to meet Mr. Wainwright junior, the relief almost made her sick.

She recognised him from a photograph she had been shown, and wondered how best to hurry him through the busy terminal. She saw Charlie Monroe looking at her, and turned her back.

There was a further delay when it was realised Mr. Wainwright junior had left a piece of luggage behind, and the red-faced chauffeur had come running onto the concourse. For a split second she did not know how to hurry them up. She sensed Charlie Monroe was about to insist they go to the back of the queue of tourists just arrived at the security check.

She didn't hesitate to use his infatuation for her to speed them along and turned to him for help. He saw the look in her eyes, which set his pulse racing. He knew he couldn't have been wrong in his dealings with her, and was prepared to do anything she asked.

When the time seemed right, David nudged Malcolm and told him it was time to start. He pulled away and snarled the word "No."

"Then I'll have to send a wire to the British police, telling them what time you'll be in Manchester, and asking them to meet us to search your briefcase, the one your chauffeur helped you smuggle through security."

"But that's your briefcase, not mine, and anyway, you can't get in touch with them from here!"

"Of course I can. The pilot's in touch with ATC and can easily relay any messages we want to send anywhere in the world."

"Ah, but you can't get to the pilot without my help."

"The purser will take a message if it's urgent."

"You've got an answer for everything!"

"Then get on with it. You know what you have to do. If you don't move by the time I count to ten, you'll regret it for the rest of your life, however short that may be," David said, digging the handgun into Malcolm's side.

"When did you get that," he demanded. "It should still be in the briefcase."

"Well it's not. I got it when you were asleep. Now don't make any more trouble. You know exactly what you've got to do, and now is the time to do it, so get a move on."

"I want the gun. Give it to me. What makes you think you should have it?"

"Sh, keep your voice down. You don't want to alert the other passengers."

"Then give it to me. I won't do anything without it."

"I wouldn't trust you with a water pistol, let alone one of these," David sneered. "Come on, or it'll be the worse for you."

"It couldn't get any worse!" Malcolm muttered.

Nevertheless, he reached up and pressed the button to call the steward. When Dave Branson arrived, Malcolm asked if he could take his friend into the cockpit. Dave said he would enquire and spoke to the purser. She thought it doubtful under normal circumstance, but Mr. Wainwright was the chairman's son and could be considered a special case. Therefore she went to consult with the pilot on the telephone that connected the cockpit with the galley.

Frank knew company policy forbade anyone other than crew from entering the flight deck at any time during a flight, and would have been steadfast in his refusal if Chrissie hadn't asked him personally.

She felt Mr. Wainwright wanted to impress his friend, and, being who he was, made him an exception.

The first officer indicated his disapproval at breaking company rules. These were made for a purpose, and the captain's first priority should be the safety of his passengers, the aircraft and all matters of security. Besides, Zac didn't want anything to interfere with his own plans, and told Frank not to let anyone in. He wondered if he would have hesitated if Dave Branson had made the request, and not Chrissie Faversham.

Frank thought of what the outcome would be if he didn't do this favour for the chairman's son. Mr. Wainwright senior could be a very hard taskmaster, and it was never good to go against his wishes, and, as Chrissie pointed out, there couldn't be any harm in letting them look round, and so, in the end, he agreed.

When Chrissie leant across him to speak to Malcolm, David was conscious of the smell of her expensive perfume, the brightness of her red hair and felt slightly uncomfortable at the closeness of her very white skin.

She asked them to follow her, and, at the cockpit door, tapped in the security number. It was 493Z. Chrissie introduced the pilot and second officer then returned to the main cabin, telling them to let her know when they were ready to leave.

"Thank you for letting us in," Malcolm said nervously, sitting in the observers seat immediately behind the second officer. "Er, you know I said there was no way hijackers could get on any of our planes? Well, um, er, I'm afraid I was wrong."

Malcolm was so unsure of himself that the captain turned round to look him fully in the face, and laughed out loud. He thought it was a joke.

That was when David took the gun out of his pocket.

"I'm afraid he's right," he said, pointing it straight at the captain's head.

Out of the corner of his eye David saw the first officer move. He raised his arm and struck Zac Powalski with the butt of the gun. He fell back into his seat, a trickle of blood running down the side of his head and a stream of abuse issuing from his mouth.

"Now that was stupid," he said, as Powalski wiped the blood away. "No-one will get hurt if you do precisely what I tell you. Do you understand that, all of you?"

"Well, do you understand?" he repeated as they looked at each other in disbelief.

"Yes," they both answered in unison.

"Yes," Malcolm echoed.

As David turned his attention back to the captain, Powalski twisted in his seat and punched him as hard as he could in the lower back, sending him crashing into the pilot and the gun flying across the flight deck. Quickly recovering, David grabbed the second officer round the neck, his thumbs pressing on the main artery to the brain. Powalski struggled, his arms and legs flailing in all directions until David lost his grip.

Malcolm picked up the gun and pointed it at the two men, his hands shaking. He started screaming to get out of the way so he could see to shoot straight.

There was little room to move in the crowded cockpit, and Malcolm made the mistake of stepping backwards. He caught his arm on the back of the seat and tripped. His attention was diverted as David made a dive and pushed Malcolm over, taking possession of the gun and knocking him to the floor.

Powalski was trying to get up as David swung round and hit him again with the butt of the gun. Blood was liberally splattered across the cockpit as Powalski lay squeezed between the observers seat and his own. The last thing he heard before he lost consciousness was Malcolm shrieking at the hijacker, and demanding the return of his gun.

"I thought you understood that I meant what I said!" David snarled. "I'll kill the next person who tries to do anything like that. And as for you, Malcolm, what do you think you're doing, trying to shoot the first officer before he's given us all the help he can."

"But I didn't. I was trying to shoot you!" he cried.

"Me? But we're in this together. Oh I see, you're trying to make it seem that you're here because we forced you, and not because you planned all this."

"I didn't! You made me come, you know you did."

"It's your word against mine," David shrugged. "Everyone knows I couldn't have done this without you, so let's see who wins in the end!"

"You can't say that. It's not true. You know you made me come. You forced me to use my position to get you in here. You know you did, and nothing you can say will alter that!"

"Well, however we did it, we're here and we're going to divert to Shannon airport, in Southern Ireland."

He got no response from the pilot.

"Now," he shouted, once more holding his weapon to the captain's head.

The pilot turned to look at David. He didn't want to do what he was told, and was trying to work out if he could afford to ignore him. He knew the safety of the passengers was his responsibility, and he really had no choice in the matter.

"That's better," David said, as he turned back to his instruments, and disengaged the automatic pilot.

"Since you've disposed of my first officer," the pilot said, "I trust you can give me the right co-ordinates to fly on."

"But of course. You didn't think we'd be unprepared for such an eventuality."

"What do you want me to tell ATC Manchester?" he asked. "They'll be following our progress, and will see any alteration to our course immediately we make it."

"Tell them you've got someone on board who's been taken ill. He must get to Shannon immediately, where he can get the necessary medication for his specific, and very rare, illness. If he doesn't receive this medication quickly, he will die. Tell them you intend to divert, and will arrange for an ambulance to be waiting to take him straight to hospital where a supply of his special medicine is always available in case of an emergency."

"What if they don't believe me?"

"It's up to you to make them believe you," David replied. "I'm sure you can convince them. It's not all that far out of the way, and seems to me to be a reasonable request."

"What am I going to tell the passengers?"

"The same, of course. Get that attractive red-head in here, and I'll tell her exactly what to tell the passengers, and when."

The pilot hesitated again. He hated having to involve Chrissie, but he wasn't in a position to argue.

Frank Proctor spoke into the phone, and soon Chrissie was squeezing herself into the cockpit. Although spacious enough for the flight crew, it was not made to accommodate three extra people, so to make more room, Malcolm was sent back to first class where Liam would be watching him closely in case he tried to do anything that could damage their plans.

Chrissie was appalled at what she saw, and tried to back away but David had anticipated her actions, and put the gun to her head. He told her that if she did everything she was told, then no harm would come to her or anyone else on board.

She nodded her agreement, and when David moved away from her, she asked Frank if he was all right. Chrissie then knelt to attend to Zac, who was beginning to come round. She wiped his face and helped him back into his seat. He was in pain and kept moaning.

She was sure he had cracked his ribs but hadn't any other broken bones. She wanted to go back to the galley for water and a first aid kit to clean him up properly, but was told he would have to wait.

As Powalski became aware of his surroundings, he tried to turn round and was stopped by a sharp pain in his chest. He groaned aloud, and was conscious of aching all over. What really annoyed him was that he had not managed to overwhelm the hijacker in spite of his best efforts, and it had all been for nothing – David was still in control.

The pilot headed the plane on the co-ordinates supplied by David, and Powalski demanded to be told where they were headed. On being told Shannon, he didn't know what to think. Was this another change in the arrangements that the IRA hadn't told him about? Did they want the money so urgently that they were prepared to hijack the plane without letting him know? If they had told him about this alteration to the original plan, he would not have been so vicious with the hijacker. What if he had overcome the man, and stopped the plane from diverting? That would have put an end to their plans, and serve them right for not keeping him informed. He felt fed up with the whole business, and wanted out. This was the last time he would do anything for the IRA if that was the way they were going to treat him.

When news of the hijack reached Richard Wainwright he took control of the situation. In his own mind he was convinced the motive was to steal the money, and his first suspicion was that Zac was involved. He had allowed himself to get too close to one of his employees, and was cursing himself for his stupidity. Always keep things close to home, his father had taught him, and do not trust anyone. He had used a tried and trusted method of shipping the money and nothing had gone wrong before. He couldn't see why it should have been different this time, unless he had been betrayed.

He called for everyone connected with Flight WF254 to assemble in the Board Room. He had to get to the bottom of this atrocity, and quickly. Every detail of the departure, passengers, security and pre-flight activities had to be gone through with a fine toothcomb. Anything that appeared different, even in a minute detail, had to be examined and the reason explained to his satisfaction.

He was faced with the loss of the largest amount of money ever raised for the IRA, and at the mercy of their secret network. He had to prove to them that he knew nothing of the hijack, and was doing his best to find the culprits. Suspicion was all the IRA needed before they acted – they weren't bothered about always getting their facts right. That they could make him 'disappear' without trace, he knew, and for the first time in his life he was truly afraid.

Richard was concerned for Malcolm, also travelling on WF254, and dismissed the suspicion that he could be involved. Richard had never left him short of money and didn't think he had the ability to organise a heist.

What did concern him was Malcolm's unknown companion. Who was he and why had they left Chicago in such a hurry? It wasn't like Malcolm to return home from the UK and go straight back. What had been so important to make him go without even cancelling his business appointments or letting his secretary know how long he would be away?

Was the unknown passenger forcing him against his will in order to steal the money? That posed another question. Who knew about the money and which flight it was going on? And why was O'Grady on board?

Richard had met O'Grady a couple of times before, and been surprised when he learned he was in Chicago. He had done as requested and met him for a few minutes. They had discussed the money, and O'Grady had said he would be travelling on the same flight to act as security guard. Richard wasn't to cause any fuss if things seemed to be going wrong and O'Grady insisted he would make sure the money got to its destination safely. Well, things had gone wrong, but could he really trust O'Grady to get the money to its final destination? He wasn't convinced!

For his own reputation, Richard had to treat it as a terrorist attack and ignore the money, but he was angry at having his plans changed, and not being kept informed of what was happening. It was as if the IRA didn't trust him any more.

On checking the flight manifesto, he saw that O'Grady's name was not on the passenger list and assumed he was travelling under a false passport.

Richard kept asking himself if he should trust O'Grady and do nothing about the money. He was in two minds whether to notify his contact in Ireland and tell him all he knew. But if O'Grady had hijacked the plane in order to get to Ireland that much sooner, then there really was nothing to worry about. On the other hand, if he let his contact know that O'Grady was on the hijacked plane, he could be in trouble for giving information about his activities that should have been kept secret.

The only other people who knew which flight the money was going on were Zac Powalski and Peter Callahan. Both had equal opportunity to steal the money, but Zac would have checked it before accepting it, which cleared Callahan.

He contacted the head of security, and asked for the surveillance tapes showing the passengers boarding flight WF254. He recognised O'Grady but could not get a look at Malcolm's companion. He didn't think he had seen him before.

It took him a while to realise that Powalski was carrying a brand new case. Why was that, when the other one was familiar to his colleagues and wouldn't rouse any suspicion? He called for the tapes from the employees' car parks, and saw Callahan's car drive in and park next to Zac's. He must have taken the money direct to the airport, where Powalski wouldn't be able to check it. Callahan must have handed the money over as the camera moved away to scan the rest of the parking area.

Richard decided to find out just what Callahan was up to. If he had taken the money then he would be dead meat, but not before the money was retrieved.

It was important to keep things running smoothly, and the routine work at O'Hare International was carried out quietly and efficiently, with flights coming and going as usual. Passengers travelling at that time were not aware of anything wrong.

— CHAPTER 7 —

After storming out of the airport, Mary took her time getting home. She enjoyed browsing round the shops and hoped the normality of this activity would help her stop thinking about Peter and what he wanted her to do. She still loved him, and the thought of going away together gave her a good feeling, but she wasn't sure she was willing to pay the price. If he could manage without her, then she thought she would be happy to share in his fortune. He was confident his plan would work, and was talking as if the money was already his. It would be easy enough to ignore how it had been obtained. After all, most passengers would have taken out sufficient insurance and those who hadn't would have learnt a valuable lesson.

When she eventually got home, she automatically turned on the radio before starting to write to Sonia. She told her sister she was thinking of going away with Peter, and hinted that he was hopeful of receiving a legacy and if all went well they would soon be in possession of a large amount of money, but not to get too excited, as nothing was settled yet!

Sonia would enjoy hearing about her latest shift, and she described in detail what had happened when the chairman's son had nearly missed the plane, and how she had been as surprised as anyone when Charlie Monroe had done as she had asked. Undoubtedly that had stopped the plane from being delayed, a very costly business, but she felt a bit guilty at having forced Charlie to do something so out of character, and thought less of him for being swayed by such a trivial trick.

She was wondering what to write next when her attention was drawn to the voice on the radio. It was describing how a plane belonging to Wright Flights International had been hijacked on a flight from Chicago to Manchester.

She sat at the table, her head in her hands, and let the tears run unheeded down her cheeks. All those people in danger, and she could have been responsible if she had helped Peter carry out his plan. For a full minute she wondered if he had gone ahead without her, but she had seen him near the security desk when she had gone to fetch the last remaining passengers, and she couldn't see any way he could have boarded the plane.

She spoke to O'Hare International, who confirmed flight WF254 had been hijacked, and everyone connected with the departure would be called in to give a detailed statement of all that had happened prior to take-off, emphasising anything that differed from the norm.

All Mary could think of was Mr. Wainwright's late arrival, and the fact that his luggage had not passed through the security check. She wondered if that could have any bearing on the case, but on reflection, realised how absurd it was to think that he could be involved. Even if he had smuggled something on board, it wasn't her responsibility. She didn't handle the passengers until after they had been through security. No, the responsibility was all Charlie Monroe's, if, indeed, that wretched piece of luggage was involved in the hijack.

However much she tried to reason with herself, she could not stop the feeling of panic that threatened to overwhelm her. She had never felt so frightened in her life, and common sense went out the window. Knowing herself to be innocent of any involvement didn't help. If all the facts were known, she could see how everyone would think she was mixed up with the hijack. She didn't know what to do, or where to turn for help.

Mary remembered Peter's saying if she wouldn't help he would go ahead without her, yet he had still been in the concourse when the last passengers had boarded. It seemed unbelievable that someone else could have had exactly the same plan for the same flight. It was too much of a coincidence. She knew Peter wasn't on board, but wondered if, after all, he had got someone else to do the job in her place.

She got no reply from his apartment.

Peter Callahan had mixed feelings when he heard about the hijack. He had already stolen the money, so a hijack by a third party would cover his tracks and he would be home and dry.

On the other hand, he knew about the way Monroe had been pestering Mary. He had seen the look that passed between them. He couldn't get it out of his head that Mary must have told Monroe about his idea and they had arranged the hijack together. He was surprised to learn she had double crossed him and gone into partnership with Monroe, but maybe he had more to offer her than Peter.

He wished he had never told her about his plan and was glad she didn't know about the money, now safely in a locker at the train station. His intention had been to leave Chicago as soon as flight WF254 had taken off, but he had decided to wait until Mary finished her shift. He knew he would have to move quickly, and tried to work out how long before the loss of the money would be discovered. Maybe a few hours, or longer if the hijackers kept the plane from landing at Manchester.

If the hijack really was a coincidence, and Mary had nothing to do with it, then she must have meant it when she said she would be prepared to run away with him. It gave him a good feeling to know that she was going along because she loved him, and not for the money, and he looked forward to going to New York where they could lay low for a few days or even weeks. Once the panic had died down, they could go anywhere in the world.

———◦———

"I've been trying to reach you," Mary said as she let Peter into her apartment later that evening. "I take it you've heard the news. I thought at first that you had hijacked the plane like you said, but you couldn't, unless you've got someone else to help."

"Of course it wasn't me! How could I, when I'm still here. I thought it was you and that Monroe guy."

"You must be out of your mind!" she cried, hardly able to believe what he was saying. "You don't think I'd anything to do with it. Don't be stupid."

"But I saw the way you looked at Monroe, and watched him take the case from the chauffeur."

She laughed and took hold of his hand.

"Do you honestly think I'd have anything to do with Charlie Monroe? You know how I feel about him, and I honestly can't see any reason why the briefcase could have anything to do with the hijack. There's no way Mr. Wainwright could have anything to do with it. He's got too much to lose if WFI's reputation is damaged. It's impossible to believe he could be involved."

She pleaded with him to believe she had not betrayed him

"What do you know about a large amount of money for the IRA?" he asked.

"What are you talking about? I know nothing about the IRA, except what you've told me and certainly don't know anything about any money. You're the one with IRA connections, and until you told me about them, I'd never given them a thought."

"Promise me you haven't mentioned the hijack plot to anyone, and particularly not to Charlie Monroe."

"I love you Peter, and wouldn't trust Charlie Monroe as far as I can throw him! I want to spend the rest of my life with you, and there is no way I would let Charlie Monroe come between us. I hate the man, and am trying to stop him from pestering me."

Peter wasn't sure if he believed her and a dreadful argument ensued. They were shouting so loudly the woman in the flat above banged on the floor to keep them quiet. Mary started to giggle and said all she wanted to do now was get away, and told Peter she was willing to give up her job and go with him. Peter realised his mistake, took her in his arms and apologised.

He told her he had abandoned the hijack plan because he'd come into some money from a different source, and intended to leave Chicago straight away. He had one or two things he still needed to do, and told her to pack a case and he would be back for her before midnight.

"But I can't go straight away. I need a few days to get everything ready, and particularly now, when I've got to report back to my boss."

"It's now or never, Mary. I can't afford to wait any longer. Either you come with me now or we forget about it."

"I want to come, Peter. I do truly, but if I go now, everyone's going to believe I was involved in the hijack. Can't we leave it for a day or two?"

"You've got until midnight to make your mind up. If you're not ready by then, I go alone."

Peter stormed out of the building.

Mary looked at herself in the mirror, and saw how pale she was. She felt dreadful; and with a big effort calmed herself down.

She didn't know what to do. Her first concern was to clear her name, and get at the truth. She needed to know that her boss didn't suspect her and to prove that she had nothing to do with the briefcase being allowed on board without the compulsory checks.

Besides, she was confident she could persuade Peter to wait for a few more days.

On reflection, she knew she had encouraged Charlie to let the briefcase by-pass security, but it was his responsibility, not hers. There was no way she could be blamed, unless someone really thought she was involved with the hijackers. She could readily see how her own actions could be misinterpreted, and once again she started to panic.

And if it were true she had unwittingly helped get a weapon on board, who would believe her? What would happen to Charlie Monroe if it were known it had been his mistake that had allowed a weapon to be taken on board? Would he try and incriminate her? Yes, she rather thought he would, particularly if it would save himself from coming under suspicion. What could she do to prove her innocence?

She nearly jumped out of her skin when the phone rang. It was her boss, asking her to attend a special meeting, and to bring with her a detailed report of everything that had happened in the lead up to the departure of flight WF254. This was her opportunity to put her suspicions in writing, and to prove herself innocent.

She started to write in earnest then. She had been told to keep to the facts, but it was difficult not to embellish them. She hoped she would have a chance to discuss the details personally, and convince her boss she had nothing to do with the hijack.

When Carol returned home, Mary was reading the final draft of her report, and was eager to discuss it. She told her everything she could remember and expressed her fears at being blamed for allowing the briefcase on board. Carol was quick to point out there was no proof a weapon was in the briefcase, and told Mary whatever method the hijackers had used, it was not her responsibility. Mary felt better and started to relax.

When the phone rang again, Carol answered and, as was their usual practice, the voice was switched to the loud speaker so they could decide whether they wanted to speak to the caller or not. Mary heard Charlie's voice, and shook her head. Carol told him Mary was out, and Charlie didn't leave his name.

"You've got to look out for that one," Carol said. "He doesn't sound very nice. I thought you said you'd told him you weren't interested."

"I did, but he doesn't want to take no for an answer," Mary said. "Don't worry though, I can take care of myself."

"Are you sure?" Carol continued. "Don't forget that you're a country gal, and not used to the wolves in the big bad city!"

"Oh yea. Do you think he's the only wolf I've had to chase off? Don't you believe it," Mary said. "I'd heard that men like girls in uniform, but sometimes it's ridiculous. Mostly it's just good-hearted fun, but you'd be surprised at the number of men who genuinely want to take me out. Most of them are travelling on business, having left their wives at home. I can't understand why someone who is just about to leave the country asks me for a date. You'd think he'd wait until he got back!"

"I thought you weren't supposed to date the passengers."

"You try and tell them that," Mary laughed. "If they're like that with us, when they only see us for a couple of minutes, just think what it must be like being an air hostess. Wonderful!"

"Like a sailor, with a man in every country! Is that what you'd like?"

"No, not really. If I hadn't met Peter, I'd choose a nice American guy. Someone who really loves me and has my welfare at heart. Someone I can rely on, laugh with, and generally have a good time with."

"I know where you can find just such a guy," Carol said, laughing.

"Where?" Mary asked enthusiastically.

"At the public library. Between the pages of a novel," Carol replied. "That sort of person doesn't exist except in a book. No-one is perfect."

"Well, a gal can dream, can't she?" Mary asked.

"Is that your version of the Great American Dream then?"

"It sure is. And Charlie Monroe doesn't come anywhere near fulfilling it." Both girls laughed.

When Charlie returned home after his double shift, he had been prepared to tell his partner to leave, but she had already gone, taking everything that took her fancy. The apartment looked empty. She must have had a removal company come and take away the large furniture. There was practically nothing left, and although the carpet was still down, the assortment of exotic rugs had gone. She had left the bed, but taken the good sheets. Charlie enjoyed cooking, and they had spent many an evening entertaining their friends to home cooked food, but he found she had taken his favourite recipe books, along with the dining table and six matching chairs. Gone was his music centre and all his favourite CD's. The good television set was also missing, and the small portable was sitting in its place.

It was one thing to tell her to go, but quite another that she'd gone of her own choice. How dare she walk out on him? She was little more than a thief! She'd taken far more than she would have been entitled to if they'd had a legal separation. He had been prepared to be generous, but now all he could think of was getting his own back.

He tried to contact her through her sister, but Charlie and the sister never had got on, and all he got from her was verbal abuse. He was pretty certain she had gone off with one of the men from work, and remembered her telling him someone was going to live in Canada. He came to the conclusion she had gone there with him.

However hard he tried, he found it difficult to put her out of his mind, and was surprised how quiet the apartment seemed. He even missed her undies drip-drying over the bath.

After a long time, he forced himself to relax. He felt uncomfortable, and remembered the incident with young Wainwright, and that cursed briefcase. Over and over again he went through the events of the day, some elusive memory lurking in his mind. Come what may, he couldn't find any logical reason for young Wainwright's behaviour. It still didn't feel right. Yet he couldn't think of anything he could do to alter the situation. He knew the plane had got off on time, but his shift had finished before it was due in Manchester, so he hadn't heard whether it had landed safely.

Charlie made a conscious effort to put it out of his mind, and showered and changed before going out for a meal. He returned to his apartment, and opened a bottle of wine. He drank the first glass quickly. The second he savoured, and tried to get interested in something on the television, but his mind was too active.

He couldn't believe he'd been so stupid. He paced up and down the room waiting for the news, and his worse fears were realised. The plane hadn't landed at Manchester. There were reports it had been diverted to another airport. Within minutes the phone was ringing, and his boss was on the line asking to see Charlie in his office immediately.

As he drove himself to the airport, Charlie wished he hadn't had quite so much wine. Red wine always did affect his stomach, and he should have known better. It annoyed him he couldn't drink as much as he used to, and felt it was a reflection on his manhood.

The interview with his boss didn't go well. It was made worse by a phone call from the chairman, demanding to know what had gone wrong and how the hijacker could possibly have gotten onto the plane. Charlie escaped at last, with orders to have a complete report on the boss's desk within the next couple of hours. Heads would roll for this days work, and he was determined he wouldn't be the scapegoat. After all, there was no other reason than his gut feeling to believe the weapon was smuggled aboard in young Wainwrights' hand luggage.

He went home and for the hundredth time went over the events of the previous shift. He wrote everything down, however insignificant, until he had a pretty fair account of what had happened. He put a lot of the blame on the chauffeur, finding it strange that he hadn't handed over the briefcase until after the passengers had gone through the security check. He wasn't as innocent as he would have them believe!

When he returned to O'Hare International for his next shift, he went to his office and read through his report for the umpteenth time. He wasn't completely happy with the result, but it would have to do. He made a note of his suspicions regarding young Wainwright not using the VIP lounge, and wished, in hindsight, he had told his boss as soon as he'd felt uneasy. He was conscious of the fact he would have looked a fool if these suspicions proved to be groundless, but perhaps it would have been preferable to the possible outcome of the situation as it was.

He had convinced himself that Mary McDowell had been an accomplice in the hijack. She had been sent to take his mind off what was happening, and to coerce him into allowing the briefcase to bypass security. Cunning. Very cunning. And it had worked! If it had been anyone other than Mary, he would not have listened, and the briefcase would not have got on board the aircraft.

It had to be Mary. She had to be in league with the hijackers. He would not believe that it was his one and only lapse from professionalism that had allowed a weapon to be smuggled on board, if it was, in fact, in the briefcase, which had as yet to be confirmed.

If it was proved she was innocent, which he very much doubted, then the blame would be entirely his, and he would be fired on the spot. There was no possibility of his ever getting another security job, and there was nothing else he could do. He had been lucky to get this one. They had been lenient with him when it was known he had served time for beating up his ex. He was too old to join the forces, and he didn't have the academic qualifications necessary for an office job. He worked hard and was proud of his advancement from junior security guard to his present position, and now it was all threatened because of her. He would have to do something about it. He felt no remorse at putting the blame at her door. If she was guilty, and could take the blame away from him, then he would make sure everyone knew it was her fault. After all, he could easily get another girl! He would have to admit he had been wrong to take the briefcase from the chauffeur, and accept any decision his boss thought fit, and hoped he wouldn't lose his job over it.

As he handed in his report, he told his boss of his suspicions about Mary McDowell. He said he hadn't written anything down because he wasn't sure what to do about it. He had nothing particular to go on, and didn't want to cause any trouble for her, until he had some sort of proof she was involved.

His boss was pleased with his attitude, and told him to make a confidential report on all his suspicions, so everything could be investigated. The source of any information received against any other member of staff would be kept confidential.

Perhaps over a meal and a bottle of wine, Mary would unwind, and tell him what had happened. With this intention, he phoned her apartment, only to be told she was out. He didn't leave his name.

His thoughts returned immediately to the hijack. Mary couldn't have done it on her own, so who was she working with? Suddenly an elusive memory came back to him in a blinding flash. The man standing a few feet away from Mary and watching what was going on was Peter Callahan, the man who had been sacked from WFI for embezzlement.

So that was it! Mary had said something about a boyfriend, and he had never dreamed she could have been in league with Callahan. It was well known he would do anything to harm the Wainwright family and Security had been told to keep an eye out for him.

And what of young Wainwright? Was he in it too? Did he know the briefcase contained the weapon necessary to hijack the plane? What was in it for him? Charlie mulled over these questions until he came to the conclusion that young Wainwright must be in partnership with Mary and Callahan.

He was surprised Mary had helped young Wainwright, and wondered where they had met. But young girls, he knew, were ambitious, and she was no exception. She must have met him somewhere, and was trying to get promotion by helping the boss's son.

Charlie ate his lunch in the staff canteen. Everyone stopped talking when he walked into the room, and he knew they were discussing what he'd done in Terminal C. There was only one topic of conversation, and he was asked a lot of questions. He left as soon as he could, and returned to his desk. He listened to the national news on his portable radio, and learned that the hijacked plane had been diverted to Ireland.

Charlie realised that Mary was his biggest threat, and he set about trying to find out all he could about her. He already knew she shared a flat on 32nd Street, and if he went now, he could be there and back before he would be missed. He didn't clock off, no point in giving up an hours pay, and everyone was used to his wandering about the terminal. Unless there was a call put out for him, no one would know he had left the premises.

Mary was surprised to hear his voice on the intercom. Even though Carol had gone out, she decided to let him in. She released the front door and told him to come up to the second floor. She wouldn't let him know of her fears, and would try and be calm about the whole affair.

She took him through into the bedroom and told him to sit on the bed whilst she continued to apply her make-up. He asked if she had heard the news of flight WF254, and she said she thought it very exciting! Of course, she felt sorry for the passengers, but she couldn't wait to get to the airport to find out more about it. Perhaps that was why Charlie was there, to tell her the latest news?

"No, it isn't!" he said. "I'm here to find out your part in it, and how they got a weapon on board."

"My part in it?" she queried, keeping her back towards him and looking at his reflection in the mirror. "You're not suggesting that I had anything to do with it, surely. All I did was process the passengers through the gate and onto the plane. I have nothing to do with their luggage or anything. By the time they got to us they had already passed through security."

"Had they?" he asked. "Everyone? Had everyone passed through security before you took charge of them."

"Yes, of course. They always have before they get to the gates."

"And everyone you saw was at the gate, were they?"

"Yes, of course. Oh, except Mr. Wainwright, but he doesn't count. Anyway, he'd already been through security when I took charge of him. He's not under suspicion, surely?" she asked.

"Why not? So far as I know, he's the only one who didn't have his hand luggage checked."

"Oh, no, surely not," she said, turning to look straight at Charlie, a frown marring her pretty face. "But it was you who took the case from the chauffeur and gave it to him. It was your fault it didn't go through the X-Ray machine."

Again she turned her back on Charlie as she continued to apply her lipstick. "I can't understand why you think I'd anything to do with it," she continued.

"Who begged me to hurry? Who's been giving me the come-on all these weeks, just so as I'd do what you ask at that particular moment."

"But that's ridiculous. I don't know what you're talking about."

"How long have you known Peter Callahan? Did you introduce him to young Wainwright? Which one of them took you to bed? Or was it both? Or was it just a business arrangement? How much did they pay you?"

"Oh no you don't, Charlie Monroe," she replied, furious that he knew of her connection to Peter. "You aren't going to try and involve me in all this. You know it was your fault Mr. Wainwright didn't put his hand luggage through the security check. If a weapon got on the plane that way, there's no one to blame but yourself, and whatever you might do or say, you won't be able to incriminate me in this business. You and you alone, are to blame."

"But what if I can prove otherwise? You've been seen talking to Callahan," he guessed, "even though WFI have instructed everyone to keep away from undesirables. What if I put a case together that's so strong there's no way out for you? What if I can prove you were involved? That you, Callahan and young Wainwright were in this together? Is young Wainwright the boy friend you keep talking about? Did he promise marriage, or were you just going off to have a good time together for a few months?"

"Stop, stop," she shouted, trying to keep control of the situation. "I don't understand any of this. Why should I want to go away with Mr. Wainwright when I've never met him before today, and of course he didn't pay me anything. Why should he? All I did was escort him and his friend to the gate. There was nothing more to it than that."

"You try and stick to that story my girl, and I'll blow a hole in it large enough to fly a jumbo jet through it! If you've only just met young Wainwright, then you must have been planning this with Callahan ever since you started working for WFI. Was it your idea I should do a double shift, and be so tired I was less vigilant than usual? Have you been giving me the eye all these weeks so I'd do as you ask at that particular moment in time? Were these all your ideas, or did you dream them up together?"

"I don't know what you're talking about. I've told you the truth when I say I've never met Mr. Wainwright before. I don't see why I should have to prove that to you or to anyone else for that matter. And what do you mean about me giving you the come-on. I've done nothing of the sort. You're the one who's been coming on to me. Why should I want to go out with you?"

"Are you denying all the conversations we've enjoyed together, and the cups of coffee? Coming it a bit too strong, my gal."

"No, of course we've talked, and had the odd drink in the canteen, but that's all. There was nothing in that, I can assure you."

"Oh come on, woman. You've been leading me up the garden path for too long now, and I accuse you of being an accomplice in the hijack."

"No, no, no, no, no," she sobbed, clutching at his arm. "You've got it all wrong. I've told you the truth, and this truly is the first time I've seen Mr. Wainwright. I even had to look at a photograph of him so I would recognise him when he got to the airport."

"That was very clever of you," he sneered.

"It wasn't. It's the truth," she continued, "and as for being nice to you, I felt sorry for you. I knew you were divorced, and thought you might be lonely. There was nothing more to it than that. Good heavens, you're old enough to be my father! I've never thought of you in any other light."

"Your father!" Charlie raised his arm and hit her across the face.

Mary started to scream, and he put his hand over her mouth. She tried to pull it away, and bit his finger. With a loud curse he let her go.

"Don't hurt me," she sobbed. "I'll tell you the truth if you promise not to do that again. Peter and I did talk about hijacking a plane and holding the passengers to ransom, but the more we looked into it, the more difficult it seemed, and we abandoned it. That's the honest truth, and we never had anything to do with today's hijack. I swear that's the truth."

"I don't believe you," he said and hit her again.

"I don't care what you believe, I know it's true. And if you're thinking Peter did it without me, you're wrong there, because he was in Terminal C minutes before the plane took off. Our plan would only work if Peter was on the plane." She rubbed her smarting cheek and got as far away from him as she could.

"You were trying to see if your plan would work, and make me look a fool! I will be the one accused of helping the hijackers if it is proved the briefcase is involvd. You are to blame for everything that's gone on today, and I mean to prove it!"

"Well you can't," she cried. "I had nothing to do with it, and the truth will come out in the end."

Something snapped inside him, and he lost his temper, as he hadn't done in years. There was enough truth in what she said to persuade him she was telling the truth. That meant the whole of the blame would be placed on his shoulders, and he couldn't bear the consequences.

He hit her again and again, seeing nothing but red and hearing nothing but the blood pounding in his ears.

As quickly as it had come on, his temper left him. He looked down at the limp body lying across the bed. He felt numb inside when he realised what he'd done. If she reported him to the police, he would be sent back to prison. He couldn't stand that. He often wondered how he had survived the last time, and knew he wouldn't survive a second term.

Her pulse was weak and uneven. He got hold of one of the pillows, and covered her face. It only took a few minutes for her to die.

Panic seized him. He looked round the apartment and wiped everything he had touched. He read the report Mary had written for the staff meeting. There was nothing in it about him that they wouldn't know from other people. He couldn't find anything that might be difficult for him to explain.

He couldn't remember anyone having seen him enter the building, and he was still clocked on at work, so no one could prove he had left the airport.

He opened the door slightly, and listened. Everything was silent as he ran down the stairs and out into the street. He returned to the airport undetected, and somehow managed to keep busy until the end of his shift.

Peter Callahan rang Mary's bell shortly after Monroe left the apartment building. He got no reply so rang the bell of the apartment immediately above hers and to his relief, the door was released and he entered the building. He didn't wait for the elevator, but ran up the stairs to the second floor and banged on Mary's door. Again there was no reply, and the door was firmly locked. He shouted to Mary, telling her to let him in, and apologising for losing his temper earlier. Feeling totally frustrated, he sat down on the floor, leaning back on the apartment door and waiting for her to return.

He started to lose his temper again. He had given her over an hour to make up her mind, and she had deliberately gone out so as not to see him. The news of the hijack had spoilt everything, and he supposed she must have been called in to work to give an account of the events leading up to the departure of flight WF254. She was more concerned at clearing her name than going away with him. Perhaps he hadn't made it clear that they would start over, with new names and new identities. He didn't want anyone to trace them, and their new identities would protect both of them from unwelcome attention.

The fact the apartment was empty was confirmed by the sound of the telephone ringing, and as no one answered, he realised there was nothing more he could do. He kicked the door in frustration, and was walking towards the elevator when the woman from the apartment above came down the stairs and asked Peter if he had rung her bell. She accused him of entering the building under false pretences, and said he would have to leave, as she had already spoken to the janitor. Peter called the woman all the names he could think of, and ran down the stairs and out into the street.

Mary McDowell was late for the meeting. That was unusual, because she had always been a good timekeeper. Her boss got no reply when he phoned, and was starting to get worried about her when the head of security came into his office. He told him of Charlie Monroe's suspicions, and the fact that Mary hadn't come into work confirmed his misgivings.

Two members of security were sent round to her apartment to find out what was wrong. There was no reply, but the janitor let them enter the building, and they looked through the keyhole of the apartment. Everything seemed to be in order.

They asked the Janitor to ring them when either of the girls returned.

Carol arrived home and let herself in. She was annoyed to see the mail still on the table. Surely Mary would have taken it when she went to work.

She went into Mary's room, and found her on the bed.

The police arranged for the body to be taken away, after giving the apartment a thorough search. They wanted to know if Carol knew of any visitors that day. The person who had committed the crime hadn't broken in. The murderer had entered by the front door, and therefore Mary must have known her killer.

Back at the airport, Charlie tried to act normally. He forced his mind to think of nothing but work, completely blocking out the events at Erskine House on 32nd Street. If he did think of them at all, he convinced himself no one knew he'd been there.

Thank God he hadn't clocked off. He had the perfect alibi. No one knew he had phoned Mary earlier, as he hadn't left his name, and the girl who shared the apartment wouldn't have recognised his voice. He was optimistic he wouldn't come under suspicion.

The shift progressed slowly. Everyone was talking and speculating on the hijack, and Mary's part in it. Had she helped the hijackers to smuggle the weapons on board? Why had she run away?

Until the plane could be examined and the crew interviewed, there wasn't much they could do at O'Hare International. Time would reveal the truth, and until then they would have to be patient.

Life at Terminal C continued at its usual hectic pace.

— CHAPTER 8 —

"I will allow the passengers to leave the plane as soon as we've landed." David said to Captain Proctor. "They will be quite safe so long as they do as they are told, and no one tries to be a hero. It is important to keep the passengers calm and the purser is to tell them the second officer has been taken ill, and we will be making an emergency landing. There is no need for alarm. They will be taken on to their destination at the earliest opportunity."

The captain contacted ATC Manchester, and although they were surprised at his request, he was able to convince them it was literally a matter of life or death. The second officer had to be taken to hospital at all possible speed.

"You promised the passengers will disembark at Shannon," Captain Proctor said after he had finished speaking to Manchester. "What about the crew?"

"They stay on board, I'm afraid." David answered.

"Along with the little Irishman, no doubt!" Chrissie remarked.

"But of course." He smiled sweetly at her. "That goes without saying. And Mr. Wainwright? Yes, definitely Mr. Wainwright. I wouldn't like to leave him behind. It would be a shame to stop him from enjoying the fun!"

"The poor man's at his wits end," she said. "It would be kind of you to let him leave."

"No, Mr. Wainwright is too useful. Maybe later. Who knows!"

"What are you doing after the passengers leave?" Captain Proctor asked.

"Take on enough fuel to get us to our final destination," David replied.

"So you don't intend to stay in Ireland?" It was more a question than a statement. "If you really mean to let the passengers go, then at least let the cabin crew go as well. Don't put them in danger."

"Sorry. We can't manage without them," David replied.

"What do you mean, you can't manage without them? What more do you want than a plane to take you to wherever it is you want to go?"

"As to that, it's on a need to know basis. And at this moment in time you don't need to know. But really there isn't any need for concern. Once our mission is completed, you can carry on as if nothing happened."

"I'll go with the Irishman Miss Faversham mentioned," Powalski volunteered, "and make sure your instructions are carried out. I can oversee what's happening on the ground, and arrange for the plane to be refuelled."

"You'll stay where you are until I tell you otherwise," David sneered.

"But I can be useful on the ground. As you know, there's a lot riding on my getting into Ireland quickly, and I'll be willing to do exactly what you say."

"What are you talking about?" Frank wanted to know. "You're not really going to help these guys?"

"Shut up Frank. You don't know anything about it."

"You bastard! You're in league with them."

"Shut up and concentrate on getting us down."

"You bastard!" he repeated. "You bloody bastard! You'd endanger the lives of everyone on board for your own ends. I've never liked you, but I didn't think even you could be this bad!"

"Shut up! You don't know anything about it!"

"Neither do I," David said. "Why should we let you go?"

"We both know it's imperative I get to Ireland quickly, and this is the result. A little surprising and unexpected, but nevertheless a good arrangement. No-one will get hurt and the job will be finished sooner than planned."

"What job? What are you talking about?" David wanted to know.

Powalski looked at him in bewilderment. Surely it couldn't be a coincidence they were going to Ireland, and this really was a hijack and nothing to do with the IRA?

"But surely you're in this with O'Grady? Isn't he the Irishman Miss Faversham mentioned?"

"What's he got to do with you?" David demanded.

"He hasn't told you?" Powalski laughed until his cracked ribs made him stop. "It's a wise man who knows his friends!" he taunted.

David was thoroughly confused. He wanted to speak to Liam, but if he left the flight deck, he would never get back in and the pilot would continue to Manchester, and arrange for the police to meet the plane and have him arrested. His only course of action was to follow their plan, land in Shannon and take it from there. Once the passengers had left the plane, he would have the opportunity to speak to Liam and find out what was going on.

Chrissie left the cockpit and called the cabin crew together. She told them what had happened and asked them to get ready for an unscheduled stop.

There was a buzz of disbelief from the passengers when she announced the plane had been diverted. The next few minutes were spent reassuring them that everything would be fine. The four businessmen in first class were shrewder. They had noted the comings and goings and knew one of the passengers was still on the flight deck. They wanted to know what was really wrong. Chrissie told them the first officer was sick and asked them not to let anyone else know. There was no point in alarming everyone.

David listened to Captain Proctor speaking to the control tower at Shannon. They were not used to receiving unscheduled aircraft, and were reluctant to allow them to land. It was only when the captain told them the first officer was ill they became more co-operative. They had flight WF254 on radar, and gave them the co-ordinates to approach.

A steady descent brought them in sight of the Emerald Isle. The land was still covered in an early morning mist, but as they got lower they could make out the green fields and beautiful golden beaches.

They could see a number of planes on the ground, and one taxiing to the end of the runway ready for take-off. The section used for passengers was separated from that used for freight, and they could see a freightliner being loaded with containers.

They had to circle the airport until the outgoing plane took off. David remained in the cockpit, sitting in the observer's seat. The plane made a good landing and taxied to the end of the runway. He needn't have worried, as it was the smoothest landing possible. Captain Proctor was a good pilot!

Chrissie picked up the intercom, and welcomed the passengers to Ireland. She apologised for any inconvenience, assuring them the delay would be as short as possible. She asked everyone to remain seated. Her voice was steady, but her hands shook as she held the mouthpiece.

ATC told them to wait in one of the lanes off the main runway until an ambulance arrived. This took about twenty minutes, by which time the passengers were standing in the aisles stretching their legs, and moaning at the delay.

A set of steps was towed out and manoeuvred into place. Chrissie opened the door to admit two medics, who went straight to the cockpit. They could see the second officer had been beaten up, and turned to look at the pilot. Frank Proctor indicated the hijacker, who was leaning against the bulkhead, the pistol held menacingly in his right hand and a balaclava covering his face.

"Thank you for coming," David said. "You will now tell the tower that you want the passengers to leave the plane before you can remove the second officer, in case his illness is infectious."

They started to argue, but Frank intervened.

"For heaven's sake, do as he says and let the passengers go. They'll be safer on the ground."

"But why?"

"Don't ask questions, just do as you're told and no-one will get hurt."

"What do you want me to say?"

"Exactly what I've just told you. You think it would be safer for everyone if the passengers left the plane before you try and remove Powalski. Tell them to send enough buses to take them to the terminal. Once they've left, you will use the ambulance to take him to hospital."

The captain asked again if one of the cabin crew could leave with the passengers, and David agreed to his wishes.

"Then let Miss Faversham go," he requested.

"Nice try, Captain," David replied, "but no. Let one of the junior ones go. How about that pretty dark haired girl? What's her name?"

"Paula Smith," Powalski replied.

"Then Paula Smith it is."

Zac Powalski was disgusted that Frank had tried to save his girl and not one of the other members of the crew. That showed how wrong it was to get involved with your colleagues. He, Zac, would have chosen the youngest person to accompany the passengers, and was in agreement with the hijacker on that one point.

"Can someone get my case out of the locker?" Powalski asked, still sure that he was about to leave with the money. "I want to take it with me when I go to the hospital."

The hijacker must have been trying to hoodwink Frank with his denial of the money, but Zac wished the IRA had let him know what was happening. An ambulance was waiting to take him off the plane, and whatever happened, he must take the suitcase with him. The IRA was going to great lengths to get the money into Ireland days before they would have received it if they had followed their original plan. They were obviously desperate to get their hands on it, and if they wanted to play games, who was he to stop them? So long as no blame was attached to him, he would go along with their games.

Once again Chrissie called the cabin crew together in the forward galley, and told them that the passengers were to leave the plane and Paula Smith was to go with them to make everything look normal. Buses had been called for and should be arriving shortly.

Paula couldn't believe her luck. The possibility of being hijacked had never been foremost in her mind, although preparing for such an eventuality was a routine part of their training.

She had been as stunned as anyone when informed of the present situation, but she had been prepared to remain on board with the rest of the crew. Now she had the opportunity to leave, and all she could think was how pleased her partner would be! She knew she would be in the front line of criticism from the passengers, but even that was preferable to remaining on board.

Chrissie handed her a piece of paper with the seat numbers and descriptions of David and Liam. She was unaware that Amy and Jack were involved. She told Paula to keep it hidden from the passengers, and to give it to the authorities. It would be helpful in finding out who the hijackers were.

As if it was the most natural thing possible, Chrissie announced over the intercom that WFI apologised for the inconvenience, but the passengers would have to leave the aircraft for a short time.

Coaches had arrived to pick them up and take them to the terminal. Some of them murmured their surprise that the plane wasn't taking them to one of the gates, and started asking each other questions.

Chrissie assured them there was no need to worry, and told everyone to leave the plane in an orderly manner, allowing the people with special needs to disembark first. She told them to leave their hand luggage, and take only what they would need for a short stopover in Ireland.

Malcolm jumped up out of his seat and pushed his way through to the forward toilet, the one nearest the exit door, and locked himself in. He knew David was still in the cockpit, and didn't want Jack to force him to stay on board. If he waited in the toilet, Jack wouldn't be able to get to him down the crowded aisles, and his way would be clear to leave.

Most of the passengers were grumbling about the inconvenience, and worrying about missing their connecting flights from Manchester. The cabin crew was kept busy answering their questions, and assuring them that Wright Flights International would compensate them for any inconvenience.

The parents traveling with children were advised to take as much as they could conveniently carry. Once again it was the FTF's who made the most noise. They had watched the steps being put in place, and wanted to know why they weren't being taken to the Terminal. The steward tried to placate them, but nothing he could say was acceptable. They were scared of what might happen to them, and insisted they never wanted to fly again. If they were made to leave the plane at Shannon, there was no way they would get back on board, and insisted they be taken to England by boat.

They were particularly nervous, and Dave Branson tried to reassure them. He said it was only a short flight from Shannon to Manchester, but they were adamant in their refusal to fly ever again. Knowing that he was not to deal with them again once they had left the plane, he washed his hands of them and went to help someone else. As he walked away, they said they would write to Wright Flights International to complain about the way they had been treated, and the unfeeling attitude of the cabin crew.

Liam had seen Malcolm go into the toilet. It wasn't his intention to let him get off at Shannon and put the whole mission in danger. He knew him well enough to know he would tell the authorities everything he could to save his own skin.

He waited outside the toilet until he heard the lock sliding open and, pushing the door, put his foot in the jamb to stop Malcolm from closing it again. Malcolm tried to shove him to one side, and would have squeezed his way to the front of the queue if Liam hadn't stopped him. Malcolm gave Liam such a look of loathing that it made him chuckle.

"Go and sit down again," he told Malcolm. "It isn't time for you to leave just yet. You can do no good by trying to run away."

"And who are you to stop me?" Malcolm asked, trying once more to push him out of the way.

"Why, I'm a friend of yours. The three of us are in this together, so there's no need to panic. We'll continue our journey shortly."

"No, you can't stop me," Malcolm replied. "I'm getting off now, and if you don't let me through I'll scream." Malcolm raised his voice, and started to get the interest of one of the passengers.

"Anything wrong, mate?" he asked.

"He's eaten something that doesn't agree with him," Liam answered, leaning towards Malcolm as if he was concerned for his welfare, but in fact poking him in the stomach until he doubled up. "I was wondering if it was something he ate on the plane, or if he'd felt ill before we left Chicago."

"I think he'll be more comfortable if he returns to his seat for now," Liam continued. "Can you let us through?"

Liam tried to get hold of Malcolm's arm, to guide him back to his seat, but Malcolm stamped on his foot, and retreated into the toilet, pulling the door shut. He locked it again and refused to come out. Liam shrugged his shoulders and sat down whilst the rest of the passengers prepared to leave.

He was ready to stop Malcolm if he tried again.

When the last passenger had left, Liam, Jack and Amy each put on their balaclavas. Chrissie and Liam went into the cockpit leaving the door open, whilst the rest of the cabin crew and the two medics were made to go to the back of the plane. Jack and Amy stayed with them, each guarding an aisle, and making sure no-one spoke. Malcolm remained in the toilet.

The coaches were shielding the plane from the main terminal

buildings, and the authorities were unaware that a bowser had driven out from the freight area and was in the process of refueling the plane.

When this was complete, the driver left his vehicle at some distance from the plane, and climbed the steps to be met by David, still wearing his balaclava. With a wink, the driver was ordered to go into the galley. Out of sight of everyone else, Callum undid his overalls and took out the rifle, the second handgun, the wire-cutters and the rope ladder that had been left in his keeping.

He was noisy in his demands for a signature for receipt of the fuel, and tried to push through to the pilot or first officer. His way was barred and he was getting ready to push the hijacker aside, when David grabbed hold of Chrissie and held the gun to her head, saying he would shoot her if Callum did not do as he was told.

When Liam entered the cockpit, Powalski recognized him from Richard Wainwright's description even though he was wearing a balaclava. Powalski acknowledged his presence with a slight nod. Frank saw the look that passed between them, and demanded to be told what was going on. Liam remained silent as Powalski tried to explain that it was nothing to do with Frank, or WFI.

If everything had gone according to plan, Frank would never have known anything about Powalski's involvement with the IRA. Usually their arrangements were meticulous, and Zac couldn't understand why this assignment had been botched from the start.

The first indication that things were not right had been at the airport, when the money had been handed over in the staff car park, leaving him no time to check the contents. A quick look had revealed bundles of notes, but he hadn't been able to count them.

Then there was the hijack. It had to be the IRA, but hadn't they trusted him enough to keep him informed of their activities? They had used O'Grady, known he was going to be on the flight, and here he was now, standing over Powalski and not helping him. When Zac asked him to explain to the pilot what was happening, O'Grady remained silent, giving nothing away, and making Zac look a fool.

In spite of his aching ribs, Powalski tried to get his case out of the crew's locker, but was pushed back into his seat. O'Grady told him to stay where he was.

They could hear Callum demanding to see the pilot or first officer, as he needed a signature for receipt of the fuel. Callum was still protesting when the two medics were sent forward, and the three of them were shoved out of the aircraft and the door closed and at the first opportunity, as Liam's attention was distracted, Frank Proctor jumped him, and would have succeeded in throwing him out of the cockpit and slamming the door if Zac had been willing to help. As it was, Frank was forced back into his seat, accompanied by a series of oaths from Liam.

"Everything OK?" David shouted.

"Nothing I can't handle," was Liam's reply.

"Why, Zac?" Frank asked. "Why is it more important to help these bastards and go against all your training? What's in it for you?"

"Shut up, Frank. It's nothing to do with you."

"You know you've killed your career. You'll never work for an airline again. Even though I don't like you, I must say that you're good at your job. Why throw it all away now?"

"I might have to work with you, but I don't have to talk to you," he replied, turning away.

"Now, now, children that's enough," Liam said. "We'll be leaving very soon now, and we need you to put your differences to one side, and fly us out of here. And there's no need to ask where we're going, because you'll find out soon enough."

"But I'm getting off here with the medics," Powalski insisted.

"In your dreams, man," Liam replied laughing.

"But that's what was said. That's why the ambulance was called, and I've got to get my case off now. Isn't that what this is all about?"

"Just do as we say, and everything will work out right in the end."

"But ..."

"I've told you, do as we say, and you'll have no more worries, oh, except trying to find a new career!"

"But ..."

"Now that's enough. I don't want to hear any more of your "buts". If you two work well together, as you have so far, then it will be good for everyone. If not, I don't want to be responsible for the outcome."

Powalski couldn't make out what was happening. If the hijack was part of an IRA plan, why hadn't he been allowed to take the money off the plane? If it was a coincidence, then what was he to do with the money? He couldn't afford to lose it, and knew the IRA would hold him responsible if it went astray. And now Frank new he was involved in something that went against WFI. That was unfortunate, and could lead to his being dismissed. That was the last thing Zac wanted, and he would have to try his best to explain things to Frank's satisfaction.

Then there was Richard Wainwright. Was he trying to double-cross him? Zac didn't trust him any more, and wouldn't put anything past him. He would have to bide his time, not get into any more awkward situations, and keep a watchful eye on what was going on.

The coaches were starting to move away when the noise of the planes' engines nearly deafened them, causing panic amongst the occupants. Some of the more nervous passengers started to scream and all of them covered their ears to protect them from the noise. When they realised they hadn't been hurt, they started to shout their grievances. Paula told them the plane was being taken away because of a fault, and as soon as it was repaired they could continue to their destination.

That satisfied most of them, until someone shouted that it was taking off. The poor girl didn't know what to say, and assured them it was necessary for the plane to go in search of the required part.

The passengers main concern seemed to be their luggage, which was fast disappearing into the distance.

Soon everyone was sitting in the terminal with hot drinks. Discussion was rife as it gradually dawned on them that the plane had been hijacked. The fact they were all safe didn't stop the hysteria, and it was a long time before they were able to relax. There was nothing they could do but wait, and mourn the loss of their luggage. They were told no one was allowed to continue their journey until they had all been interviewed, and only then would alternative transport be provided.

An announcement would be made at Manchester to the effect that the plane had been diverted. People meeting passengers would be advised of the estimated time of arrival later in the day.

All available airport employees were called in to help deal with the passengers, and one by one they were taken away to be questioned until a picture of the days events started to emerge. They hoped to get a description of the hijackers, and some indication as to where the plane was going, how many people were on board, and the reason why the plane had been hijacked in the first place.

Paula told them everything she could remember, and tried to describe the hijacker. As she hadn't spent much time in first class, she couldn't give an accurate description. He had boarded the plane with Malcolm Wainwright. The plane had been delayed a couple of minutes, but not long enough for them to miss their take-off slot. She had seen nothing unusual on the flight, until it had been diverted. She had understood it was something to do with the second officer being taken ill, until the purser had told her the true situation.

She handed over the paper Chrissie had given her, and the information made it easier for them to get descriptions from people sitting near the hijacker.

Paula didn't know of anyone else who might have been involved, and was surprised to learn that an Irishman and a young couple had also remained on board. She knew about Malcolm Wainwright and the purser's speculation that he was being forced against his will.

By comparing the passenger list with the people in Shannon and the information supplied by the purser, they were able to name the four missing passengers, and as they were unable to find any information about them, it was assumed they were travelling under false papers.

When questioned about Mr. Wainwright, Paula said she believed he had persuaded Captain Proctor to let him take his friend onto the flight deck. After they had landed, he'd gone and locked himself in one of the toilets, and she'd seen him come out when the passengers were getting ready to disembark. He had spoken to someone, and Mr. Wainwright had turned back and locked himself in again.

She was asked to describe this other passenger, and gave a fair description of Liam.

Paula felt sure that none of the cabin crew had any idea of what was going on before the actual hijack. Until then it had been a quiet routine flight. If they had suspected anything was wrong, then there was no way anyone would have opened the door leading to the flight deck. A telephone was used to communicate with the rest of the crew, and when meals were being served, a code number had to be used to allow the door to open. Only the person in charge of the cabin crew knew the code, which was changed with every flight. Paula couldn't say why the two passengers had been allowed access to the flight deck, and could only guess that it was because of Mr. Wainwright's position in the company.

ATC notified all other airports, and a watch was kept for the pirate plane and from then on it was tracked for the whole of its journey.

It was inevitable the press should hear of what was going on, and it was soon on the national news. They confirmed that the passengers were safe and unharmed. Speculation was rife as to the final destination. Only time would reveal the true location, and the authorities spoke confidently of apprehending the passengers who had remained on board. It was with their usual sensationalism they announced that one of the hijackers had been identified as Malcolm Wainwright, the son of the chairman of Wright Flights International.

This last piece of news reminded them of the boast made a few days earlier, that WFI were the safest airline to fly with. This put a whole new light on the situation, and, together with the fact that the passengers were all safe, there was renewed speculation this had been done to spite the chairman, rather than for any other, less acceptable reason.

Some of the papers were making light of the situation. They played down the fact that the hijackers had been armed, since the weapons had only been used as a means to an end, and hadn't been fired. They speculated on how they could have been smuggled on board. Why had the hijackers demanded coaches to take the hostages to the terminal? Was it to help them? Was this another means of showing that they were acting in a humane way, and making a statement rather than a criminal act?

They interviewed a man from the Freight Company, and Callum was loud in his condemnation of the hijack. He said he'd been working in the garage, when he'd been told to take fuel to the unscheduled plane. Yes, it was unusual, as his company usually only dealt with freight planes, but the situation was not normal and he could understand why they didn't want the plane to go anywhere near the main terminal if there was someone on board with an infectious illness. He had received instructions over the phone, with no accompanying paperwork, so had risked the infection to get a signature on his delivery note. That was why he had entered the plane, quite unaware of the danger he was putting himself in. He hadn't seen anyone well enough to identify them, and the one person he had contact with had been wearing a balaclava. He hadn't been able to take his eyes off the handgun. It was all a nightmare and he wanted to put it out of his mind.

The door to the flight deck had been open, and he'd seen the pilot and co-pilot in their seats. He guessed there was someone else with them, but couldn't see who it was. Everyone else was sitting at the back of the plane, and he was quite sure two of them wore balaclavas. The medics would have had a better sight of them. He'd been surprised to be allowed to leave the plane, but as he hadn't seen or heard anything he didn't think he was a threat to the hijackers.

He also said he had been told to put enough fuel in the tank for a long journey, and wanted to know who was going to pay for it.

In hindsight, he wished he hadn't gone anywhere near the plane, and refused to supply the requested fuel, but he would do everything in his power to apprehend the hijackers, and offered his full co-operation to the Garda.

— CHAPTER 9 —

David Renfrew gave the captain the co-ordinates to fly away from Ireland, and he put the plane back on automatic pilot. The cockpit door was fastened open and David, Liam and Jack took it in turns to stay on the flight deck to stop a recurrence of the trouble with Zac Powalski.

Liam handed the second hand gun to Jack. He was told to stand guard over the pilot and first officer as David wanted a private word with Liam. There was no need to tell him not to use it except in an emergency.

"What the devil do you think you're playing at?" David demanded once they were out of earshot of the people on the flight deck.

"If you told me what you're talking about, then maybe I could tell you," Liam replied.

"What are you and Powalski up to?"

"Is he the co-pilot?"

"You know bloody well he is! Stop trying to get out of it! You're up to something, and I want to know what."

"Well now, what makes you so sure?"

"He asked if you were on board."

"Did he now! How exactly."

"He called you O'Grady, and asked if you were the Irishman the purser had mentioned."

"Did he now! Well, well. And how did he know I was here, and me with a false passport and all."

"That's what I want to know."

"Who'd be telling him it was me? That's a surprise then, him knowing who I am and why I'm here."

"So there is something I don't know about! Tell me or I'll bloody strangle you, you shagging bastard!"

"Calm yourself down, me friend. There's nothing for you to bother about."

"Nothing for me to bother about? When you're plotting something with him that I know nothing about?"

"That's it, me friend. It's best if you do know nothing about it."

"We can't have secrets on a mission like this. Come clean, or I'll ..."

"Or you'll what, me friend?" They stood facing each other, their voices raised and attracting the interest of everyone else. "Shoot me? Blow me brains out together with the whole plane. I don't think so." He dropped his voice to little more than a whisper. "We're here to rescue Pam Crichton, and for no other reason. Don't you go and spoil what we've achieved so far. There's no need for you to know about me other interest, because the less you know the better for you and I swear it won't interfere with your plans."

"Come on, Liam. We shouldn't have any secrets from each other, particularly now. What could you possibly be doing with that creep over there?"

"Well, if you insist, we're just delivering a little contraband."

"Who to?" David wanted to know.

"Now, that I wouldn't like to say," Liam replied, turning round and trying to walk away.

David grabbed his arm and swung him round until they were facing each other.

"Why not? It must be something serious if you're not willing to tell me about it."

"Because, me friend, the less you know the better for you," Liam said looking him straight in the eyes.

"How can you even think of doing something underhand when Amy and Pam are involved?"

"Well now, as I see it, these are two completely different jobs. There's no reason for one to stop the other. We can collect Pam first, then after we get back to Manchester we can deliver the goods as arranged."

"What can you possibly be smuggling into the UK? All that I can think of is diamonds. Is that it?"

"Nay, diamonds have to be sold on, and on the black market don't fetch their full value. No, this commodity is more easily disposed of."

"Not drugs? I know how you feel about them. I can't believe you've become a drugs pusher."

"Quite right. I can't abide those who ruin other peoples' lives for their own profit. No, it's not drugs, tobacco or anything like that."

"Then it's got to be money! But who would want you to bring cash into the UK from the States? Good God, don't tell me it's for the IRA. You don't want to get mixed up with them."

"But I am, and have been for many a year. We have our contacts in the States, and they're able to supply us with the necessary funds for our work. It just happens that we've got a shipment on this flight, that's all."

"That's all? You'd risk your life, all our lives, to help those shagging bastards?"

"Now, there's no need to get nasty. You wouldn't understand, even if I tried to explain. It's inbred, something that goes back a long, long way. I don't get involved on the front line any more, but am useful in other ways."

"I don't believe you! Are you telling me that when you were in the army, you were working for the IRA? Even when we were posted to Ireland?"

"Well, that just about says it all. I might have passed on certain information, but I never put me mates in danger. What sort of a person do you think I am?"

"I'm beginning to wonder," David could hardly believe what Liam was saying.

"Oh man, don't let your temper divert you from the main purpose of this mission. We've got to continue and not let anything stand in our way."

"Where is it? This stuff you're smuggling?"

"Powalski has it somewhere."

"Where?"

"Now, that I'm not sure of. But when he tried to get off at Shannon, he wanted to take his case with him. What exactly did he say?"

"Something about having to get to Ireland quickly and knowing who your friends are."

"Sounds about right for him."

"What does it all mean?" David asked. "You've got to tell me if we're going to finish this job together."

"OK I'll tell you. Don't say I didn't warn you. You won't like it, but we, the IRA, have a big job in hand and need the cash to pay for it. That's where our American friends come in. They raised the cash and arranged to send it over in one consignment, and, purely coincidental, chose this flight. Powalski was given the money and managed to get it on board. Most probably in his case. He was to take it to a contact in the UK, who was going to pass it on to me. It's my job to get it into Ireland. That's all."

"You're joking. The last thing we want is to get involved with them. How could you let this happen?"

"I saw the funny side of it! Here I was, waiting for the money and not knowing when it would be delivered, and there you were, wanting a plane. You chose WF254 not me," he lied, "and when I went to see my contact last night, he'd also chosen WF254. Surely you can see the funny side."

"No I can't. All I see is more complication that you could have avoided. We're supposed to be mates, and I don't even trust you now."

"Be serious, David. You can trust me on this. After all, I did get Amy and Jack into the States. Without my help, this whole project would've come to nothing. Besides, if Powalski hadn't been so foolish, you wouldn't have known anything about it. I would have received the money as planned, and you'd be none the wiser."

"I'm not happy about this."

"I can see that, me friend, but the best thing you can do is forget it. Come on man, don't let your temper distract you from the main purpose of this mission. We've got to continue and not let anything stand in our way. You can't stop what's already happened, and it's not advisable to meddle in the affairs of the IRA. Powalski's a fool and should be shot for this days work. He's not supposed to know my identity, let alone blab it about the place. There was only one person who knew I'd be on this flight, and he must have told Powalski. I'll have to sort that out later, but in the meantime I'll make sure Powalski doesn't bother us again and cause any more trouble."

"You do that, and remember, I'll be right behind you, and, friend or no friend, I'll put a stop to any more secret dealings!"

The cabin crew was told to sit at the front of the main cabin, far enough away from each other to prevent conversation. The curtain dividing first class from tourist was pulled open so they could see each other, and Malcolm remained locked in the toilet.

Thirty minutes into the flight, David issued a new course. This time they were flying on a direct line to Italy.

"What will happen to us?" Captain Proctor wanted to know. "Do you intend to let us go, like you did the passengers?"

"That depends entirely on you and the crew," David replied. "If you do what we tell you, then you won't have any problems. Don't get me wrong, though. If any one of you tries to become a hero, or to overpower us again, then we'll have to retaliate. We're prepared to sacrifice the crew to get our own ends, and we'll do so without hesitation."

"And what of Mr. Wainwright? He seems to have his own ideas. Is he going to spend the whole time in the toilet?"

"He'll come out soon enough when he starts to get hungry," David replied. "Meanwhile he's as well off in there as anywhere. I take it he can't do any damage from in the toilet?"

"No," Powalski replied. "If he did, he'd set the alarm bells off. Are you worried about him?"

"Not in the least," David said casually. He couldn't afford to let anyone think they could get at him through Malcolm.

He glanced into the first class cabin, where Liam, Jack and Amy were discussing the day's work. So far so good!

Jack wanted to know what David and Liam had been arguing about. Liam refused to tell him, and David told him to mind his own business.

"But it is my business!" Jack responded. "We're in this together, and we've all got a lot to lose if things go wrong. Is it anything to do with Liam meeting Richard Wainwright last night?"

"What the devil do you know about that?" Liam demanded.

"I'd gone out for a walk when I saw you across the street. I saw Richard Wainwright get out of his car and stand talking to you for a few minutes before he drove off again."

"Why didn't you tell me about this earlier?" David wanted to know.

"You were in the cockpit. This is the first chance I've had to speak to you. I've kept an eye on Liam, and don't think he's done anything else, but I want to know why he's made contact with Malcolm's father, and what they were talking about.

"I thought we could rely on you, Liam," Amy said twisting her hands together to stop them from shaking.

"You can," Liam assured him.

"I thought it suspicious you were so willing to come along and now you've betrayed us!"

"You're wrong. I came because I believe in what you're doing, and I wanted to keep an eye on things in case you didn't meet up with

David. You couldn't have managed on your own. If it wasn't for me, you'd still be in the UK."

"No we wouldn't. We'd be on a plane out of Manchester at this moment. We're not entirely dependent on you! We can do things on our own!"

"We can spend all day speculating on what might have happened!" David interrupted. "I think you'd better tell them, Liam. They've a right to know."

"No. Just understand it's got nothing to do with the hijack. It's completely separate and it won't affect us in any way. It's something I've been planning for a while, and it's purely coincidental that flight WF254 has been used for more than one purpose."

"What purpose? Why won't you tell us?"

"Because there's no point in giving you information you shouldn't have. Information that could harm you if certain people found out."

"People like Richard Wainwright?" Jack wanted to know.

"There, you've hit the nail on the head! Take my advice, and don't get involved with him. Keep out of his affairs or you'll regret it."

"You think it was him who shopped you to Powalski?" David asked.

"No-one else knew I'd be here. It has to be him. When we finish this job, you can leave him to me. I'll make sure he doesn't bother any of us again!"

Jack had to be content with what he had been told, as it was obvious David and Liam were not going to tell him any more. He resented being kept in the dark, and determined to find out what they were up to. After all, it could be useful to him in the future.

Richard Wainwright had told Powalski that O'Grady would be keeping an eye on things, yet he had not been allowed to deliver the money when they were in Ireland, and he wondered what O'Grady was playing at. He was obviously one of the hijackers, which didn't make sense unless the money was unloaded with the passengers. Was he planning to keep it for himself? If so, Zac would do all he could to stop him. In the meantime, he would do as his captain told him, even though it made him feel physically sick. He thought it wrong for the captain to co-operate so fully with the hijackers. Not only was he prepared to make polite conversation, but was trying to joke with them as well! He had only made a half-hearted push to overpower them and had tried to get his girl off the plane instead of that lovely young stewardess, Paula Smith.

He thought the hijacker had shown one weakness. Malcolm Wainwright. He would have to think how he could turn that to his advantage.

"Tell me what drives a man to do what you've done," Frank waned to know as they sat back in their seats, leaving the auto pilot to fly the plane.

"I've done nothing to endanger lives, if that's what you mean," Powalski replied.

"But you're up to something with the hijackers, and it's obviously gone wrong. Why else would they beat you up?"

"It's nothing to do with that. OK, I wanted to get something into Ireland, but we're not there now and I don't know where we'll end up."

"Do you give me your word you've nothing to do with the hijack?"

"Absolutely."

"What about this man, O'Grady?"

"He's a double crossing bastard. OK, we've got something we're doing together, but not this and I don't know how he could let his partner beat me up."

"I'm glad he did! After what you've done, I'd do it myself, given the opportunity!"

"You wouldn't, if you knew what's really going on!"

"Then tell me."

"OK, so I'm taking something out of the US and into Ireland, but it's never caused any problems before."

"You fool. How can you get away with it without involving the rest of the crew, or WFI for that matter?"

"I've been successful before."

"Not on my flights, I hope."

"Whenever necessary."

"Who are you working for?"

"You don't want to know."

"Come on, Zac. Can't you hear the hijackers arguing? It sounds to me the left hand doesn't know what the right hand's doing. Is this O'Grady man involved in something with you, that the others don't know about?"

"It looks like it. I'm beginning to think we really have been hijacked, and my smuggling's got nothing to do with it."

"We've got enough on our plates at the moment and I need you to help me get through this hijack safely, but let me assure you, Zac, that as soon as we return to Chicago I'll do everything in my power to have you grounded."

"I wonder what made them do something as stupid as this?" Frank asked after a long pause. "What could be so important that he's prepared to sacrifice himself and his friends?"

"I've no idea, and care even less," Powalski replied. He ached all over and could hardly concentrate on what he was doing, let alone make speculative conversation.

"They've not even bothered to cover their faces, except when the medics and the mechanic were on board. They appear to know exactly what they're doing, and everything's been well organised. And the double-dealing Irishman? Do you think we're taking him somewhere? Could he be the reason for this hijack? What do you think?"

He got no reply.

"Do you think he's an IRA terrorist? Are we going to take him somewhere where he can't be extradited? Or do you think they could be doing this to disprove Mr. Wainwright's boast that WFI is the safest airline in the world? I know the Board were afraid someone might take it as a challenge. Have you any explanation?"

"No," Zac replied, indicating he had even less interest. "If it's their idea of a joke, and they're doing it to prove WFI wrong, then I for one don't think it funny!" Zac continued, closing his eyes and wishing himself elsewhere.

"Do you think it could be that? I did wonder at first. That would account for the passengers being left behind. If they've done it for that reason, then Richard Wainwright will be furious, and take it out on anyone foolish enough to get within shouting distance. No wonder Wainwright junior locked himself in the toilet!"

"I can't believe anyone would be so foolish, just to prove a point." The captain continued after a few minutes silence, "they've got too much to lose if it goes wrong, and when we eventually get back, they can be easily identified and face a long prison sentence."

"I don't know, and care even less. All I want is to get back to Manchester as quickly as possible."

"So do I, but we can't change course without them noticing. Listen, Zac, for the sake of the crew we've got to do as they say, and we've got to work together. I'm in charge and you'll do as I say, when I say it. Forget about smuggling for now, we can sort that out once we're back in the States, but in the meantime, we must support each other."

"I think it's our duty to do everything we can to stop them," Powalski replied. "Whatever it is they're up to, it's not right. If it were legal, they wouldn't have had to go to these lengths. I don't like being beaten up, and even less do I like having a gun thrust in my face."

"Now then, man, don't do anything foolish," Frank implored. "You know what happened last time. I don't like being manipulated either, and have never found myself in such a hellish situation, but we can't risk the lives of the crew. We have no option."

"I'm sure we could do something if we tried."

"Listen Zac," Frank said. "Don't even think of doing anything like that again. You don't think I'm happy doing this, do you? Did you see the way that bastard held Chrissie? I could kill him for that, but we've no choice. We can't afford to risk even one life by crossing these people. I don't mind admitting they've scared the shit out of me, but I'm not going to risk my life, or the lives of those entrusted to my care, for some bloody upstart with more power than sense."

Powalski made a derogatory noise in his throat, and the conversation came to an end.

"Interesting theories Captain," David said from the doorway. "You'll find out soon enough which are correct."

———◆———

It had been agreed that Jack and Amy were to make sure the aircraft remained on the ground at Osijek whilst David and Liam supervised Pam and the refugees. They hoped Captain Proctor and First Officer Powalski would help once they knew what was going on, but Jack was to remain on board to keep them in check. The gun was to be used to gain their co-operation if they tried to take off and leave anyone behind.

Jack wanted to locate Pam and help her aboard. After all, he had been involved right from the start, and felt he should be able to choose and not be told by someone who was trying to take over his position. It took some persuading to get him to agree.

He went to talk to Amy and asked her to walk down the plane with him. He tried to persuade her to speak to her brother as he wanted more excitement, but Amy was in full agreement with David. She explained that Liam and David had been trained to move about in enemy country and with the minimum of noise.

"Then if I can't get any excitement later, how about some now? Come with me and we'll join the mile-high club."

"But I can't. Not in front of the others."

"They won't even know. They're too busy playing the big shot. Come on Amy, you know it's what you want. Now's your chance. We can make love here, and it'll be even more exciting knowing your brother is only a short distance away."

He took her into a centre row at the rear of the main cabin, and pushed her down across the seats. He started kissing her, his hands caressing her body and his tongue exploring the depth of her mouth. She tried to push him away, but the more she struggled, the tighter he held her.

"No, Jack, not here," she managed to say as she turned her head away. "I can't do it, not with David and Liam so close."

"Grow up Amy and stop behaving like a stupid schoolgirl." Jack held her in a vice-like grip, his mouth kissing hers so hard that it hurt. "You know it's what we both want," he whispered in her ear.

"I've told you it's not what I want here, with everyone so close."

"But think how exciting to join the mile high club. I know you'll regret it all your life if we don't take this opportunity. All your friends will be jealous when they realise we're going out together."

"You're very sure of yourself!"

"Well, what competition do I have? Would you rather I was Joe?"

"Don't mention that creep to me."

"Then you'll agree I'm the best catch in the village!"

"Maybe the car has something to do with it," Amy said spitefully.

"Whatever the reason, you've got to admit it's true."

"That doesn't alter anything. I'm going back to the other," she tried to slide from beneath him.

"If you refuse I'll have to look round for another girl when we get home. You know you won't like that."

"Please don't be cross, Jack," she gasped as he changed his position. "I just can't do it here, that's all. Please wait until we're home again and on our own."

"I may never have another chance to do it in a plane. Come on, Amy, don't be a spoil-sport."

He tried to kiss her again and forced her back onto the seat. The more she struggled the more he tried to force her, and she started to feel frightened. Was he really going to rape her? If she shouted, would anyone hear her? When he reached to undo his zip, she managed to push him to the floor and get away from him.

Pulling her clothes straight, she hurried back towards the others. Jack gave her a contemptuous look before sitting down as if nothing had happened.

Amy wanted to know what there was on the plane that could be of use to the refugees, and started looking through the luggage in the overhead lockers. The first class cabin was made ready for any casualties, and anything she thought would be useful was stored on the seats.

Clothes, nappies and baby things were left in the main cabin, and the arms between the seats raised so the seats could be used for sleeping.

Toys, books, writing paper etc. were left at the rear of the plane, turning it into a play area for the children.

She asked Belinda Page and Effie Constantine to help but they refused. Under the circumstances she didn't blame them, and didn't insist. It gave her something to do, and she knew better than they did what might come in useful.

Liam was furious at the way things had changed. The two jobs should have been kept completely separate, and no one would have been any the wiser. As it was, he had been exposed by Powalski, a crime in itself, and now everyone on the plane knew his real name and his connection with the IRA. Richard Wainwright should have known better. He had no right to tell Powalski he would be keeping an eye on the money. If it weren't for Amy, Liam would still be in the UK, making his way to the contact to receive the money and Powalski would not have seen him or known his name. He was no longer safe, making it even more imperative that he should make a new life for himself, well away from his beloved Ireland, and the influence of the IRA.

Amy had a lot to answer for and he was almost wishing she had been sent to Holly in New York instead of coming with them. Yet he had known that he couldn't afford to have her running tame knowing he would be on flight WF254. One false word and she could have undone all the years of work he had accomplished with the IRA. One way or another he had to stop her from talking.

Liam had already decided that he would keep the money and make it look like Powalski had taken it. That way he would be in the clear, and get back at Powalski for what he had done. He would have enough money to start over and make a decent life for himself, Bridie and the children.

At best they could go to live in Ireland with new identities, knowing the IRA network was working to keep them safe. At worst, they would have to take on new identities and move away. He felt cheated, as his main ambition was to return to Ireland and spend the rest of his life there with family and friends.

But Powalski and Wainwright were the enemy now. It was obvious they were in league with each other for some nefarious activity, as it was against Wainwright's character to confide in a subordinate, so, with a bit of luck, Powalski would incriminate Wainwright, thus paying off two scores at one go. He could see Powalski was nervous and guessed his intention to interfere. He knew he had committed the crime of exposing one of his colleagues and would try to turn the situation to his own advantage. Powalski knew that if he could dispose of Liam, that would be the end of it, and the IRA probably would not even hear about the betrayal.

It was like a game of cat and mouse, each keeping a close eye on the other. It was a game Liam enjoyed, but by the attitude of the first officer, Powalski hated every minute of it.

Liam regretted having told Wainwright of his plans, yet he had hoped by telling him he would be flying on flight WF254, he would not take the threat to the money too seriously. He had made the decision with the intention of making it easier for his friends, and it had back-fired on him.

Chrissie managed to talk Malcolm into returning to his seat. He avoided looking at the others and was soon asleep.

— CHAPTER 10 —

It was with a mixture of trepidation and relief that Pam Crichton walked back to the tent in the refugee camp at Tuzla. She had spoken to Amy and arrangements had been made to meet David at Osijek, but she feared for his safety, and her own ability to make the journey with the people in her care. She was worried they wouldn't all get away, but knew she had to try.

Her first thought was to consult with Kajic. After his nights sleep, he had apparently managed to put the hurt of his sister's death behind him, and concentrate his efforts on helping the others. He took on the responsibility of looking after Dina's baby, and called him Dino after his mother. Kajic fashioned a sling out of some strips of material, and carried baby Dino on his front, the baby's head just a few inches below his chin. He attended to all his needs, and dropped a kiss on his head when he became fractious.

He agreed they should be able to get to Osijek within the stated time, but it would be hard going if the roads were as congested as they had been on their journey to Tuzla. They must be well prepared for the journey, taking everything they would need, as they couldn't rely on help from any of the towns or villages they would pass through.

People were too concerned about looking after themselves without having to worry about a bunch of refugees.

Fuel was going to be a problem. They still had enough to fill the tank, but he would feel better if they could fill the containers they had brought from the orphanage.

Pam was allowed back into the camp, and asked to speak to the Duty Officer. She explained it was imperative for her to get to Osijek, and asked if he could arrange for her to have enough fuel. He wanted to know the purpose of her journey, and she said it was for medical reasons. She had been asked to treat someone in the camp, and had diagnosed a serious complaint that could only be treated at Osijek hospital, and they had to get there straight away if his life was to be saved. The officer agreed to let her have what fuel he could spare.

The rest of the time was spent in acquiring what they might need. Clothes were bartered for bandages; dressings were changed and wounds attended to in exchange for food and water. Kajic returned triumphantly carrying a detailed map of the area they would be travelling through. When asked what he had given in return, he smiled and refused to say.

They worked out a route together, and as soon as they had eaten the food provided in the camp, packed everything into the truck. No one stopped them taking down the tent, which was stowed with the rest of the gear.

A woman came to them, carrying a child of about two years of age. She handed the girl to Pam, and begged her to take care of her daughter. The mother spoke good English and explained that she wanted Melita to be brought up in a modern democratic country and asked Pam to promise she would take responsibility for her, and make sure she was looked after in England.

Pam refused to take the child, saying she would be better off with her mother in spite of the troubles, but the mother intended to return to her home, and it was too dangerous for little Melita. She thrust an envelope into Pam's hand, before disappearing into the crowd.

Kajic called to Pam to help him with one of the children from the orphanage, so she pinned the envelope inside Melita's coat pocket, and told her to sit down. Melita did as she was told, and Pam was relieved she could understand English.

Even though they hadn't told anyone what they were doing or where they were going, people seemed to know, and two young women and their three children joined them and started helping in the preparations for the journey. Pam was grateful for their help when, shortly before they were due to depart, six more children were added to their number. They were all from one family, and their mother told them it was their only chance of staying together. She intended to return to her home and find her husband. The children were to contact her when the country had returned to normality.

The mother told the oldest, Pietre, he was now responsible for his younger brothers and sisters, and gave him all the money she had. She also gave him the address of a relative living in London, and told him to take his brothers and sisters there, and to place themselves in the care of her cousin.

They hadn't wanted to leave their mother, but she told them she couldn't cope with them any more, and it was better for them to part. The children tried to cling to her, but she pushed them away, telling them she didn't want them any more and trying to keep her tears hidden. It was a tearful group who moved out of the camp later that day.

Pam sat in the front of the vehicle with baby Dino and Melita whilst Kajic drove. Pietre sat in the back with his brothers and sisters, and the adults looked after the other children.

The journey was slow, and they were forced off the road many times by the volume of traffic making for Tuzla. As they got further from the town, the on-coming traffic changed from refugees heading for the air base, to military vehicles, and when these approached, they were forced to move off the highway and onto the verge, regardless of the conditions of the road. They had to bounce the vehicle over rough ground, and on one such occasion a slow puncture delayed them even more.

The spare tyre was worn and the jack unreliable, but Kajic managed to raise the vehicle off the ground, and the older children found enough rocks to force under the truck.

By nightfall they had covered less than a quarter of the journey, and the children were hungry and fretful. Melita had started crying for her mother, and nothing they could do would calm her.

It was too dark to continue but if they could feed the children and settle them down to sleep, then the adults, too, would be able to relax and prepare for the following day.

After consulting the map, they took a turning off the main road that would take them through a valley, before re-joining the main highway a little further on. This diversion should offer them somewhere quiet to spend the night without taking up too much of their precious time.

Kajic pitched the tent in a hollow between some rocks where it was sheltered from the light wind that had started to blow as the sun set. The truck was left on higher ground at the side of the road, and when the tarpaulin was fastened, it was cosy enough.

Kajic saw to the re-fuelling of the vehicle whilst Pam sorted out what food there was available. It had to be rationed to last another two days, and she decided the best thing to have that first night was hot soup and bread.

The older children were sent off to collect firewood, and soon they were all comforted by the sight and sound of the fire. Milk was heated for the younger ones, and some cans of soup opened and their contents mixed together. Loaves of bread from the camp were broken up and handed out. Once they were fed and warm, the children seemed more content, and were able to settle down for the night with full stomachs.

The older children slept in the tent with Kajic, and the rest in the back of the truck. Baby Dino also remained with Kajic, sleeping peacefully in the same blanket, and not being disturbed by his movements until it was time for his feed.

It must have been about two in the morning when it started to rain. The first rain they'd had in weeks. It started gently, but soon the raindrops were hammering on the tent, waking the occupants. Kajic looked out and could hardly make out the shape of the truck.

Pam was also wakened by the storm and untied the tarpaulin, battling against the strong wind and rain. She was horrified to hear a gushing noise which grew louder with each second until it blotted out the sound of the storm. A flash of lightning lit the scene, and was followed almost immediately by the deafening sound of thunder. The rainwater was gushing down into the hollow, bringing loose stones and scree with it. The ground was so hard the water wasn't able to soak away, and had formed into a small torrent. It was heading straight for the tent. What had seemed like a safe shelter for the night was the worst place they could have chosen in a storm!

Pam shouted at the top of her voice, but the wind whipped the sound away. She pulled a blanket round her shoulders and stumbled towards the tent, her torch, reflecting back from the rain, was of little use. She was thankful for the brilliance of the lightning, which prevented her from falling over one of the guy ropes. Kajic stepped out of the tent just as the water reached them.

They were both washed off their feet, and the tent collapsed in a writhing mass of arms and legs as those inside tried to escape the engulfing water and soggy canvas. Their screams could be heard above the storm.

Kajic was the first to find his feet, and he grabbed the canvas and tried to pull the tent to one side, out of the gully and onto the road. Pam helped, but their strength was nothing compared with the water, and the canvas ripped. The tent was washed downstream before it snagged on a boulder.

Kajic and Pam ran towards it, their torches searching for signs of life. The rumble of thunder was constant and the lightning flashes closely followed one another. This proved to be a blessing, lighting up the area enough to help them find the children. They were all shivering as the relentless rain soaked through their clothing. Their fingers were numb, which made it difficult to sense what they were touching in the dark running water.

Those who were able to escape from the canvas unaided joined in the search for the others, but baby Dino and Pietre were still missing.

They had to shout to be heard above the sound of the storm, and those who were fit enough continued searching until they were exhausted. The lightning lessened, but the rain still poured down, making it impossible to remain in the open. Eventually the search had to be abandoned as the bad weather continued.

Four of them had suffered serious injury. One of the girls from the orphanage had broken her leg and dislocated her shoulder; another had a broken arm and two of Pietre's family suffered from cracked ribs. They were all suffering from shock, and minor cuts and bruises. It was a miracle so many had been found, and were still alive.

Pam and Kajic attended to their various needs, turning the cab into a consulting room, whilst the women took care of the others. Splints and slings were made out of what was available, but it was daylight by the time the last of the children had been treated, and they could turn their attention to each other.

Kajic had a dislocated finger, and he never even flinched when Pam treated it. She hadn't received any physical injury herself, but was quite exhausted, and longing for a hot drink. This had to be denied, as there was no dry wood available to build a fire.

The children were silent. Pam looked into the back of the truck, and saw them sitting closely together, trying to get warm under the dry blankets. Those with injuries were the only ones lying down, the rest were huddled together in an attempt to get some warmth from each other.

Kajic took one of the boys with him when he went in search of the two missing children, whilst Pam handed out what food she could find that had escaped the wet. It had stopped raining by the time they had eaten, and she made all those who could, get out of the truck and jump up and down in the road. Gradually they started to get warm, and she tried to get them to play games and turn the exercises into a fun time.

As the sun rose, they could feel its warmth, and Pam organised the children into two groups. She gave each group a blanket, and they had to wave it up and down in the sunshine. The team with the driest blanket had won. The children were fully occupied by the time Kajic returned to the truck. They had located and buried the two missing children.

They were on the point of leaving when they heard a vehicle coming up the valley towards them. Kajic said to stay where they were, and went to the bend in the road to see who was coming. From the direction of Tuzla, following their route, an old bus chugged up the road. It was full of refugees. An old man was driving and stopped the vehicle when he saw Kajic, and there was much discussion and arm waving.

Pam asked them why they had followed her, and they said they had heard rumours in the camp at Tuzla she was going back to England with the people in her care. They didn't know how or where the story had started, but many people believed it.

They insisted on joining the group, preferring an unknown future in an unknown country to the horrors they had already experienced. They needed to get away from the danger, hurt by the hatred engendered between their neighbours and friends, made homeless with only the things they could carry, being separated from their friends and not even knowing when they would eat again.

They were prepared to risk everything in an attempt to get away from Bosnia, and had left the air base shortly after Pam and Kajic. They had tried to catch up with them, but been delayed on the road. By the time they realised the doctor was no longer ahead of them, they started asking questions and were told that a truck had been seen leaving the main highway so they had turned round and followed the track until it was too dark to go any further. They had stopped for the night, and pleaded with Pam to let them go with her.

She didn't know if she could help them, but if they insisted she couldn't stop them. She made it plain she wouldn't stop to help if they got into difficulties, as she wouldn't jeopardise her group, and they had no time to spare. They would have to keep going as long as the light held, with only a short stopover at night if they were to get to their destination on time.

The group was threatening to grow out of all proportion, and

Pam hoped she and David would have the strength to cope with that number of people.

They set off once more in the direction of Osijek. Kajic led the way, and the old man, Osbih followed close behind. There was a long delay as they tried to rejoin the main highway. A military convoy was heading towards Tuzla, and they had to wait until all the vehicles passed before they could continue north.

A stream of refugees cluttered the road and made their progress slow, too slow for Pam's liking and she was getting more and more concerned as the day advanced. The continual bumping on the uneven road did nothing for her, and before the day was over she had a blinding headache, her body felt bruised, and she was hungry.

"The bus has stopped," Kajic announced. "Do you want me to go back to see what's wrong?"

"I suppose you'd better," Pam replied.

"I didn't think you meant it when you said you wouldn't wait for them," he said, grinning at her.

"They've run out of fuel," he reported back. "Can we spare any for them?"

"Don't ask me," Pam snapped. "You're the one who knows how much this thing does to the gallon. As long as we've enough to get to Osijek, they can have the rest, I suppose, but if we only have enough for our needs, don't give them any."

"I guess we can spare a can. It won't be enough to get them all the way, but we may be able to pick some up in Brod. It's the next town, and it has a military base, so they may have some to spare. We'll have to count up the money we have between us, and hope it'll be enough to buy some food as well."

The refuelling done, the vehicles continued laboriously on their way, Kajic following a route he had worked out from the map instead of keeping to the main road. He tried to keep to minor roads, and even though they had to travel further, their progress was continuous, and Pam began to be hopeful they just might get to Osijek on the appointed day.

It was better travelling on the minor roads, as it was the men of military age who were particularly vulnerable, and Pam was concerned for Kajic's safety. She hoped if they were stopped, she would have enough influence to keep him with her. She guessed most of the troops would be corrupt, but they didn't have enough money to bribe their way through any roadblocks.

When they saw a platoon of soldiers camped at the side of the road Pam's heart sank. She had heard too many stories of refugees being stopped and disappearing into the countryside, never to be heard of again. She urged Kajic to drive on, and she smiled and waved at the soldiers. Intent on what they were doing, they took little notice of the two vehicles, and stepped aside to let them pass.

Their progress was slow over the mountains, and in order to save fuel, they let the vehicles free-wheel downhill. On one such occasion they went round a bend, and Kajic struggled to keep the vehicle under control without running down three young men sauntering down the middle of the road. Osbih's reactions were not as quick, and he ran into the back of the truck. When both vehicles stopped Kajic jumped out to see what damage had been done.

The young men had scattered, two to one side of the road and one to the other. One of them fell badly cutting his knee. He tried to follow his friends, limping after them, but he fell again when he put his weight on his injured leg. Pam went to the injured boy and helped him back to the truck where she cleaned and stitched the wound. There was no sign of his friends.

The people in the truck were not badly hurt and the women tried to keep the children calm, assuring them they were alright and rubbing bruised knees and elbows.

Kajic and Osbih examined the damage, and were relieved to find it was superficial, mainly damage to the bodywork, and they were able to straighten the nearside rear mudguard on Kajic's truck by hand. The tyre was still inflated, and they hoped it hadn't been punctured, as they didn't have a spare.

One of the women from the bus went to help Pam, and was able to interpret for her. The young man said his name was Janni, and begged them not to hand him over to the military. They promised to help him and, to gain his confidence, told him where they were going, and why.

Once reassured he called to his friends. They walked gingerly towards the truck, and Pam held out her hand in welcome.

Their names were Nedzad and Mahmutovic and they were from the same village. They had been close friends since school days and were now at university together. They were completely opposed to the present troubles, particularly when they found themselves on opposing sides in a war they thought pointless and futile.

They had always done everything together, and were determined not to join in the fighting, with the possibility of killing each other. They decided to run away, and were trying to make their way to Hungary, where they hoped to remain until there was peace once again in Bosnia. Nedzad spoke English well, whereas the other two only had a limited knowledge of the language.

Janni wasn't strong enough to continue walking, and Pam wanted to keep an eye on the wound to make sure it didn't get infected, so she offered them a lift. After talking it over, they agreed to accept a ride as far as Osijek. They were squashed into the back of the truck and were wonderful with the children, keeping them entertained and playing childish games with them. Many a time Pam smiled as the sound of their laughter penetrated the cab.

They had been on the road for another half-hour before Kajic's fears were realised. The steering was getting harder, and he knew they had another puncture. He stopped the truck to investigate. The rear tyre was completely flat.

Once again they had to empty the vehicle of all its belongings, and to jack it up at the side of the road. On examination the tyre was seen to have a long deep cut where the mudguard had eaten into it. The bus had a spare, but it was larger and wouldn't fit. They hadn't had time to mend the first puncture, and there was nothing for it but to change back onto the tyre with the slow puncture, and hope it would stand up to the journey to the next village where they hoped to get it fixed. They had to keep stopping to use the foot-pump, and everyone did their best to keep their spirits up.

Nedzad and Mahmutovic were willing and eager to help, and were not averse to taking the toddlers into the bushes whilst the women changed the babies' nappies. They found enough dry material to make a fire, and everyone was grateful for a hot drink, and another sustaining bowl of soup.

They were unable to get a spare at the next village, but managed to mend the slow puncture, and as soon as it was ready, they set off once more.

They reached Brod at dusk, and had some difficulty in finding the right road. Kajic parked and waited for the bus to catch up with them. He consulted with Osbih, and they had just decided which way to go when they were surrounded by soldiers with rifles, demanding to be told who they were and where they were going.

Kajic told them they were evacuating a hospital, and everyone was ill and in need of medical attention. They had been separated from the rest of the convoy when they'd had a puncture, and were now trying to make their way to the hospital at Osijek, where they were expected. He told them they had an English doctor travelling with them.

Kajic translated what he had told the soldiers and it was obvious they didn't understand English. He told Pam they must hide Nedzad and Mahmutovic, as the soldiers were particularly interested in males between the ages of 15 and 40. Janni, with his bandaged leg, would be taken as one of the patients.

The soldiers ordered everyone out of the vehicles, and as Pam tried to stop them, they pushed her out of the way. She tripped and fell, bruising her arm and grazing her knee. She shouted out in protest, and one of the soldiers raised the butt of his rifle, threatening to hit her with it. Even though he was an old man, Osbih wasn't going to stand by and watch the doctor being hurt, so he pushed the soldier to one side, and helped her to get up.

The soldier spat at the old man, and turned his attention to the first of the two vehicles. By the light of a powerful torch, they could see the occupants cowering together. Janni had his injured leg raised and his back to the light, Mahmutovic had his head rather inexpertly bandaged, and Nedzad wore his arm in a sling. The women had been busy whilst the others had been talking to the soldiers!

Melita had been asleep in the warmth of the cab, and chose that moment to wake. Her cries filled the air, and Pam opened the door and leaned into the cab. She grabbed her make-up and liberally covered Melita's face with it. The effect was all she desired. Melita looked as though she had a high fever, but the child stopped crying as soon as she saw Pam, and she had to pinch her a couple of times before she started to cry again.

The more she pinched her, the louder Melita cried, and the soldiers backed off. They weren't interested in sick children, but they forced Kajic to go with them. They marched him to a building in the town centre. Pam and the old man followed, demanding to be allowed to enter.

The soldiers didn't know what she was shouting, but they knew from their colleagues that she was an English doctor, and they stood a little in awe of her. They indicated she was to follow, but wouldn't allow Osbih to enter the building. He returned to the others whilst Pam was shown into a small room where they left her for over an hour. She tried the door, and to her consternation it was locked.

She made such a fuss that eventually the door was opened and a young soldier entered the room. He spoke to her in English, and she was quick to explain who she was, and to demand the release of her colleague. She also demanded they be allowed to leave, saying how outrageous it was for an English citizen to be detained against her will in a foreign land, particularly when she had chosen to help that country by offering free medical advice. She started to relate all she had given up in order to help strangers and this was all the reward she got, to be locked up like a common criminal!

When the soldier started to hesitate, Pam knew she had made the right move. He left her alone once more, but this time the door was left open, and someone arrived with a cup of tea. She had finished drinking it by the time the soldier returned, and asked her to follow him. She was shown into a large office.

An officer sat behind the desk, and Kajic stood with his back to the door, two soldiers standing to attention, one on either side. The officer spoke to her in English, and invited her to take a seat. Kajic turned towards her and Pam saw he had been beaten about the head, his right eye was swollen and closed, and he was bleeding from his nose and mouth.

"I most strongly protest at the way you've treated my colleague and me," Pam said, taking a high hand and refusing to sit down. "I am an English doctor, and this is my colleague. We are escorting patients to the hospital at Osijek, and there is no reason whatsoever why we should have been detained. I demand that you allow us to continue our journey immediately."

"What proof do we have that you are who you say you are?" the officer asked.

"What more proof do you need?" Pam replied. "Just look at the patients. And if that isn't enough for you, ring the hospital at Osijek and they will confirm everything I've told you. It isn't our fault we got separated from the rest of the convoy and lost our way."

"We have already done so," the officer replied quietly. "They say they have no knowledge of any evacuation, and are not expecting any new patients."

"Who did you speak to? One of the receptionists? You can't expect everyone to know hospital business. If you speak to the right person, they'll confirm our story."

"Who do you suggest I speak to, Dr. Crichton?" he asked.

"Dr. Milbourne," Pam answered without hesitation, praying that he wouldn't be on duty, or if he was at the hospital, that he would realise the trouble she was in.

Although she had only met Dr. Milbourne once, she was certain he would help her in her present predicament. He had been at Osijek for a couple of months now, and in close contact with the team at the hospital in Sarajevo. In all probability he would know Pam had been separated from her colleagues, and would accept that she was trying to make contact with him.

"I'll speak to him if you get him on the phone," she continued.

"There is no need, doctor. I will speak to him myself," the officer answered.

"Dr. Milbourne?" he asked when he was connected to the hospital. "I am pleased you are there, and wish to confirm that you are expecting some patients evacuated from Tuzla hospital, and under the guardianship of an Englishwoman, Dr. Crichton."

"You are? That is good," he continued after a short pause. "I wish to let you know that the two vehicles separated from the rest of the convoy are safe, and will be continuing their journey as soon as it is light. They will be sheltered and fed here in Brod, and no harm will come to them overnight. Good-bye."

He put the phone down, and smiled at Pam.

"Really, there was no need to confirm with Osijek," he said. "Only an Englishwoman would demand her rights under such circumstanced. And I am going to ask for your word as an Englishwoman that you are not hiding any men of military age. That is now a criminal offence for which you will be severely punished. All men over 15 years of age are required to report for duty at the nearest military establishment. If they do not they will be shot."

"We are not sheltering any able bodied men over 15 years of age," she lied. "We've an old man driving the bus, and some women helpers. The rest are patients, all of whom require medical attention, and everyone is exhausted. The only able bodied man we have with us is my driver, and he is part of the medical team. We can't manage without him, and his medical expertise is more important in the hospital than anything he can contribute to the war effort. He's better at treating bullet wounds than making them!"

"Ha, ha. Better at stopping bleeding than starting it, eh? I am pleased you have not lost your sense of humour, doctor. It is something sadly lacking at this time. So, you may both leave now. I will make the schoolhouse available to you for the night, and you will leave by 6 o'clock tomorrow morning."

He picked up some papers from his desk and started sorting through them. He took no more interest as the two guards pushed them towards the door. They were escorted back to the vehicles and told to follow the soldiers.

The schoolhouse was cold and dark, but at least it was dry, and they were taken into a large room and left alone. Kajic found the boiler house, and managed to get the heating going. They would be able to dry everything that had got soaked the night before. About an hour later, someone arrived with enough bread to feed everyone, and milk for the children, and for the second night running they settled down to sleep with full stomachs.

They were woken at dawn with yet more bread, and told to move on as soon as they had eaten, and were on the point of leaving when the officer from the night before walked into the schoolhouse and took Pam to one side.

He told her he had heard through his connections at Tuzla, that an English doctor was evacuating refugees, and he asked her to confirm it.

Pam was reluctant to admit to anything.

"If it is true you are escaping to England, then I want you to take my wife and children with you," he said. "You must know how dangerous it is for me to make this admission, and if it is known, then I could be shot as a traitor. Please help me, Dr. Crichton."

"I don't know what to say," she replied. "You can understand my position. I have friends whose lives depend on me. I wouldn't betray them for anything in the world."

"Good. That confirms my suspicions. You would have denied it if it were not true. My wife and children will be waiting for you at the bend in the road, about 2 kilometres from here. I will be with them, and will do all I can to make it easy for you to get away. Good luck!"

"Before you go," Pam called after him as he started to leave. "We need a new tyre for the truck before we can continue our journey. We also have a puncture in the spare that needs mending as well as fuel for the bus. It is practically empty and we don't have enough to get both vehicles to our destination. Can you help us?"

A slight nod indicated that he had heard, and within an hour the tyres were fixed and a jeep arrived with sufficient cans of fuel to take both vehicles to the end of their journey.

Even at that early hour it was busy in the streets, and they made their way through the crowds of pedestrians and out onto the road that would take them to within a few kilometres of Osijek. The road was busy with on-coming traffic heading for the market at Brod.

True to his word, the officer was waiting with his wife and children. He kissed them all and lifted the children into the truck. His wife was reluctant to leave but he insisted, and she climbed into the vehicle and put her arms round the children, tears running unheeded down her cheeks. The officer stepped aside and watched as they continued on their way.

Kajic hardly spoke during that long days ride. He was completely withdrawn and couldn't even be bothered with the children. Pam knew he must be tired and hurting from his beating. When they stopped to eat, she tried to get him to feed Melita, but he said he had to check the two vehicles to make sure they were roadworthy, and they must hurry if they were to get there on time. He didn't even look at the child.

Once again the map proved to be useful, as they were able to find an alternative route away from the main highway. Another delay was caused when the bus ran out of fuel, and the old man supervised whilst Nedzad and Mahmutovic filled the tank from the containers. They were pleased to be of use and very grateful to the Englishwoman who had risked so much to save their lives.

The officers' wife and children sat quietly, not talking to anyone and not even attempting to help with the other children. They accepted a drink when it was offered, but refused food.

It was early afternoon on the third day when their route brought them back onto the main highway. They hardly saw any other vehicles, which was just as well as there were few places where it was safe for them to pass. With each mile, they were moving ever nearer to

Osijek but they expected to arrive in the early hours. Pam prayed David would wait for them and not leave them stranded in a strange and hostile country.

— CHAPTER 11 —

Captain Proctor and First Officer Powalski were surprised at their instructions to head the plane towards Hungary. They had expected their destination to be Italy, and the new heading took them completely by surprise.

"Is that our final destination?" the captain asked.

"Probably not," David replied.

"Don't tell me we're going into Bosnia," he said.

"Then I won't."

"I can't think of any good reason why you'd want to go there unless it's to continue the war."

"Surprisingly enough, our reasons are peaceful and humane."

"So far you've not done anything to convince me of that," Powalski commented.

"Time will tell, and you're quite right, captain. Flight WF542 has now become a rescue flight, and we are heading for the former Yugoslavia."

"Don't you know there's a war going on?"

"That's why we're going there. Our mission is to land at Osijek Airport, collect a group of refugees, and take them back to the UK."

"You must be mad. Do you expect us to fly into a country at war, and out again, without even being challenged? It isn't a game, you know. These people are deadly serious."

"I know that," David replied. "And we, too, are deadly serious. We intend to land at Osijek, which is approximately 50 miles away from the Hungarian border. We believe it is far enough away from the fighting not to cause too much of a problem, and we hope to be in and out again before they realise what's happening. Do you think you can do it, Captain?"

"If it's a large enough runway, I can certainly land at Osijek, if that's what you mean. But what happens if we're intercepted?"

"We'll have to deal with whatever they throw at us, but so far as I'm aware, the United Nations has control of the air-space within a fifty mile radius of Sarajevo, and we're flying far enough outside that area to be clear of their radar. I'm hoping they'll not look twice at us if we let them think we're going into Hungary. We need only change our course at the last minute. I hope Osijek is near enough to the border for us to get away with it."

"Hm, maybe you could just be right, but there are two points I want you to be honest about. Give me your word that we aren't taking arms, or doing anything to continue this war?"

"I do give you my word, for what it's worth," David replied.

"And the Irishman, O'Grady I think Zac said? Is he going to return to the UK with us, or are you intending to leave him behind? I won't take part in any scheme that'll take a terrorist, or anyone connected with the IRA, into Bosnia."

"You've no need to worry. He's as much against this war as any of us and is no more connected to the IRA than your colleague here," David replied, laughing and digging Powalski in the back.

"Are you trying to tell me they are both in the IRA? Is it true, Zac?"

"This has nothing to do with them, as I'm sure your new friends will confirm," Powalski replied sarcastically.

"I don't like the way this is going," Captain Proctor continued. "I might as well fly into the mountains, then it'll be over for all of us."

"But not for the refugees. They're waiting for us at this very moment, and trusting we'll get them away from the war within the next few hours. If we don't get there, they will be in an even worse position than before. In fact, the Irishman is a friend who's come along to help. I've been quite open with you, Captain, but I must remind you that I am in charge of this flight, and you'll do what I say."

"I could still crash the plane," the pilot replied.

"True. But would you like to be responsible for killing all those on board?"

"What are a dozen lives compared to the devastation caused by arming untrained and undisciplined men to kill and maim their neighbours, and help them continue ethnic cleansing?"

"I do appreciate your point of view, Captain, but as I said, I've told you the truth, and we're going to land at Osijek, where, hopefully, a party of refugees under the guardianship of an English doctor will be waiting for us. If they aren't there, we'll wait for them. They have a long way to travel but should be there by now. If not we'll wait for them on the runway, and hope the ground staff will leave us alone."

"Why Osijek and not Subotica?" the first officer asked after consulting his map. "It's much closer to the Hungarian border."

"Because of the distance they have to travel. We had to choose Osijek as being the easiest place they could get to. It would have taken them a lot longer to travelled the extra miles, and with each day it makes it more dangerous for them to remain in the country."

"Let's hope the authorities don't object."

"Let's hope so, indeed," David responded. "Have you any experience of Osijek, Captain? Have you been there before?"

"No" he replied shaking his head. "Have you, Zac?"

"No, sir. I've flown into Split and Pula, but never further inland."

"Same here. Let's hope it's a large enough runway. Let me know, Zac, when we reach the nearest point to Osijek, and give me a new course to take us directly there."

"I'll leave it in your capable hands," David said, after checking they had turned onto the right course. "Let me know when you need to make contact with the aerodrome. I'll be within shouting distance." He was relieved at their acceptance of the situation.

"Do you think he's telling the truth?" Powalski asked when David left the cockpit, not taking any notice of Jack, sitting in the observer's seat, his handgun ready for any emergency.

"Yes I do. I can't see any other reason why we're here. When I've seen the pictures on the TV I've often wondered if I could help in any way, but the only thing I could think of was to give a cash donation to the charities. I never expected to be involved like this. I'll be prepared to help all I can if he's assisting some of the refugees to escape to a better life but I wish he'd gone about it a different way."

"I'm not so sure," Powalski replied. "I don't trust him. Even if he's telling the truth, why did he have to be armed?"

"I wouldn't have diverted to Shannon at his request, even if he'd told me why he needed a plane. I wouldn't have put the passengers in danger, or the aircraft for that matter."

"I suppose that's one point in his favour, that none of the passengers was hurt, but I still don't like it, and think we should try and put a stop to all this nonsense. If we could overpower them as soon as we land and they're busy with the refugees, we could take off and be back in the UK in a few hours."

The captain frowned at Powalski, indicating Jack listening to everything they said.

"No," he continued. "If there really are refugees waiting for us, then we'll take them back to Manchester. After all, we've come this far, so we might as well go with it to the end."

Powalski's first concerned was to get rid of the IRA money. He had made a mess of things by naming O'Grady, but was powerless to do anything about it for the moment.

On leaving the flight deck, David sat in the nearest seat. One look at Liam was enough to tell him he was impatient to get moving whilst Amy sat nervously biting her fingernails. Malcolm was blissfully unaware of what was going on, having drunk his way through a large and varied quantity of alcohol found in the duty free. The rest of the crew sat back in their seats, resigned to await their fate.

Chrissie asked if she could serve some food, and was told to organise drinks for everyone, and it seemed strange sitting drinking coffee as if on a regular flight. It gave the whole thing a strange air of normality.

David felt it was time to let the rest of the crew know where they were going, and what they intended to do. He called everyone into the first class cabin, and told them in detail why they had hijacked the plane, and their reason for going to Osijek.

He explained they had done everything in their power to make the journey safe and assured them there would be no danger for those remaining on board the plane. It was highly unlikely anyone would fire directly at the plane in case they killed one of the crew. They would only fire if they were certain they could kill the hijackers.

They listened in silence as David asked them to be prepared to help an English doctor and some refugees fleeing from the war, and asked for their co-operation on the flight back to the UK. He emphasised that he didn't want them to do anything whilst they were on the ground, and stressed the point they shouldn't leave the aircraft under any circumstances. If they did, he wouldn't be responsible for the consequences. Unless they were told otherwise, they were to remain in the main cabin and it would be better for them to keep well away from the windows.

In the meantime they could sit together, but he stressed if he had any trouble from anyone, they would be separated and tied into their seats until they were ready to fly home.

It was early in the afternoon when the pilot announced he was on direct approach to Osijek. So far they hadn't been challenged, but they were entering the area covered by Osijek air traffic control and requested permission to land. It was refused.

Captain Proctor told ATC armed men had hijacked his plane, and he was powerless to do anything other than obey orders. When someone with a better command of English was found, David took the intercom and told them he intended to land, with or without permission. They would circle the aerodrome twice, and then come in on the third approach. It was up to them to make sure the runway was clear, and any resultant accident would be entirely their responsibility.

As soon as the airport came into view, the plane circled at a fairly low altitude whilst Captain Proctor decided on the best approach.

There were vehicles moving on to the runway, blocking the way, and making it impossible for them to land. David spoke to ATC and told them they still intended landing on the third approach, and if they didn't clear the runway immediately, they would be responsible for the lives of the American and British citizens on board.

By the end of the second circuit, the vehicles were still parked on the runway and they could see the faces of the drivers staring up at them. Some stood outside their vehicles, and others leaned out of the windows.

On the final approach, the undercarriage was released and the wheels locked into place. Their approach was as slow as the pilot could manage without actually stalling, and it seemed as if there would be an almighty pile up as they almost floated towards the ground.

Sticking firmly to his course, Captain Proctor went through the landing routine as if the runway was perfectly clear and ready for a normal landing. His hands remained steady, and he was completely in control. He could imagine the devastation if the vehicles didn't move out of the way, but he stuck to his course, every second taking them nearer to disaster.

The people in the cockpit were holding their breath, mesmerised by the sight of the cluttered runway. Up until the last moment the first officer, too, had remained calm. But the prospect of a pile up was too much for him, and he shouted to the pilot to pull out. It was a tense time for everyone.

Captain Proctor took no notice, every part of his mind and body concentrating on making a good landing. He was playing a macabre game of 'dare' with the drivers, and by the look on his face he wasn't going to be the one to turn away.

The wheels had almost touched the ground when one of the drivers jumped into his vehicle and drove onto the grass verge. This movement triggered a reaction from the others, and soon all the vehicles sped away, leaving the way clear for the plane to land.

Captain Proctor had not shown any sign of nerves, but the tension could be seen in the whiteness of his knuckles, and the determined expression on his face.

Frank Proctor turned the plane round to face in the direction he would need for take-off, taking the plane as near to the perimeter fence as he could manage. His instructions from ground control were that the plane was to stay away from the airport buildings. They did not want it anywhere near the terminal, or any area frequented by their staff or passengers. David told him to turn off his radio so that there was no further contact with the people on the ground.

David, Liam and Amy walked the length of the plane, looking out of the portholes, checking as much of the surrounding area as they could see, but there was no sign of Pam or her party. They were exposed where they were, and if one of them left the plane they would be an easy target for the snipers who would undoubtedly be looking for an opportunity to shoot. There was no doubt that armed guards would be keeping a close watch for any movement and it would make it impossible for them to board the refugees as it was certain the authorities would not stand by and watch what was going on. It would be foolish to try and leave the plane in daylight, therefore the alternative was to wait until it was dark, and hope they could move about undetected.

David told everyone not to close the shutters to the portholes, so that they could see all round the plane. He hoped the people on the ground would be content to let them remain on the runway, and wait until they made the first move. All they could do now was sit it out and wait until it was dark enough to contact the refugees.

Liam took Powalski to the back of the main cabin where their conversation could not be overheard. He wanted to know exactly what Powalski had said to implicate him, and where the money was.

He said the case was safe with the flight crew's luggage, and it had been a slip of the tongue to mention his name. He regretted it as soon as he'd said it. But surely O'Grady could understand his anxiety? The money was hot, and if found by the wrong people could get them all into trouble, more trouble than they were in at the moment.

After some persuasion, Powalski confirmed it had been Richard Wainwright who had told him O'Grady would be on the flight.

Liam had to let it go at that, assuring Powalski he hadn't heard the last of it, but advising him to help with the refugees. Once back in the UK he could dispose of the money as originally intended.

The crew sat together in the centre seats in the main cabin, talking about what had happened. Chrissie served drinks as she thought fit. The only one who sat slightly apart, and didn't join in their conversation, was Zac Powalski. Malcolm also sat away from the others, completely oblivious to what was going on around him.

At the first opportunity, Powalski went and sat next to Malcolm and tried to talk to him. Malcolm was in such a state it was doubtful he even knew he was being spoken to.

Powalski was disappointed to find he wouldn't be any use to him, as he had hoped to find an ally. Between them they might have overcome the others. As it was, he realised he was entirely on his own unless he could persuade O'Grady to see sense. At the next opportunity, he would have a serious word with him.

They had been sitting on the runway for over an hour before the authorities made their first move. Effie Constantine called out that she could see a jeep moving towards the plane.

David told Jack to watch the first officer and keep his handgun ready whilst he went with Liam to see what was happening. Sure enough, a jeep was moving slowly in their direction, a machine gun mounted on the front, and pointing menacingly at the plane. The vehicle stopped a good distance away, and one of the three soldiers spoke through a loud haler.

He wanted to know what their demands were, and why they had come to Osijek.

Liam headed towards the cockpit, and David quickly followed. The window next to the pilot's seat was the only one that would open, and there was no way they were going to open the door in order to speak to them. Liam opened the window and pointed his rifle at the man who was speaking.

David took hold of the handset and spoke to the people in the tower. He told them to back off and leave them alone. They were not doing any harm, and if left alone, no one would get hurt.

He waited until his message had been relayed to the soldiers in the jeep, and could see them discussing what to do next. Again David told them to back off. Again nothing happened.

He nodded to Liam, who took careful aim and fired at the jeep. His first shot took out the front nearside tyre, and his second the front offside.

The driver reversed the jeep, and limped back towards the terminal building.

That was the last they saw of them in daylight.

As soon as it started to get dark David pulled on his balaclava. He opened the emergency exit door over the wing on the far side of the plane from the airport buildings. This was also the shortest distance to the wire fence that formed the perimeter of the airport.

He attached the rope ladder and left the plane jumping down onto the runway, his handgun gripped firmly between his teeth, and the wire cutters protruding from his pocket.

Once on the ground, he crouched low and ran towards the fence, falling flat on his stomach as soon as he reached the grass verge. He lay there for some minutes, expecting a reaction from the terminal, but there was none. He crawled slowly towards the fence, keeping his face turned away from the moonlight.

He found a place where the ground dipped, and the lower half of the fence was hidden from the sight of anyone in the airport buildings. He decided this was the best place to make a way through, and started cutting the mesh with the wire cutters provided by Old Josh. He was a long way from the Bank of England!

When the hole was large enough, he pushed his way through and out onto a narrow dirt road, more of a farm track really, which ran parallel to the fence. Crouching low, he ran in what he hoped would be the direction Pam would come from, but he could see no sign of any likely vehicle. The track veered to his left, but he couldn't make out where it was leading. He stayed close to the fence and cut across the farmland until he reached a hedge, forming a border with a tarred road. He could hear a vehicle approaching from his right, and waited until it passed before pushing through the hedge. There were no places to hide if any more vehicles were using the road that night. He would have to rely on lying flat on the grass, and hoping he would not be seen.

He walked cautiously up a slight slope until he came to a T-junction on the brow of the hill. This road was busier, and he had a good view of the main entrance to the airport some distance down the road to his right. It was well lit, and there were a lot of people standing around in small groups. He could make out a soldier on duty, with a rifle held loosely in his hand. He wasn't surprised airport security had called on the Military to help in this emergency.

At the junction, he turned to his left, away from the airport, until he thought it was safe enough to cross the main road without being seen. He then doubled back, on the opposite side of the road. Another hedge ran parallel to the road, and he pushed his way through this, to find himself in the airport car park.

There were civilian guards as well as soldiers keeping watch at the main entrance, and he was disturbed to see that one of them had a guard dog. He didn't fancy getting involved with that!

The car park ended with yet another hedge, which he tried to push through, but it had grown up through a wire fence, and it was impossible to penetrate. Barbed wire ran across the top, and on inspection he discovered the only way out of the car park was the way he had come, or through the gate that led back onto the main road immediately opposite the main entrance and the soldiers. It was impossible to leave that way without being seen.

Using the mudguard off an old car, he began to dig a hole through the bottom of the hedge. This took longer than he had anticipated, but eventually it led him onto the grass verge. He lay in a slight ditch that ran the length of the road but it offered poor protection.

A little further on a military jeep was surrounded by soldiers. They were smoking, talking and laughing amongst themselves. If they had been posted there to keep a look out, they weren't doing a very good job!

David remained in the ditch, and slowly crawled his way passed them. He was grateful they did not have a guard dog with them, and that they were an undisciplined group. If they had been fully alert, they must have seen him, but as it was they did not even turn when he was within spitting distance.

Continuing in a northerly direction, he came to the edge of the airport. A utility road led across the end of the main runway, and once again there were more soldiers. They too, were completely unaware of his presence.

When he heard a vehicle coming from the south, he remained in the ditch, not moving a muscle and hardly daring to breathe. He watched the soldiers stop and search the car, and question the occupants. They did not appear to be particularly interested and soon waved it on its way. David had just started to crawl away, when he saw one of the soldiers heading in his direction.

The man climbed over the gate into the field, and almost trod on David as he stood up against the hedge to relieve himself. David heard the noise of his zip when he had finished and waited for him to go back to his colleagues, but he remained where he was, and David had the feeling he was being watched. It would take someone with very sharp eyesight to distinguish his outline from the undergrowth. He moved his head slowly until he was facing the soldier, and they looked into each other's eyes.

David's reactions were quicker than his. By the time he had raised his rifle, David was already upon him and had tackled him to the ground, his hand firmly clamped over the soldiers' mouth. The man kicked out with his legs, catching David in the chest, knocking the breath out of him and making him lose his grip on his weapon. He fell awkwardly, but in a matter of seconds had picked himself up and threw his whole weight on top of the soldier, stifling any sound that could alert his colleagues. It took a lot of effort to keep his hand clamped over the soldier's mouth whilst his fingers clawed at David's face and eyes. His free hand searched the ground for something to use in his defence. His fingers closed on a rock and before he knew what had hit him, the soldier went sprawling on the ground. It was a vicious and bloody fight both men kicking out with booted feet and clenched fists, and it was touch and go who would come out the winner. But eventually David saw an opening and using all his strength managed to overcome his opponent and send him crashing to the ground where he lay unconscious, his face resting in the pool of his own urine.

David daren't leave him where he could easily be found when his colleagues started looking for him. He picked him up and carried him away from the road and through another gate into a field full of wheat. He carried him round the field until they were far enough away for his cries not to be heard. He then tied the soldiers' hands and feet together with his own belt, and formed a gag out of his handkerchief, which was stuffed in his mouth. When David left him he was starting to come round.

He picked up the soldier's rifle and slung it over his shoulder before returning to look for his own gun.

Another patrol was skirted before he reached the farm track that he guessed would take him back to the plane. It was closed off from the road with a wooden gate but he continued for a short distance, until he reached another junction, and yet another jeep. They were watching the tarred roads that encircled the airport. There was no sign of any more traffic and he was getting worried they would start to look for the missing soldier. He could not afford to hang around any longer, and made his way back to the plane.

He was concerned Pam would not make it that night. He did not want to keep the plane standing on the runway during the following day, and prayed they would be able to leave before dawn. He hoped Pam would have enough initiative to approach the airport cautiously and did not fancy their chances if they were stopped and searched. He hoped they would leave their vehicle some distance away and approach the airport on foot, but he and Liam would have to go in search of them in case they did not know what danger they were heading into.

Blood and mud liberally coated his clothes and body, and he was so wet and filthy by the time he climbed back into the aircraft that Amy ran to him and did all she could to clean him up.

Liam was already wearing his balaclava and on the point of leaving. David explained where each patrol was situated, and the only chance they had of getting the refugees on board was by using the farm track which ran right up to the airport perimeter. Situated as it was, the plane should hide their activities from the people in the terminal buildings and make it a bit easier for them to board.

A few minutes later David dropped down from the wing carrying the rifle he had taken from the soldier and, closely followed by Liam, ran to the hole in the fence. They were not challenged, and hoped their activities had not been noticed. They walked together to the point where the track turned left, and Liam took the left fork, whilst David continued on his previous course. He joined the road, and returned to the crossroads, turning left away from the airport entrance. A few miles up the road, he waited in the darkness. Each time a vehicle approached, he tried to see who was in it, and hoped he would be able to recognise, and make contact with, his cousin.

Jack and Amy remained on board the plane to make sure everything was made ready for their passengers. Jack carried the handgun and was ready to use it if anyone caused trouble. He paid particular attention to what Zac Powalski was up to.

If he heard shooting, or found that Liam and David had been taken, then he was to try and contact Pam. If he found her, they were to depart immediately everyone was on board, but if she, too, was captured he was to instruct the pilot to leave Osijek and return to Manchester. Under no circumstances were they to wait for anyone who had been captured.

Chrissie and Frank were sitting together in first class holding hands, and speculating on how worried their families and colleagues would be. They hoped Fiona would still be waiting for them when they eventually returned to Manchester, and they would tell her they were going to be married straight away. Life was too unpredictable to wait.

Zac Powalski was watching Jack. He was virtually the only hijacker on board now that Malcolm was no use to anyone, and he dismissed Amy as being a mere child. If the others would co-operate, it should be possible for them to over-power him, and regain control of the aircraft. They could then take off and be back in Manchester in a few hours time.

He walked over to the captain, and was disgusted to see him actually holding hands with one of the crew. Powalski would have to report him when they returned to Chicago. It was against company policy to be intimate whilst on duty, and because they had been hijacked was no excuse.

When he explained what he intended to do Captain Proctor didn't agree. He didn't want to risk anyone being hurt if Jack had the nerve to shoot, or what his reactions would be if they tried to get away. Besides, if there were some refugees waiting to be flown back to the UK, then he could see no harm in it, and that was what they would do.

Zac could hardly believe his ears. Was Frank really going to sit back and let the hijackers dictate what he should and shouldn't do? Well, he wasn't such a coward. He'd show them. He knew his duty, and, if he got the chance, he wouldn't hesitate to stop them.

With this in mind, he went and sat in the seat nearest the emergency exit. Jack watched him move, and stood over him, waving the handgun menacingly, a look of excitement in his eyes.

— CHAPTER 12 —

After saying good-bye to his wife and children, the Officer remained at his desk at headquarters in Brod. He waited until he was off duty before contacting the airport at Osijek. He was told that a plane was standing on the runway, with its crew and hijackers still on board. There had been no communication between them since the plane landed, and all they had done was to ask the military for assistance. Soldiers had been posted at strategic points round the airfield, and guard dogs were patrolling the perimeter at random.

The officer asked to be kept informed of any activity from the plane, and suggested they let the hijackers make the first move. It wasn't diplomatic to start any confrontation, particularly at this time when they didn't want to get America or Britain any more involved in the war than they already were. He recommended they did not interfere with the hijackers, and suggested that only if it could be proved they were bringing illegal arms into the country should they be stopped.

It was little enough he had done, but he dare not compromise himself any more and hoped the telephone call would have eased the way for his family.

It was well past midnight by the time Kajic announced they were almost at the airport, and wanted to know if they were to drive into the aerodrome or leave the vehicles outside and approach on foot.

"No, don't drive in," Pam said. "We must be careful. Is there a road we can take that gives us a view of the airport? Let's stop and look at the map."

They found a road that wound up the hill, taking them away from the airport, but which should give them a view of the whole area. They would decide what to do when they got to the top and had seen whether the plane was waiting for them or not. They took a right hand turn shortly before they would have passed David on the main road.

They left the truck and looked down on the airport complex. The main buildings were lit but the runway was in darkness. Kajic wished he'd had the forethought to bring some binoculars.

It all looked very peaceful, but if a plane was waiting for them, he could see no sign of it. For the first time he felt discouraged. If the doctor had been let down by her friends, what were they going to do with all these people? Would they really be allowed into the hospital at Osijek? At least Dr. Milbourne had been told they were on their way. Perhaps he would be able to help.

It took some persuading to make Pam stay with the truck whilst Kajic and Nedzad walked off into the darkness to find out what they could. Mahmutovic had also wanted to go with them, but been persuaded that, as the only able-bodied man left, it was his duty to stay behind in case the doctor needed him.

Kajic and Nedzad moved slowly down the hill until they came to another road. They turned in the direction of the airport, keeping well into the shadows, until they heard a vehicle coming up behind them. They crouched down as the vehicle sped past. As it approached a bend in the road they saw its brake lights come on. Kajic whispered to Nedzad to stay where he was, and ran on ahead until he could see what was happening round the corner.

There was a military jeep parked at the side of the road, and one of the soldiers had stopped the vehicle, and was talking to the driver whilst another soldier casually inspected the car.

Kajic ran back to Nedzad and signalled to him to keep quiet. He whispered that they would have to return the way they had come, and try and find another way into the airport.

They doubled back until they came to a narrow, unmade road that looked as if it were used by farm vehicles. It seemed to be going in the right direction, so they decided to climb over the gate, grateful for the protection of the hedge. After a short distance the track turned sharply until it reached the perimeter of the airport. It then followed the line of the airport fence.

As they walked further down the lane, they could make out the outline of a plane, parked close to the track, and at the very end of the runway.

"That must be it," Nedzad whispered. "How do we get in touch with them? What do we do if it's not them?"

"It's got to be them," Kajic replied. "They'll be keeping a watch for us. We must let them know we're here. Let's get as close as we can, and hope they'll see us."

They were almost at the hole in the fence when they heard a slight noise from behind. They turned and saw Liam standing there, his balaclava hiding his face and a rifle pointing at them in a business-like way. They stood quite still, not knowing what to do. Nedzad took hold of Kajic's arm, and tried to stand in front of him, protecting him from Liam.

"Who are you?" the man asked in an Irish accent, strange to their ears.

"We're just out walking the dog. He's run off somewhere, and we're looking for him," Kajic replied in English.

"And what sort of dog would that be?" Liam asked.

"An English setter," Kajic replied.

With a sigh of relief, Liam lowered his rifle.

"It's all right then, me friends, there's no need to worry," Liam said. "Where is Dr. Crichton?"

"Thank God you've come," Kajic replied, relieved to have made contact and mistaking Liam for David. He pushed Nedzad to one side. "Dr. Crichton's just up the road, and there are a lot of people with her. It's good to meet you, sir. She's told me a lot about you, and we knew you wouldn't let her down," he continued, holding his hand out in welcome. "My name is Kajic, and this is Nedzad. We didn't know if you were enemies. We've had lots of trouble getting here, and we hoped you would have waited for us."

"Of course we've waited for you," Liam replied. "I'm a friend of the doctors, and her cousin is waiting up the road. Take me to Dr. Crichton and we can collect him on the way. We can decide what's the best way of getting you all to the plane once we've seen where they are."

When they reached the main road, Liam told them to wait in the quiet of the field whilst he went to find David.

"Liam tells me you've left Dr. Crichton with the transport," David said. "How far away is she, and how many of you are there?"

"Two vehicles, mainly full of children but with some adults. We left them at the top of the hill."

"Can they walk to the plane?"

"Not all of them. It would take the young children a long time, and there aren't enough adults to carry them. Also some of them are wounded."

"Right, then we'll have to bring them down in the cars. To avoid the patrols we must cut across the farmland until we reach this road. We'll have to keep the lights off, and, if necessary, have someone walk in front of each vehicle to show the way. We must hurry, but we can't afford to risk an accident at this stage."

"We've got a truck and a bus, not cars," Kajic said, trying to make everything clear. "Do you think this track's wide enough?"

"It'll have to be. This is not the time to worry about the paintwork!"

"I'll lead the way back," Nedzad said, eager to please, "but if we return the way Kajic and I came, there's no need to cut across the field. We can follow the road until we come to this track, and if we open the gate, the vehicles can drive through. On our way here, we had to turn back once because of the soldiers, but then we didn't know the road. Now we can go straight back. There was no-one about when we came down."

"Then lead on, young'un," Liam said falling into step beside him.

It took them less than half an hour to get to the top of the hill. Pam and Mahmutovic were both listening out for the slightest noise, and when Kajic gave a whistle, it was echoed by Pam, and soon the two parties were greeting each other. Pam threw her arms round David and cried with relief.

Liam told Kajic to tell everyone to get back into the vehicles. They were to be completely quiet, and it was important for the children to remain silent. No one was allowed to smoke, in case the glow from their cigarette was seen.

Having been woken up, the children were fractious and it took a lot of ingenuity and imagination to keep them quiet. Little Melita was reluctant to let Pam out of her sight, and cried whenever she was put down, so she sat contentedly in the cab, playing with one of the buttons on Pam's blouse.

David told Kajic to drive slowly as he climbed onto the sill by the drivers' door and clung onto the outside of the vehicle, the soldier's rifle still in his hand, the safety catch off.

They drove with dipped headlights until they thought their lights might be seen, and then switched them off. Nedzad guided them to the track that led back to the plane.

The vehicles edged slowly forward at walking pace, going down the middle of the track and being guided on their way by the intermittent moonlight. When the clouds obscured the moon they had to rely on their night vision, and, miraculously, they arrived at the perimeter fence with no mishaps.

They turned to the right, following the fence and heading for the gap. They hadn't gone very far when they saw a vehicle parked in front of them. It was the jeep that had challenged them on the runway, its two front tyres replaced, and the machine gun pointing towards the plane. It could not have been there long, because the bonnet was still hot from the heat of the engine. David indicated for everyone to stay where they were, and, crawling flat on his stomach, moved slowly and silently forwards.

He could smell their cigarette smoke seconds before the soldiers came into view. There were four of them crouching by the perimeter fence, with their backs turned towards him. They were pointing at the plane, and talking in whispers. He couldn't tell what they were saying.

He sensed, rather than heard, a movement behind him, and turned sharply onto his back, legs and arms raised in an attempt to protect his body from attack. He swore under his breath when he realised it was Liam.

The soldiers had stopped short of the gap, and Liam indicated he would go round them so they could attack from both sides. He would signal when he was ready.

David lay still, waiting for the signal and hoping the soldiers would not return to their jeep before he was ready. At last he heard it, the sound of a nightjar, a pause of ten seconds, then the sound repeated.

On Liam's signal, David stood up and raised the rifle, shouting to the soldiers to stand still. He could see the white of their faces reflected in the moonlight as they turned to see where the sound had come from. One of the men stood up, but even before he could raise his own rifle, Liam had jumped forward, and knocked him to the ground.

David bent almost double and ran as fast as he could towards the two soldiers nearest the fence. They were still crouching down as he threw himself on top of the nearest one. Together they rolled on top of the other man, and David heard the crack of a bone breaking.

They fought like animals, kicking, punching and biting each other until David had him in such a position that one sharp move would have broken his neck. It was only then that he was able to look round, and see that Liam had already tied up one soldier, and another lay unconscious on the ground. The man they had fallen on had broken his upper leg, and in spite of the tremendous pain he must have been in, was dragging himself towards the jeep. He would have reached it in another second if Liam had not stopped him.

He pulled the trousers off the man David was holding, and soon he was trussed up and unable to move. The injured soldier suffered the same fate.

They dragged them back to the jeep and sat them down, tying their own clothing round their necks, and securing them firmly to the vehicle. The more they struggled, the tighter their bindings became. They would be completely immobilised until someone came to rescue them.

David emptied their weapons, and removed the ammunition from the machine gun. Liam took a razor sharp knife from one of the men, and slipped it down his sock.

They decided not to destroy the radio. If someone tried to contact the soldiers and found it had gone dead, they would become suspicious and send someone to find out what had happened. If they got no reply, they would assume they had left the jeep to reconnoitre the area. It could give them those extra precious minutes to get everyone on board the plane.

They pushed the jeep off the road, and David told Mahmutovic to stand guard, and let him know if he heard any sound from the radio. He was told not to touch anything, but to run and tell them straight away. He waved as they drove past and parked beside the hole in the fence.

Liam climbed the rope ladder on to the wing of the plane and put his head in through the open door.

"We've got them," he said triumphantly. "Stand by to receive your new passengers, Captain."

He was nearly knocked over by Amy in her rush to greet Pam!

Janni and Nedzad put their weight on the bottom of the rope ladder, making it firm for the others to climb up, but it was a slow process, and some of the children were frightened of falling. Liam searched the ground to find the abandoned wire cutters, and opened the fence to the very top. Osbih then drove the bus through the gap, and parked under the wing of the plane. He climbed onto the roof and the children were helped up to him. He was then able to lift them on to the wing, where David and Liam were waiting to take them into the safety of the aircraft.

Jack asked the crew to help in lifting the children into the plane. Chrissie looked at Frank for guidance.

"Please yourself, then," he said, as Melita was left standing in the aisle, rubbing her eyes and quite bewildered at finding herself in a strange dark place, with unknown people staring at her, and being separated from the doctor. She started to cry, and Chrissie picked her up and tried to console her.

They didn't know whether it was the noise, the movement or just coincidence, but they had almost emptied the truck when the searchlights were turned on, and the activity round the plane was visible to everyone. Liam grabbed the nearest rifle and crouched in the shelter of the wheel arch. He fired at one of the lights but it remained obstinately lit.

"Damn this shagging rifle," he said, throwing it down on the ground. "Pass me the one we got in London, and I can do the job properly."

David handed him Old Josh's rifle, and his second shot took out one of the lights. The result was exactly what they wanted. The lights were switched off, and the place was plunged into darkness once more. They were able to continue getting the refugees on board.

Mahmutovic came running towards them, saying they were trying to contact the soldiers on the radio. David told him to forget about it. Everyone on the plane started to help then, and in a very short time most of the people were sitting in their seats. Janni, Mahmutovic and Nedzad remained outside and were talking to Kajic.

"Come on," David shouted. "We've no time to lose. The sooner we're away the better. What's keeping you?"

"The boys only asked for a lift to Osijek," Kajic explained, "but want to know if it's possible for them to go with you to England. Will they have the chance to finish their university education, and start a new life there, or will they be made to return to Bosnia?"

"Of course they can come," he shouted. "Tell them we'll do all we can to help them, but hurry!"

With his wounded knee, Janni found it impossible to climb up the rope ladder, but there were plenty of willing hands to lift him aboard, and soon the three friends were seated together in the aircraft.

David asked Chrissie to secure the door and turned to Captain Proctor.

"Captain, we are now ready to return to Manchester," he said, giving him a mock salute.

"Yes sir," he replied. "And there's nowhere I'd rather go than Manchester!"

Only then did they realise that the first officer was missing. Zac Powalski was not on the plane.

Zac Powalski had taken advantage of the fact that everyone was concentrating on getting the refugees on board, and his movements went un-noticed. If he could get the IRA money and leave now he was certain he could bribe his way into Hungary. He could then start a new life for himself away from the USA and it was time to make a new start. Alert to take advantage of any opportunities available to him, he couldn't believe his luck when he saw the handgun Jack had carelessly left on the seat when the refugees had arrived. He slipped it into his pocket, casting a furtive look round to make sure nobody had noticed.

The first opportunity he had to leaves the plane was when the old man was manoeuvring the bus under the wing, and everyone's attention was diverted. He crawled to the wing tip and dropped the case onto the ground, and on the pretext of helping, climbed down the ladder. It was easy to slip away un-noticed.

Crouching low, Powalski ran down the lane until he came upon a jeep with four soldiers securely tied in their seats. A young man was keeping watch over them, so he moved out into the field and decided to lay low until the coast was clear.

On learning of Powalski's disappearance, Liam's first thought was the money. He asked Dave Branson to show him where the crew stowed their luggage, but there was nothing belonging to Powalski.

Cursing himself for not keeping a closer eye on him, Liam said he would have to bring him back to the plane. He couldn't have got far and his case would have delayed him further. It was then Jack realised the handgun was missing, and assumed Powalski had taken it.

Cursing Jack for an incompetent fool, Liam called for the emergency exit to be re-opened and was soon on the ground. He reckoned Powalski would have remained in the field until things settled down, and after a few minutes found his tracks heading away from the airport. Following the signs of someone dragging a heavy case, he soon caught up with him, squatting in the field with his back to the airport.

Trying not to make a sound, Liam crept nearer. His intention was to jump Powalski before he had time to fire Jack's handgun. He had almost reached him when Powalski heard a noise and turned round to see Liam bearing down on him, a look of hatred in his face.

His instinct was to run, and he stood up and ran as fast as he could holding his cracked ribs with both hands. When he remembered the handgun, he took it out of his pocket and pointed it at Liam just as he caught up with him and tackled him to the ground.

Powalski fell awkwardly, and couldn't move for a few seconds. That gave Liam the advantage, and he soon had him in a position where Powalski was unable to move, with the knife Liam had taken from the soldier cutting into the skin of his throat.

"Trying to run out on us, you shagging bastard!" Liam's mouth was close to Powalski's ear. "You know what happens to those who betray their friends and steal their money? I'd knee-cap you right here, but I don't want to bring the soldiers down on us."

"Come on, O'Grady, we're in this together. We can help each other. I've got the money here. We could share it, fifty fifty. No one in Ireland need know anything about it. If you help me get into Hungary, I'll make sure you're set up for the rest of your life."

"Why should I trust you?" Liam wanted to know.

"I could give you names. Richard Wainwright is the main man in Chicago, and I've managed to get a lot of other contact numbers from him. It would be easy for a young man like you to find out their identities, and there could be wealth beyond your wildest dreams paid to keep their names secret."

"Why you shagging bastard, you'd sell your mother to save your own skin."

"We can be partners and work together. It could be good for both of us."

"I wouldn't work with you if you were the last man alive."

"Sh, there's someone coming."

Liam had also heard the noise, and with a quick movement of his hand, slit Powalski's throat.

He turned to see David staring down at them and shaking his head.

After taking the gun out of Powalski's hand, Liam pushed the limp body to one side, wiped the blood off his knife and returned it to his sock.

"I had to stop him firing and bringing the soldiers down on us," he explained.

"And sorting your other problem at the same time, no doubt?" David replied, watching Liam search for Powalski's case.

"That too, of course," Liam replied. "We'd better get back, there's nothing more we can do here."

"We can't leave him here."

"Why not?" Liam wanted to know.

"Because it's an unwritten law that we always take our dead home."

"Please yourself, but what will you say when they want to know who killed him?"

"I could tell them the truth," David replied, trying to pick Powalski up in a fireman's lift.

"I think he was knifed by the soldiers sent to find out what was happening to the truck."

"Why did he take his case?"

"How do we know? It's not our business to know what's in his mind."

"I must be mad to agree to that," David said, heading back to the plane as fast as he could.

Neither man spoke until they were back on board. Liam told the others he had been too late to save Powalski. It appeared he must have run into some soldiers. Liam had found him lying in the field with his throat cut. He had found Powalski's case nearby and decided to take it home for his next of kin.

Captain Proctor was devastated. He couldn't believe what Zac had done. He'd been told not to leave the protection of the plane, and warned what could happen. It was his own fault for disobeying his orders, but it didn't make his death any easier.

"I'm sorry Captain but there's no point in risking another life to retrieve his body. Unless we're going to let them pick us off one by one, we'd better move," David said, putting his hand on the pilot's shoulder.

The pilot boosted the engines in preparation for take-off, but before the plane began to move, Jack entered the cockpit.

"He's not the only one who's missing," he shouted. "Have you seen Malcolm? The last time I saw him he was asleep in first class."

"When was that?"

"Just after you followed Powalski."

"Damn him," David said. "Have you checked the toilets?"

"He's not there. I'm certain he's not on board."

"Damn him," he said again. "If they've not killed him as well, I'll have to go back and look for him. Stop the port engine, Captain, or you'll fry me alive."

The noise of the engines had made the people on the ground more active. A number of vehicles were heading towards them and the airfield lights were switched on.

They could see Malcolm sitting on the grass leaning against the fence, a bottle in one hand and a cigarette in the other, completely oblivious of his surroundings.

"Open the door again," David said. "I'll have to go and get him."

"No," Jack shouted, trying to hold him back. "Leave him here. You'll never make it. He's an American. They won't hurt an American!"

"And what do you think the first officer was?" he said, pushing Jack away. "Of course they'll kill him if they get the chance."

Liam had already opened the door, and climbed out onto the wing even before the engine stopped. David followed, and they jumped onto the roof of the bus, and down to the ground. Liam knelt behind one of the wheels, and fired his rifle under the belly of the plane. The vehicle nearest the plane stopped.

Bent almost double, David ran to the fence and picked Malcolm up in a fireman's lift. A bullet whizzed past within a few inches of his head, quickly followed by the sound of Liam's weapon. The sniper fired again, and this time David felt the bullet hit Malcolm. The impact nearly knocked him over, but he managed to hold on, and was soon back under the shelter of the wing.

They managed to lift Malcolm's unconscious body onto the roof of the bus. The steward was leaning over the wing, and he reached down and dragged Malcolm into the plane.

Liam looked at David and shook his head.

"Look at us," he shouted. "Risking our lives for that shagging bastard. And do you think we'll get any thanks? Not in a million years."

"Come on," David shouted, pushing him in front. "This is no time for thanks."

David grabbed hold of Liam and pushed him ahead. Before he could follow, he heard a noise that made his blood turn to ice. He looked to his left and froze. A dog was streaking towards him, its teeth bared and a wild look in its eyes. He could hear a fierce growl, and the sound brought him back to his senses. He tried to jump away, but was gripped by fear. He felt Liam's hands trying to get a grip on his clothes, but they were wet and slippery from crawling in the ditch, and he fell back onto the runway.

The dog was on him before he could move, its teeth sinking into the flesh of his right arm, and the weight of its body pinning him to the ground.

Liam jumped down on top of them, and plunged the knife he had so recently used, into the animals' neck. It gave an awful howl, and turned towards him, but before it could attack, he slit its throat, and, tossing the body to one side, somehow managed to lift David off the ground. Using all his strength, the little Irishman hauled him back into the safety of the plane.

"Go, go, go!" he shouted as soon as they were inside, and even before the G-force of take off forced him back into his seat, David had lost consciousness.

— CHAPTER 13 —

It was such a lovely day that Grandpa decided to leave the milking to Joe for once, and take his gun out to see if he could shoot some rabbits for the pot. He couldn't understand why the key to the gun cabinet was missing, as he was always particular about keeping it safe. He kept a logbook to show who had used it and when, meticulously recording dates and times, and according to that, it should be hanging on its proper hook.

When asked if she knew where it was, Granny said she hadn't seen it, and started to worry. She was afraid it could have got into the wrong hands.

"Don't be daft, love," Grandpa laughed at her concern. "It couldn't have been taken by anyone but the family. Nobody else could have found it, or even know what it unlocks if they did happen to see a key lying about. It's been a secure system all these years, so I can't believe it would fail us now. Someone must have opened the cabinet and forgotten to put the key back, however unlikely that sounds."

"You've used it since Matthew was home, and I don't think David's used it for years, and Amy wouldn't take it without your knowledge. Anyway, what would she want with it in Yorkshire?"

"Well, it certainly isn't Pam, you or me, so that only leaves Amy. It isn't like her to take it without permission. Why don't you give her a ring and ask if she's any idea where it could be?"

"That'll be it. She's been invited to take part in a shoot, and was so excited she forgot to fill in the book. I'll give her what for when she gets back. It's too bad of her to take it without permission."

"I can't help feeling that something's wrong."

"Don't fratch, love, there must be a logical explanation. Give her a ring then and if she's taken it you can stop worrying."

When Granny spoke to Amy's friend, she was upset to learn Amy wasn't there. They hadn't seen each other for months.

Granny couldn't think of any reason why Amy would go away secretly and take the shotgun with her. Amy was aware of the law on firearms, and knew the consequences of carelessness or abuse. She also knew that, as the licence holder, any misuse of the shotgun would be the responsibility of her Grandpa, and it wasn't like her to do anything that would get her family into trouble. But Amy was so high-spirited and headstrong that she would do things on impulse without considering the long-term consequences.

She expressed her concern to her husband. Grandpa pooh-hooed the idea that Amy had anything to do with the missing key, and decided that he must have mislaid it last time he went shooting. He started looking for it in earnest, but as the day wore on, and there was still no sign of the key, he started to lose his temper.

His attempt to ring Pam in Sarajevo was a cause of more concern. Her colleagues had lost touch with her, and no one knew where she was or what she was doing. A small comfort was derived from the knowledge that she had her driver-cum-interpreter with her.

His next call to the camp was equally frustrating when he was told that David was on leave for at least another week. He was generally pretty good at letting them know his movements, so why all the secrecy now? Where could he be and what was he up to?

Matthew was the only one of his grandchildren he managed to contact. He said he hadn't heard from his sister or cousins, but he was getting a bit worried about Pam. The reports of the escalation of the problems in Bosnia were disturbing, but as he didn't know of anything he could do to help, he was quite capable of putting it to the back of his mind.

He was more interested in talking about his new girlfriend. It had been love at first sight, and he was looking forward to introducing her to his family. He was certain they would love her, and he would take the first opportunity of bringing her down to the farm and showing her where he had spent the majority of his childhood. He liked to tease her about the advantages he had over someone brought up in a major city in America.

Grandpa brought him back to the question of Amy's whereabouts, but Matthew could not remember when he had last heard from either Amy or Pam, but thought it must have been two or three months ago. He was not a good correspondent, and the girls seemed to be too busy to bother writing to him.

"Amy and Pam have been in touch with each other a lot within the last few days," Granny said when Grandpa put the phone down.

"That's not unusual. They've always stayed in touch," Grandpa replied, "but Pam wouldn't involve Amy in anything dangerous. If she was in trouble surely she'd ask David."

"But David's away," Granny pointed out. "Could Pam have asked Amy to contact him? Do you think that could be it, and she's gone off to look for him?"

"But why take the shot-gun? It's ridiculous to think she'd have to use it to make him help Pam. Knowing him, he'd jump at the chance, and enjoy every minute of it! No, there's got to be more to it than that."

"We mustn't get carried away. After all it's only the key that's missing. It could have fallen behind the dresser, or been put back in the wrong place."

"No. I've searched everywhere and it's not in this room. Before I contact the police, I've got to know for certain whether the shotgun is here or not."

"What if it isn't?"

"Then we've got to report it missing. It's my responsibility to keep them informed, and if I don't, and they find out, they won't renew my licence. After all, it could have been stolen, but I've not seen any sign of a break-in."

"If that was the case, surely the cabinet would have been damaged? There's no sign of any scratches, and the lock looks to be normal."

"Talking pays no toll," Grandpa replied. "Help me break into it now, before I lose my temper again."

"It's supposed to be burglar-proof," Granny replied with a sigh, but she was willing to help.

The special firearms cabinet had been built with the purpose of making it impossible for anyone to open it without the key. An hour later the cabinet remained obstinately shut. They had not made any impression on the solid structure and Grandpa was in such a temper that Granny left him alone to cool down.

When she took him a cup of tea he was standing by the window, staring out across the farmyard to the fields beyond.

"I can't wait to get my hands on that girl if she's done this to me," he said, running his hands through his grey hair and shaking his head.

"Well, we still don't know if she has anything to do with it, and I've been wondering why, if she did borrow the shotgun, she didn't put the key back. It's so seldom you take it out these days that it could have been weeks before we realised it was missing. She knows enough not to lose it, so perhaps she put it safe somewhere. Have you looked in her room to see if it's there?"

"Of course not. I never go in her room unless she specifically invites me. It doesn't sound hopeful to me, but we might as well look."

They had just about given up hope of finding anything when Grandpa discovered Amy's jewellery box concealed under a jumper at the bottom of her wardrobe. The key to the gun cabinet had been wrapped in a tissue and placed at the bottom of the main compartment.

———◦———

Their worst fears were realised when they opened the empty cabinet. The only thing inside was a note from Amy stating that she had taken the shotgun to help bring Pam home from Bosnia.

They were still deciding what to do when news of a hijack was first broken.

"We're getting news of an airliner that's been hijacked on its way from Chicago to Manchester," the newsreader said. "First reports say it's been diverted to Ireland, and we'll bring you more news as it comes in."

"Well, that can't be her," Granny said, a note of relief in her voice. "She's not in America that's for sure, and she wouldn't want to go to Ireland either."

"Don't be so absurd, as if she'd even think of hijacking a plane! You do have some funny ideas love," Grandpa laughed.

"Well there are times when I wouldn't put anything past her. She doesn't think things through before jumping in with both feet."

"But not anything as serious as hijacking a plane! She wouldn't have the nerve, or the know-how. It's so absurd I don't know why we're wasting our time discussing it."

"If she had managed to contact David, I'm sure he wouldn't have let her get involved, so who would she ask?"

"You know her friends better than I do."

Not wanting to let her husband know of her concern, Granny asked Joe when he had last seen Amy, and was told he had seen her with Jack Palmer driving out of the village together. He hadn't seen either of them since. She knew Amy had a crush on Jack, but there was something about that young man she didn't trust. But was that a good enough reason for Amy to lie to her? If she had wanted to go off with Jack for a few days, then surely she could have told them of her plans, but Granny knew she would have done everything she could to stop them.

"It has to be Jack. Jack Palmer. Joe said he'd seen them driving out of the village. They must have gone together."

"I can't see him doing anything to help anyone else or for that matter any reason why he would want to help Amy. It's not as if they're going out or anything."

"I know she's infatuated with him. You've got to admit he's very good looking, and owning a car like his can only add to his charm."

"I hope she's not that worldly!" Grandpa snapped.

"She's very young! Girls of that age are impressionable, but I think we're barking up the wrong tree. If it really is them, firstly, why would they need to hijack a plane, and secondly, why would they go to America to do it?"

"I don't know. It does seem to be a co-incidence, but, yes, you're right. We cannot afford to jump to conclusions and guessing pays no toll."

"If she has found out that Pam is not with the rest of the team, surely she wouldn't have gone out there to find her?"

"Of course not! She wouldn't be that foolish," but even as the words were spoken, they both realised that it was the sort of thing she just might do.

"Well, even if she did think of going, she wouldn't need to take your shotgun. There must be some other explanation."

"Pam is in the care of the medical team, and it is their responsibility to get her home, not ours. Besides, there's no reason for Amy, or anyone else for that matter, to go to Bosnia to meet her. That would be asking for trouble, and I cannot see it being any advantage to Pam either."

"I'd like to know how Jack Palmer is mixed up in her disappearance."

"Then let's go and see his mother, perhaps she can throw some light on the situation."

"We're now in touch with our correspondent in Ireland," the announcer said at the next news bulletin. "Can you tell us exactly what the situation is at Shannon?"

"Earlier this morning, a plane belonging to Wright Flights International was forced to divert to Shannon in Southern Ireland. We believe there were at least two hijackers on board. They gained entry to the flight deck and forced the pilot to land. The surprising thing is that all the passengers were made to leave, and were left on the runway."

"Are all the passengers safe then?"

"Yes they are, but they aren't very happy at being stranded, particularly when their luggage is still on the plane. I haven't been able to speak to any of them yet, but I understand they haven't been in any physical danger. Arrangements are being made to fly them on to Manchester, and they should be leaving Shannon within the next few hours."

"Do you know if the hijackers were armed?"

"Yes. They left a member of the crew to help with the passengers. She said one of the hijackers had a gun which he threatened to use if the pilot, Captain Frank Proctor, didn't follow his instructions."

"Thank you very much," the newsreader said. Looking straight into the camera, she continued, "we will bring you a further report from Manchester as soon as the passengers get there, and in the meantime we are trying to find out the identity of the hijackers. It is understood that Malcolm Wainwright, the son of the chairman of Wright Flights International, was on Flight WF254, and is thought to be still on board. We will let you know as soon as we have any further information."

News of the hijack was the main item on all the news channels, including live coverage of the passengers arriving at Ringway International Airport, Manchester.

A barrage of photographers greeted them and a number of people were interviewed. They all gave the same account; they had been told to leave their hand luggage behind, except for what they would need for an hours stay at Shannon, and it was whilst they were getting on the buses that the plane had taken off. They didn't expect to see their possessions again.

Many of them were angry, and liberal in their complaints, and were quite open about what they would do to the hijackers if they could lay hands on them, yet relieved they had escaped unharmed from such murderous and dangerous people. A number of passengers said they felt sure they could identify the people involved.

There were moving pictures of reunited families and friends crying and kissing each other. One man said he was thankful they were all safe, and the worst thing for him was picturing what might have been. He was grateful no one was hurt, and wanted to put the incident behind him.

An interview with the stewardess, Paula Smith, confirmed that Malcolm Wainwright was on board. He had certainly arranged for one of the hijackers to visit the flight deck, but whether from choice or because he was forced to do so, she couldn't say. He had remained on board, together with two male passengers and the rest of the crew. Everyone else had left the plane at Shannon although two young adults were unaccounted for, and believed to be still on the plane.

She then gave a list of the names of all the crew, and said there really was nothing further she could tell the press.

A short time later Mrs. Palmer was telling them that Jack had gone to London for a few days, but she didn't know how long he would be away. She thought he was alone, but he hadn't actually said so.

Not wanting to tell her of their fears, Granny and Grandpa made light of the truants and expressed the hope they would be back soon.

Mrs. Palmer then enquired how Pam was coping in Bosnia, and if she was planning to return home. She had been concerned for her, and was following the news reports with added interest.

She also stated how strange it was that one of the people on board the hijacked plane was a friends of Jack's. So far as she knew, they had not been in touch since their school days, but both Jack and Amy had been excited at seeing him interviewed by the BBC about the hijack in Tokyo. How strange that he should be on one of his own planes when it was hijacked! She had discussed the situation with Jack and Amy, and had been impressed by their knowledge of what was going on. She hadn't heard exactly what they had said, but from the tone of their voices she knew they were getting very excited. Yes, she could confirm that was the night before they left.

And now, within days this friend was once again in the news, also connected with a hijack. It seemed very strange to her, and she had wanted to ask Jack what it was all about, and wondered if her neighbours had any thoughts on the matter.

They couldn't think of any, and laughed it off as being a coincidence. Finding it hard to keep their emotions in check, they returned home, anxiously listening to the car radio for any news that could allay their fears.

The only explanation, however unreasonable, was what they had first thought, that Pam had asked Amy to contact David, and when she had not been able to do so, headstrong Amy had decided to take matters into her own hands.

They couldn't understand why she hadn't confided in them, as they would have done anything to get Pam home, but Amy had turned to Jack for help rather than her grandparents, and they felt hurt and embittered. The pain of seeing his granddaughter turn away from him was almost physical and a deep resentment towards Jack Palmer welled up inside him. Grandpa sat in his favourite chair staring into space. The sparkle had gone out of his eyes, and he looked old and tired.

Various thoughts jostled one another in Granny's head. If Jack's school friend had been made to help in this second hijack, and two young people were also involved, was it unreasonable to suppose that they could be Amy and Jack?

She could understand that it would be impossible to use a commercial flight to get to Bosnia in the current situation.

When they had been looking for the key, Granny had noticed a letter addressed to Amy in Pam's handwriting. She went upstairs to get it, and as she read it the tears rolled unheeded down her cheeks. All her fears and anxieties were confirmed. Silently she passed it to her husband to read.

"So it looks as if Amy and Jack really are the two young adults referred to," Grandpa said sitting down and holding his head between his hands.

"I've been thinking about this," Granny said, breaking the long silence. "If Amy and Jack are involved, and it was your shotgun used in the hijack, then who were the other two? If she had managed to contact David and he was one of the hijackers, I'm sure he wouldn't have let her go with him. So who could the two other hijackers be?"

"Don't be silly, woman," Grandpa tried to console her. "I don't know what they're up to, but Amy wouldn't do anything so dangerous, and even if she had managed to find David, he would soon put a stop to such nonsense. If the truth be known, they've probably gone to London to meet Pam, and decided to give us a surprise by bringing her back here unannounced."

"Then why take your shot-gun?" Granny wanted to know.

"How do I know?" he snapped. "But there's got to be some other explanation."

"Do you honestly believe that?"

"No," Grandpa had to admit.

Since the accident when the four children had gone to live together on the farm, Amy had been particularly close to Pam, and there wasn't anything she wouldn't do for her. Perhaps if David had been at home, things would not have been so bad, but David wasn't at home, and Granny knew that would not stop Amy from doing all she could to help her cousin.

It was reported that the plane had been tracked to Hungary, before changing course and heading towards Bosnia.

Reluctantly Grandpa admitted that if Amy had managed to hijack the plane, and was going to collect Pam and her colleagues, then that would answer all their questions.

Their anxiety turned to fear as the grandparents listened to the reports. They felt numb with shock, and dare not think of the outcome.

Yet Granny thought it was just like Amy, impulsive and daring, to go and do something outrageous to help her cousin.

"How can she be so stupid," Granny said for the umpteenth time. "Doesn't she know how dangerous it is? What will we do if she doesn't come back?"

Grandpa put his arms round her. It was as if they had been bereaved all over again.

— CHAPTER 14 —

Lieutenant Keith Walton was called to apartment 21 Erskine House on 32nd Street, Chicago. Homicide had a fascination for him. He got a lot of satisfaction from finding the killers, knowing they deserved everything the courts handed out to them.

He was always disturbed at the sight of young murder victims, and this case was no different. He was determined to find out who had brutally attacked this young girl, and make them pay for it. Mary McDowell had everything to live for. She had a good job with prospects, a nice apartment which she shared with a friend, Carol Comyn, and a loving family back home.

At first there didn't seem to be any motive for the killing. An autopsy revealed it wasn't a sexual attack, and it appeared the girl did not have any enemies. He set his team to work, sifting through everything, checking fingerprints, and finding out how the murderer had got into the building.

Gradually a picture started to emerge. The door hadn't been forced and, therefore, the victim must have known her killer. She had let him, or her, into the building and opened the apartment door herself. She must have known her visitor well enough to let them in when she was alone.

Everyone living in Erskine House had to be interviewed. Those who had already left by the time of the murder were eliminated as soon as it was confirmed they were where they claimed to be, and the remainder were questioned in detail, and asked to remember everything they had seen and heard that day. It didn't matter how small or insignificant, they were to let Lieutenant Walton know.

Keith Walton didn't believe in coincidence. Everything had a purpose and nothing was left to chance. Therefore, when he learned that Mary McDowell had been killed on the same day as flight WF254 had been hijacked, and that she had been involved in loading the passengers on that particular flight, he concentrated his enquiries on events at O'Hare International.

His friend and colleague, Lieutenant Tom Ford was in charge of the hijack investigation, and was willing enough to discuss the two cases. Gradually the two investigations merged together, as they realised the murder could well be connected to the incident at the airport.

He learned that Mary had been sent to escort a VIP at the last moment, and the plane had been delayed slightly. Under normal circumstances the police would not have been interested in that piece of information. There were always delays at airports, and even the passengers were amazed if they took off on time. No, on its own that didn't seem to be significant, except for the involvement of Malcolm Wainwright. The fact that he had behaved in a way different to his normal routine attracted their attention. True, there had been the odd occasion when he had not used the VIP lounge, but why hadn't he done so on that particular day, and why was he so late in getting there?

Another difference was that he had left his briefcase on the pavement whilst his colleague had carried his. Why? Was it so that the chauffeur would give it to him after they had passed through security? They heard how Charlie Monroe had allowed that particular piece of luggage to by-pass the X-Ray machine. He had taken it from the chauffeur and given it to Mr. Wainwright personally.

For a brief moment Charlie had wanted to deny it, but there were too many witnesses. He told the police the reason why he had not taken it through the security arch was that he was carrying enough metal on his person to set the alarms off, and he was completely sure in his own mind that Mr. Wainwright would not be a party to a hijacking. The most important thing at that moment had been to get the passengers boarded quickly and not to delay the plane any longer than was absolutely necessary.

Yes, he'd had instructions to be more vigilant, but on this occasion he had done what he thought was right at the time. He was sorry if he had done anything wrong.

After his visit to the airport, Lieutenant Walton returned to Erskine House and the janitor let him in. Apartment 21 was guarded by a young policeman and he opened the door for the Lieutenant to enter. He sat down, trying to absorb the atmosphere of the place and to picture what had happened that fateful day. He was sitting quietly when he heard the policeman knock on the door before letting Carol Comyn enter.

"Oh, it's you, Lieutenant," Carol said. "What are you doing here!"

"I'm trying to get a feel for the place," he replied. "I'm sorry if I frightened you. I was intending to come and see you later, but if you can spare the time, I'd prefer to talk to you here."

"I've just come to collect some more clothes. You know I'm staying with a friend for the time being?"

"Yes. But tell me, can you think of anyone who might have wanted to speak to Mary that day? A boy friend or someone who wanted her to get hold of some duty free cigarettes? Anything like that?"

"Well no, not really."

"But ... Come on, Miss Comyn, there was a definite 'but' in your hesitation."

"Well there was one person, but it's absurd to think he might have come here when she told him she wasn't interested."

"Go on."

"Well, there's this man at the airport. His name was, is, Charlie Monroe." Lieutenant Walton's interest heightened. So there was a connection between Monroe and the murdered girl. "He's quite a lot older than Mary, and yet he seemed to think she might want to go out with him. Mary was a kind-hearted girl, and someone had told her Charlie was divorced, and she felt sorry for him. I'm convinced there was nothing more to it than that. She was getting a bit fed up with him always trying to sit with her in the canteen and he was often waiting for her in the car park and walking her to her desk. She found him a bit of a laugh really."

"And he asked her out?"

"Yes. She told him she never even thought of him in that light, but he still insisted on pestering her. He rang her here on the day she was killed. I answered the phone and told him she was out. He didn't leave his name, but I know it was him."

"What makes you so sure?"

"It was his voice, being that bit older, and I switched on the loud speaker so that she could listen, and Mary said it was him."

"Then there's no doubt."

"No, none at all."

"And then what? Do you think she changed her mind?"

"No, I'm sure she wouldn't have done that. She had a boy friend, and she wouldn't have gone out with anyone else. She wasn't that sort of girl."

"Monroe was on duty at the airport at the time of the murder, so he couldn't have been here as well," the Lieutenant said, thinking aloud. "Tell me about the boy friend."

"They seemed quite keen and saw each other most days."

"Have you met him?"

"Very briefly when I got home from work one day. They were just leaving, so we only spoke for a few minutes."

"Do you know his name?"

"Yes, it's Peter Callahan."

"Tell me everything you know about him. Take your time, there's no rush."

"It's funny really, but he said he was a distant cousin of the Wainwright's. Evidently they're both descended from an Irish family who emigrated to the States a long time ago. With the growth of Wright Flights International, Mr. Wainwright's side of the family did well, as you know, and is now a well-established and well-respected family, one of the wealthiest in this part of the States, whereas Peter's family are struggling. He seemed to resent that, and I know he asked Mary a lot of questions about them but she was only an employee and wasn't able to tell him much."

"Think hard, Miss Comyn, and try to remember every detail of what Mary told you. It could be very important."

"I don't want to seem disloyal to Mary, but I wasn't too happy when she told me Peter had plans for making money, and wanted her to go away with him. They discussed where they would go if he pulled it off."

"Could he have asked her to help in some criminal act? Or if he was involved in the hijack, do you think he could have asked Mary to help smuggle arms onto the plane?"

"Good God, you don't think Mary had anything to do with that, surely."

"I don't know. It's a possibility and would give us a motive for the murder."

"I'm sure I'd have remembered if she'd said anything about that! But no, she definitely didn't mention it to me. It seems impossible she'd even consider helping the hijackers, it's so out of character."

"That's often the case. It's sometimes the quiet ones who are tempted. If this Peter Callahan could persuade her there was no danger to herself and she'd get a share in whatever money he could raise, do you think she'd have been tempted?"

"My first instinct is to say no, but truly I don't know. And I don't think it's fair of you to ask me. She was my friend, and I can't, won't, think ill of her."

"I'm sorry Miss Comyn. I was thinking aloud. In my job I've got to think of everyone who has an opportunity if I'm going to find out who murdered Mary and why."

"Do you think it was connected to the hijack then?" Carol wanted to know.

"I don't honestly know at this time. It's only speculation at the moment and just another avenue to go down. You know where to contact me if you think of anything else. We need all the pieces to fit into the puzzle before we get an overall picture of what really happened."

"Is Peter a suspect?"

"I've only just heard of his involvement. At the moment I'm more interested in Monroe. Do you know if Mary has told anyone else about her dealings with him?"

"You should ask Sonia, Mary's sister. She wrote to her all the time, and she told Sonia everything. I'd be surprised if she hadn't told her about that phone call, and the way we laughed when he rang off."

"Surely that was just before she was killed. What makes you think she wrote to Sonia then?"

"It was her letters. They were still on the table when I got home. It was the sight of them that made me suspect something was wrong. She always took them to the mail on her way to the airport, and on that day, they were still here."

"Where are they now?" he asked.

"In my purse. I put them there with the intention of mailing them when I went out later that evening, but when I found Mary, they went out of my mind, and they've been there ever since. Did I do wrong?"

"Don't worry about it. Can I have a look at the letter now? Did you say there were two? Who was the other one for?"

"It was a bill. We take it in turns to pay the Hydro, and it was that."

"Thank you, Miss Comyn, and don't worry about the letter. I'll make sure Sonia gets it after we've finished with it. Do we have a note of where you are staying?"

"Yes, I left the address with the police-woman. In fact, she helped me move in, so she's been there."

"Good. If you think of anything else, let me know."

Lieutenant Walton read the letter through a couple of times. It made fun of Charlie Monroe and confirmed everything Carol had said about him. It also hinted that Mary could soon be in possession of a large amount of money, but then went on to say she was just kidding, and not to take any notice. She asked Sonia not to tell anyone.

His team was told to find out all they could about Peter Callahan. This was easier than expected as he already had a police record. On leaving school, he had claimed kinship with the wealthy businessman and been given a job with Wright Flights International, but he had been caught stealing from the company, and a nasty argument had received a lot of publicity in the press. He had been involved in more than one incident with the police, and sworn to get even with WFI and particularly with the Wainwright family.

Peter Callahan was on the point of leaving his apartment when he heard someone at the door. He hoped it would be Mary, come to make up after their quarrel. He was shocked to see Lieutenant Walton and learn of her death.

Who could have done such a thing? And why? She was the only girl he had ever loved, and now she was dead! He would have to go away without her, but it wouldn't be the same!

"Planning to leave, are you?" the police officer asked, looking at the piles of clothes.

"Yes, we, Mary and I, were planning to go away together. I was supposed to pick her up later tonight."

"Is that what you were rowing about?"

How did he know about that? He would have to be careful. Had he said too much already? Perhaps it would have been better not to admit they were leaving, but he wasn't thinking clearly. He must be more careful!

"It was just a lovers tiff. Nothing important," he replied. "I can't believe she's dead. When did it happen, and how?"

"We've not established the exact time of death, but she was beaten up and suffocated."

"Dear God, who could do that to her? She is, was, such a sweet girl and I loved her more than anything. I can't believe it!"

"I'd like you to come down to HQ and answer a few questions. The car's waiting."

"What now? Can't it wait until later. I don't feel up to it at the moment."

"Come along, sir. It won't take long."

Before interrogating Peter at the police station, Lieutenant Walton was handed a statement from Ms. Emily Gammage. Ms. Gammage lived in Apartment 31 Erskine House, directly above the one occupied by the two girls. She was eager to tell them she had heard Mary arguing with her boy friend on the day of her death, and that she had distinctly heard raised voices. She had not been able to make out the exact words, but was adamant the quarrel was a serious one. She had banged on the floor, but they hadn't taken any notice. She had been so concerned she had gone down the stairs in order to make sure Mary was not in trouble. No, she hadn't used the elevator as it made too much noise, and, after all, it was only one flight of steps and far more convenient.

She was about to knock on the door when she heard them talking normally. Not wanting to interfere, she had returned to the stairs and gone up the first few steps, out of their sight, just as the door had opened. The young man left the apartment and swore in impatience at having to wait for the elevator. She didn't think he had seen her and as she didn't want to appear nosy, she had gone back to her own floor, knowing Mary was alone and not being threatened any more. The police wanted to know what time that had been and she was able to tell them the exact time as she had written it in her diary.

From her sitting room window Ms. Gammage had a good view of the street and could see most of what went on. She spent much of her time sitting and watching the world go by and sometimes she got frustrated because the only place not visible from her window was under the canopy when people were actually standing at the main door. She liked to watch the comings and goings of the residents of Erskine House, as she regarded them as her family. She generally knew if anyone was in or out of the building. Some of the residents understood and thanked her for keeping an eye on things, but others called her a busybody and she hated the idea they might think her nosy. She was interested in them, that was all, and it gave her something to do and a purpose in her life if she thought she was helping in some small way.

If anyone had mislaid their key they all knew to ring her apartment and she would let them in. That was what she thought had happened later on that particular day. Someone had rung the outdoor bell and she had pressed the button to release the lock. She waited to hear the sound of the elevator but whoever it was hadn't used it, which meant they must still be on the lower floor. She hoped she hadn't let a salesman into the building, and felt she should ring the janitor, but she hadn't wanted to, as he had been quite nasty when she had opened the door on previous occasions and she didn't feel up to explaining that she had been pleased to help her neighbours and hadn't even thought about security.

She had dozed off in her chair, so couldn't be positive whether Mary was in the building or not, but she began to feel uneasy and decided to give her a ring. Ms. Gammage had phoned Apartment 21, and got no reply. Wanting to make sure she hadn't let any undesirables into the building she once again went down the stairs to the second floor. She heard a door bang and saw the same young man walking away from Mary's door. They stared at each other before he turned and ran down the stairs and out of the building. Again she was able to give them the exact time.

Emily Gammage was shown a photograph of Peter Callahan and was able to identify him. As an afterthought, she was shown a picture of Charlie Monroe, and she said she was certain he, too, had visited Erskine House that same day.

Carol left a message for Lieutenant Walton at police headquarters. She remembered Mary telling her she had seen Peter talking to Charlie

Monroe in the car park. She had been surprised they knew each other, but when Mary asked about it, Peter said they had just met and were only passing the time of day.

As Ms. Gammage had stated that Monroe had been to the apartment on the day of Mary's death, the lieutenant decided it was time to speak to him and had him brought to the precinct for questioning. There was something in his eyes and the way he acted that roused Lieutenant Walton's suspicions. He asked Tom Ford to sit in on the interrogation after giving him all the known facts.

Charlie knew the old feeling of hopelessness. He had been so certain no one knew he had been interested in Mary McDowell, but it now appeared some of his department had been laughing at him behind his back and making bets as to whether he could succeed in attracting the young girl or if she would refuse to go out with someone of his age and reputation. It was intolerable.

Yet on that fateful day, he had left the airport unobserved and had his time card to prove he was on duty at the time Mary was killed. He was certain no one could prove he had left the premises and that would be the best alibi anyone could have.

He did not enjoy the interview with Lieutenant Ford and Lieutenant Walton, but didn't think he had said anything to arouse suspicion. He admitted he had been interested in Mary but she had refused to go out with him and he had accepted her decision. He had not tried to push her into any other, or stronger, relationship. He was a responsible person and wouldn't do anything to upset a vulnerable young girl. He admitted talking to Callahan in the course of his duty as WFI had requested airport security to keep him away from their planes. When he had seen him in the car park he had asked him to leave and a nasty argument had ensued, resulting in Callahan being escorted off the premises.

Tom Ford was certain the link between Monroe and Mary was connected to the incident at the airport, and the briefcase. He was already in possession of Charlie's prison record and knew all about the way he had beaten up his wife. He was amazed a corporation like O'Hare International had taken on an ex-offender in such an important position where he was vulnerable to temptation and an easy target for blackmail.

The next step was to find out if Monroe was an accomplice and had deliberately helped the hijackers to smuggle the weapons on board, or if he had been duped by them. If Monroe had done his job properly, the weapons would not have gotten on board the plane, assuming they had been in the briefcase.

Having discovered everything that had happened to Monroe over the past few days, how his girlfriend had left him, how he had been turned down by Mary and then been used by the hijackers, would all contribute to a lowering of his self esteem. He wasn't the sort of man to allow these things to wash over him, and they could all have contributed to his anger. He had a history of violence and the Lieutenant felt he was quite capable of killing Mary in a fit of temper.

Lieutenant Tom Ford set his team on interviewing everyone who was at the airport at the time of Mary's death. He wanted to know exactly where they were, what they were doing and who they were with. This way people confirmed where their colleagues were and yet no one admitted to being with Monroe. There was a period of a couple of hours when no one could confirm he was even on the premises.

Lieutenant Walton had been interested to learn of the connection between Callahan, Monroe and Mary. Callahan's involvement in the hijack wasn't altogether unexpected. They were able to prove he was at the airport at the time of the hijack. He had been seen following Mary to the security area in Terminal C when she had left her post to go and escort the VIP's. What was needed now was proof he had used Monroe to get the briefcase on the plane without it being checked. He had been caught leaving Chicago, yet his landlady said he had just paid the rent for the next quarter, so why was he leaving in such a hurry? Was he running away? The fact he had been seen at O'Hare that day and at the apartment later, was enough to make him a firm suspect in the murder. If he had organised the hijack with Mary, then they must have needed the help and co-operation of Monroe to get the briefcase through security.

Keith Walton had the reputation of being a tough cop and he had no sympathy for Callahan, and it was his intention to get him to admit his part in the murder of Mary McDowell. He was sure Callahan and Monroe were working together.

Peter was strong in his denial but could see how a case was being built up against him. He had been seen with the murdered girl on the day she had been killed, and snatches of their argument had been overheard. He'd also been seen when he had returned to the apartment, but that old bat upstairs had said she had heard the door slam shut. She had got that wrong! He had not been in the apartment but he remembered kicking the door in frustration, and that must have been what she heard. It was her word against his, but he was convinced no one was prepared to believe him. Things were not looking good. He would do anything to get away. He had got the money to enable him to disappear, and he could hide until the real killer was found.

Richard Wainwright wanted him behind bars, and he would not put it past him to have Mary killed and put the blame squarely at his door. He was aware of the influence Wainwright had, and rightly guessed at his determination to keep him locked up and out of harm's way. When he eventually found out that the IRA money was not in the case when Powalski delivered it, he would know Callahan was the only person who could have taken it.

He would end up in prison, and didn't think they would let him out for a long time, but if he co-operated with the police now, they might be lenient with him. He admitted he had gone to Mary's apartment to find out about the hijack after he had heard it on the news. She hadn't heard anything more, but was writing a report of everything she had done that shift. She intended to go to a meeting at the airport later that evening when she should have been leaving Chicago with him. That was what they had argued about. He did not want to go without her, but she wanted to wait for a few more days.

He swore that was all, and she had been alive when he left. He had returned later to apologise but she had not let him in. He heard the phone ringing out and as no-one answered he knew the apartment was empty.

In frustration he had kicked the door, and that must be what the woman upstairs had heard. He had definitely not entered her place on his second visit, and she had been very much alive when he had last seen her, and he had not killed her.

Richard Wainwright had been kept fully informed of everything, including his son's activities prior to the hijack. He would do anything to keep Malcolm's name out of it and minimise his involvement, so when he heard Peter Callahan had been taken in for questioning he had been delighted. He would do everything he could to put the blame on him.

He believed Callahan had arranged the hijack in order to get the IRA money. Only he, Powalski and O'Grady knew it was on WF254, and he could trust Powalski and O'Grady. But why involve others when he'd had it in his hands already? It didn't take Richard long to guess that Callahan had already got the money, and the hijack was his way of letting the IRA think he wasn't involved.

Richard hadn't reached the top of his profession without being ruthless, and he was quite prepared to sacrifice Callahan. It would mean a lot to get that bastard behind bars, where he couldn't threaten them any more. He wasn't interested in getting the real hijackers, only in stopping Callahan from causing problems for the Wainwright family.

He wanted to know what he had done with the money, and decided to search his home for any clues to its whereabouts.

He took his minder, Parker, along and when they got there he found the place practically empty, and two suitcases standing in the hall waiting to be collected. A third case was open on the bed, half packed with his clothes. It looked as if he had been interrupted and left in a hurry.

Parker emptied the cases on the bed and sorted through the contents.

There was nothing to indicate where the money could be hidden. The half-packed case followed the same fate, and again there was nothing of interest. He found Callahan's passport in a drawer in the bedroom, together with his personal documents. His bank statement did not show details of a large deposit so he must have put the money somewhere else.

Richard helped himself to pretzels and beer as he waited for Callahan to return.

Lieutenant Walton didn't have enough evidence to keep Peter any longer, and allowed him to return home, with the warning that he must not leave Chicago. When Peter opened the door he saw immediately that his apartment had been trashed. He was amazed to see Richard Wainwright and another man sitting on his Chesterfield and drinking his beer.

"What are you doing here, and how did you get in?" he demanded.

"Where is the merchandise you should have handed to Powalski?" Wainwright asked, getting right to the point.

"What are you talking about? I handed it to Powalski as ordered."

"No you didn't. You waited until it was too late for him to check the contents, and handed it over in the staff car park."

"How do you know?" Peter asked, hoping the panic he was feeling would not sound in his voice.

"I've got it on tape."

"That doesn't prove anything. I gave Powalski the case, and he took it on the plane."

"True. But I would like to know what was in the case."

"Exactly what was given to me."

"Then why the hurry to leave town?"

"I've been planning this for a long time. Anyways, there's no reason why I shouldn't leave if I want to."

"You can go with my blessing, but not with my money."

Wainwright nodded to Parker, and before Peter knew what was

happening Parker stood behind him, and got him in a bear hug. Callahan was not strong enough to prevent the larger man from squeezing him and could feel the breath being forced out of his lungs until it felt as if his eyes were about to pop out of his head. Parker let go as Callahan lost consciousness.

Callahan's pulse was weak and erratic, and Wainwright waited until he stirred and started to come round. Parker picked him up from the floor and pushed him into a chair. Callahan shook his head to try and clear the buzzing noise that drowned out all other sounds and coughed until he was sick.

"You bugger, you nearly killed me," he said in a hoarse whisper.

"He will next time if you don't tell me where the money is," Wainwright responded.

"I've told you, I don't have it," Callahan persisted.

"I don't believe you."

"But you must, it's the truth."

"We've searched everywhere, so it's not here." Wainwright continued. "If you help me to get it all back, then I'll let you go. If not, Parker knows what to do."

"But I keep telling you I don't have it," Peter pleaded.

"And I keep telling you I don't believe you. What other reason would there be for you to leave in a hurry? No, you've got it hidden somewhere, and I intend to find it, one way or the other."

"If I did have it, which I'm not saying I have, you wouldn't be able to find it," Callahan said.

"You wanna bet?" Wainwright sneered. "Now where could you have put it so we couldn't find it. Somewhere you can get it back in a hurry, no questions asked. You'd want to get rid of it quickly, so the obvious place is the left luggage desk at the airport. Let me have the key, and I'll send Parker to get it."

He saw the sly look in Callahan's eyes and thought he was laughing at them.

"No, that's too easy," Wainwright continued. "How about I try at the train station?"

Callahan tried to make Wainwright believe he had hit upon the right place, and started to whine. If he could get Parker to leave, he would have a better chance of getting away from Wainwright.

"No, it's not there," he said, suddenly realising that was an admission that he had the money.

"Make him talk Parker and get the key from him."

Callahan cringed as Parker crossed the room and forced his arms behind his back. Wainwright ruthlessly searched in his pockets. Callahan was still too weak to put up any resistance but he knew there was nothing there.

"If you don't co-operate you will have wasted your life for nothing." Wainwright told Callahan

Callahan knew him well enough to know that he meant what he said. He could see no way out, and hoped that if he did as be was bid, then Wainwright would let him go. He would have to start a new life, as he had planned to do with Mary, but this time he would be on his own and without the money. At least he would still be alive, and able to look out for another opportunity to get rich.

He decided that it would be the better of two evils to hand the money back, and told Parker to go into the bathroom and look at the soap in the shower. Parker found the key to the left luggage locker, pushed into the soft bar of soap.

Callahan was being sick again as they left his apartment. Some time later he was woken from an exhausted sleep by the phone ringing. Richard Wainwright told him he had retrieved his property, and that his Irish colleagues were going to take care of him. They had no mercy for anyone who betrayed their cause, and their revenge would be short and sweet. He laughed as he put the phone down.

Richard phoned his colleagues in Ireland and told them the money was still in the US, and that he would take it to Ireland personally. He told them not to trust Callahan any more and explained what he had done. Richard gave them as much information as he could to help them find him and was told to leave it up to them to deal with Callahan.

Leaving the rest of his belongings unpacked, Peter left Chicago and drove straight to New York. He sold his car and rented a small room in a sleazy part of town. He dare not go out in case he was recognised, and waited until he had a full beard and long hair before he dared be seen in daylight. Even then, he kept looking to see if he was being followed.

Everything had gone wrong. He had lost his girl, and had no money and no prospects. He knew it would only be a matter of time before the IRA found him, and his life was nothing more than a living nightmare.

Ms. Gammage admitted she had not physically seen Callahan come out of the apartment, and said that she could have been mistaken. The noise made by kicking the door was exactly the same as if it had been slammed and she could have been confused, but they had definitely been rowing earlier.

As the case against Peter lessened, the one against Charlie Monroe strengthened, and a few days later Monroe was arrested for the murder of Mary McDowell.

He never did get to court. He hanged himself on the morning his case was due to be heard.

— CHAPTER 15 —

At the command to "Go, go, go," Captain Proctor started the right hand engine, and moved the plane slowly forward.

The people on the ground stood and watched the hijacked plane gather speed; thankful it was leaving and was no longer their concern. The pilot spoke to the tower and told them he was ready for take off. They confirmed the way was clear to leave.

Within a few minutes the engines had reached maximum thrust and they were able to speed down the runway and lift off unchallenged.

Malcolm had been shot in the neck, and was still unconscious. The bullet entered at the base of his neck by his left shoulder and travelled down towards his right lung. It was so deeply embedded Pam decided it was too big an operation to perform on the plane. She strapped him up so tightly he was unable to move. It was doubtful whether he knew what had happened to him.

Amy offered to help Pam attend to Malcolm, but Dave Branson had been trained in first aid and was willing to assist, so Amy took charge of the refugees, making sure they knew where everything was, and helping the children to find toys to play with.

She spoke to the cabin crew, asking for their assistance, and was pleased with their response. Only Belinda Page and Effie Constantine refused to help in any way. They sat together discussing the day's events and speculating on what would happen to them. All they wanted was to return to their shared apartment and forget about their troubles. Both girls seriously considered giving up flying and taking a ground job.

Hannah Watson stayed close to Chrissie, helping where she could, but only doing as Chrissie requested, and ignoring Amy. She was willing enough to serve drinks and what food they had left, and felt reassured at the normality of the flight.

Sue Howser did all she could to assist and encourage Chrissie, and kept in close contact with Captain Proctor, telling him where everyone was and what they were doing.

Jack sat in Powalski's vacated seat, and any attempt he made at conversation with the pilot was answered curtly. He soon got bored and started plotting how he could gain from the present situation. He knew he would not be able to get any more money out of Malcolm, and wanted to wait until Martin was more secure in his profession to guarantee a good income in later life, when he would make good use of the tapes again.

He worked out a way of blackmailing all the hijackers without harming himself. Liam would be easy. He had used his business to help them get into the States, and Jack knew he would rather pay up than go bankrupt. David would lose his position in the army if it were known what he had done, and was ripe for plucking. Amy was too young for financial gain, but he would find a way of using her for his own pleasure. Apart from the fact she was attracted to him, she would do anything to save her brother and cousin.

Then there was Pam. He wasn't completely sure she could be banned from practicing medicine because of this episode, but intended to find out and, as doctors had a good income, he would be set up for life. If she didn't co-operate, he could always threaten to tell the authorities exactly who had been involved and what they had done. It pleased him to dream about his future wealth.

When everyone else was busy, Liam forced Powalski's case open. He couldn't believe his eyes when he found most of the money had been replaced by wads of paper! Some bastard had stolen the money! His money! Now he would have to wait for another opportunity, and the chances of that happening again were almost nil. As he started to think more clearly, he realised that Powalski couldn't have known that the money was not in the case. Why risk his life for a case full of rubbish? No, it must have been taken before it reached the plane. Who and how were questions that he could leave for his IRA colleagues.

Being in charge of the operation stateside, it was Richard Wainwright's responsibility to make the necessary arrangement for ensuring the merchandise reached Ireland without a hitch. He would have a lot of explaining to do.

David's arm throbbed, and he suddenly started to panic. There was nothing frightened him more than a mad dog! He could feel the weight of its body on top of him, and the wetness of its tongue on his face.

In his worst nightmare, he lashed out with his good arm – and sent Chrissie Faversham crashing to the floor. Liam came running and held him in a vice-like grip, shouting that it was alright, the dog was dead, and he was safely back on the plane.

David became aware of the noise and the vibration. He was lying in one of the reclining seats in the first class section, his arm bandaged and raised on a pile of blankets. Chrissie had been leaning over him and sponging his face when he started to come round. She picked herself up from the floor, and rubbed her arm.

"If that's all the thanks I get for trying to help, I won't bother," she said, but the look in her eyes contradicted the tone of her voice.

She accepted his apology, and said something about not wanting to cross him in a row! He slept then, the sleep of someone who'd had an exhausting night, and was content to relax in the security of a safe place.

When he awoke, he couldn't remember where he was. He saw Liam talking to someone, and called out to him.

"That's right," he answered. "Tell everyone me name, why don't you."

David started to apologise, but was interrupted.

"Sure now and its not important. What's a name between friends?"

"Waking up, are you?" Chrissie said, walking up to him and taking his pulse. "You'll be alright now. As soon as she's finished with her patient, the doctor will attend to you."

"Did I knock you down?" he asked, not sure whether he had dreamt it or not.

"You sure did," she replied, "but I understand you thought I was the dog. Mr. Irishman killed it. You've no need to worry."

He tried to sit up, but she pushed him back into the seat.

"Oh no, you don't! You've lost a lot of blood and must keep your arm raised. I've managed to stop the bleeding for now, but you must keep still or it may start again. Here, Mr. Irishman," she said turning to Liam. "Don't let him move more than is absolutely necessary. I must go and help with the children. We'll try and give them a hot drink and settle them down to sleep, and some of them may be hungry."

With that she left Liam hovering anxiously over his friend.

"That other business, Liam? What's going to happen about that?"

"You'd best forget it. There's nothing you can do now, and if we stick to the story it was the soldiers who killed Powalski, then we've no cause to worry."

"Do you think the captain might be suspicious?"

"No, why should he?"

"He knows something is going on between you and Powalski, even if he doesn't know what it is."

"Then he's probably pleased it's been sorted without him being involved."

"Hm, maybe! What are you going to do about the IRA shipment?"

"Nothing that will involve you or anyone else on the plane. In fact, it has all gone pear-shaped, and you'd laugh if I told you! There's been some sort of conspiracy and the money's not in the case after all. Someone must have got it before it was given to Powalski. That's all you need to know, me friend. It'd be the worse for you to know more."

"So it's all settled."

"In a manor of speaking. There's a score I have to settle with Wainwright senior, but I'll bide me time. It could take years before I have the opportunity, but it'll come one day, and he'll never know what hit him."

"Will his fate be the same as Powalski's?"

"That's for me to know, and you to find out," O'Grady replied.

"You're turning into a ruthless killer, and I'm not sure I want to be associated with you any more."

"But if it wasn't for me, you'd have been eaten alive by that great hairy monster."

"Don't remind me," David shuddered.

"Does that mean we're still mates?" Liam wanted to know.

"We've always looked out for each other," David replied after considering the matter.

"Of course. Didn't we save each other's lives just now? Now that was a stupid thing to do, throwing me up on the wing like that. There's no call for a big man to pick on those smaller than himself."

"And who'd be lying here now if I hadn't?"

"And it would be meself, not you with a sister and cousin to consider."

"And what of Bridie, and your brood?" he asked.

"I tend to agree with our young friend," Liam replied, ignoring the last remark. "It was a complete waste to risk your life for that shagging drunkard over there."

"Malcolm! I'd forgotten him. How is he? I felt the bullet hit him, but he seemed to be still breathing. He's not dead, is he?"

"No, he's not dead, though near enough to make no difference. It's taking the combined skills of the doctor and steward to keep him alive. They wanted to get the bullet out, but it was in too deep, so they've had to patch him up, and hope he's still alive when we reach the UK."

"How long since we left Osijek?"

"Almost an hour. Most of the passengers are either sleeping or playing, and the crew is doing a wonderful job with the children. We've been lucky there!"

"Help me up," David said, pushing the blankets off. "I must speak to the captain. Has he been contacted by ATC, and what's he told them?"

"Now then, be still. You're not the only person who can think! We've got it all under control. Jack is keeping the captain company in the cockpit. He can keep an eye on things when the automatic pilot is engaged. We'll be back in the UK before we know where we are. We don't expect any problems with ATC, or at least not until we get to the UK."

"Thanks Liam. I'd love a brandy if Malcolm hasn't drunk it all!"

"I'll go and find some," he said and made his way to the galley.

"What are you looking for?" Chrissie wanted to know as he started rummaging through the various lockers.

"Brandy, or something to help make him more comfortable."

"Oh no you don't," she replied, pushing Liam out of the galley. "Alcohol is the worst thing you can give someone who's bleeding. It makes the heart pump faster, and they bleed even more. I've not spent the last hour patching him up so you can start him bleeding again. Really he'd be much better off with a cup of hot sweet tea."

"You take it to him then. I don't want it flung back in me face," he said, winking at her.

She smiled at Liam, and told Hannah Weston to give him a drink of strong tea with plenty of sugar. When David complained, she told him not to make such a fuss, and to drink it up, as he needed all the energy he could get.

Whether it was the relief of knowing they would soon be back in the UK, or the fact that she and Frank were going to be married soon, Chrissie wasn't sure, but now the immediate danger was over, she was enjoying herself. She loved looking after the passengers, and always tried to make their journey as enjoyable as possible.

She also loved helping with the children, and on this flight there were more children than adults, and she had the time and space to sit with them, and to attend to their immediate needs.

She was pleased to be able to help the refugees to a better life, and determined to do all she could to help the children once they landed in the UK. She tried not to dwell on the fact that Zac Powalski had been killed, and Mr. Wainwright injured, but she knew that if they hadn't left the plane, no harm would have come to either of them. It would have been much easier to leave without them, but the hijackers had risked everything in an attempt to save their lives.

When she had finished attending to Malcolm, Pam went to see what she could do for David. He had a number of cuts, bruises and bites from his struggle with the soldier, as well as the damage caused by the dog, and was developing a spectacular black eye! She was more concerned at stopping infection from the bites from the human than from the dog! She had heard of more troubles arising from human bites than from animals, and she was particularly conscientious in cleaning and disinfecting his injuries. She was thankful the army made sure their soldiers were up to date with their tetanus injections.

He had been badly bitten, the animals' teeth ripping through the flesh leaving a tear that needed stitches. Chrissie had stopped the bleeding, and Pam carefully unwrapped her bandages. She thoroughly cleaned and stitched the wound as David tried to keep his mind off what she was doing, but there were times when he swore at her! She laughed and told him not to make a fuss, as she had never done a better job!

He said he never wanted her to treat him again. Call herself a doctor! A butcher, more like. But the result was good, and when the bandages were back in place, he felt a lot better.

Pam went to examine the patients with minor injuries and decided she couldn't do anything more for them. The broken bones would have to be attended to in hospital and she asked the pilot to radio ahead for ambulances to be available as soon as they landed.

———◂o▸———

The children settled down remarkably well. The old man was feeling exhausted, yet he managed to play with the remaining children from Pietre's family, and tried to keep their minds off the death of their eldest brother, and the fact that with him had gone the name and address of the people they were going to stay with in London. Consequently they had no one to go to, and their mother had no means of contacting them.

The women sorted through the toys and clothes left by the passengers, and did all they could to keep the children entertained. There was room for everyone to lie down, and some of the children slept peacefully, warm and secure after their long exhausting journey.

Pam brought the little girl, Melita, to sit with David. She couldn't settle, and was frightened of the noise and confusion. She must have felt lonely without her mother, and even though she only understood the odd word in English, he talked to her until she fell asleep on his lap.

Janni dozed in first class, the pain in his leg only temporarily relieved by painkillers. It was a long uncomfortable flight and he would be pleased when it was over.

Nedzad and Mahmutovic settled down to discussed what they would do when they got to England. They felt nervous at the prospect of a totally different culture, language and religion, but hoped they could all stay together.

———◂o▸———

Once the patients had been seen to, Amy and Pam were able to spend some time together. Pam wanted to know why Jack was there. He had never been a particular friend of theirs, and since he'd won that sports car, he had tried to lord it over the village, with every girl for miles around swooning after him. Much as she loved Amy, she couldn't see Jack chasing after her. She was too young and innocent. Holly Branson was more in his line!

Amy started to giggle at this suggestion, and told Pam why she hadn't been able to get hold of David. He had been in New York with Holly!

Jack had a mean streak, and Pam wondered if he was trying to get back at David by helping Amy to do something he knew David wouldn't approve of. But Amy was able to reassure her that it wasn't so. Jack had told her he had admired her for a long time and wanted to go with her to protect her from harm. She didn't tell Pam that he had tried to rape her on the flight to Bosnia, but that could have been her fault, as she could have given him the wrong impression. She knew she had encouraged him, and slept with him in Chicago, so he must have assumed that she would be a willing partner.

In a rush of confidence, Amy told Pam how kind and helpful Jack had been and she couldn't have managed without him, particularly his contact with Malcolm. That had been the reason for going to America, and the only way they could have got a weapon onto the plane. Without Jack they would still be in England and Pam in Bosnia.

Once she was back home, Pam would keep an eye on things between Jack and Amy. She didn't want to upset her cousin, but she wouldn't trust Jack as far as she could throw him!

There was no need for further conversation, and they soon slept after the fatigue, both mental and physical, of the last few days.

David thought his pride had been hurt as much as his body. Nevertheless, he slept most of the time, drifting in and out of sleep, and vaguely aware of what was going on.

Once he opened his eyes to see Liam standing over him. He put his hand on Melita's head, trying not to wake her.

"Will you do as you're told, and stay still. I've only woken you because the pilot is doing his rounds. He's inspecting the passengers, as a good captain should, and will be here in a few minutes."

Captain Proctor had left the cockpit, and given Jack instructions to call him if he thought anything had changed. He walked the full length of the plane, looking at his new passengers, and talking to those who were awake. The officer's wife had a good command of English, and went with him to interpret.

He was thanked many times for risking so much by flying his plane into a hostile country just to help them. He was an answer to their prayers, they said, and would be blessed.

It was the plight of the children that touched him most. Some were separated from their families and among strangers who didn't even speak the same language, yet they sensed the kindness of the adults, and knew the comfort of hot food and somewhere warm to sleep.

When Captain Proctor went to talk to David, Liam lifted Melita off his lap and laid her down on a nearby seat, covering her with a blanket. David tried to sit up and was amazed how weak he felt.

"Don't move on my behalf," the captain said, his firm grip forcing him back into the seat. "Are you badly hurt?"

"Only a flesh wound," David replied. "I'll be alright in a day or two."

"Well, you've lost a lot of blood by all accounts," he said shaking his head. "It's a pity. I was looking forward to knocking you down for what you've done to us, and particularly for holding that gun to Miss Faversham's head. I give you fair warning if we do meet again, I'll not hesitate!"

"Needs must when the devil drives," David replied.

"Well, I can't do it whilst you're in this state, so consider it done for now. But circumstances change, and I've been talking to the passengers, and after what I've heard, I'm more inclined, at this particular moment in time, to shake you by the hand. Your good one, that is!"

He held out his hand and David gripped it, each understanding the other.

"We'll be crossing the English coast soon. They're expecting us at Manchester, and will have a welcoming committee waiting for you, I've no doubt."

"Have you told them about your first officer?"

"No not yet. I'll have to tell them he wouldn't have been killed if he'd obeyed my orders and remained on the plane. I don't know if that will help you, but it is the truth."

"Thank you. I don't know how we'll come out of this, but I hope the media will be on our side, and people will see the good we've done, and forget the bad."

"I can't speak for the rest of the crew, of course, but for myself, and Chrissie Faversham, we'll do all we can to stop WFI from pressing charges. After all, there was no need for you to risk your life to save young Wainwright. I'll personally tell Mr. Wainwright exactly what happened."

"Thank you," David said, gripping his hand for a second time. "There's one more thing you can do for us, Captain. I want you to let us off at a private airstrip in the southwest of England."

"I thought you wanted us to go to Manchester?" he replied, not at all pleased with this change in plan.

"I do. But first I want you to let us off. We don't want to be on board when you get there. As you said, there'll be a reception committee waiting, and we don't particularly want to meet it."

"Are you sure a private runway is large enough?" he asked. "We need a lot of runway to take off again."

"Yes, you shouldn't have any trouble."

"And what exactly do you want us to do when we get there?"

"Take the plane as near as you can to the main hangar, and let us off. That is the five of us. Malcolm will have to stay on board as he needs to be hospitalised. You'll then take off again and head for Manchester. What you do after that is up to you."

"What is there to prevent us from staying with you?"

"You wouldn't want to disappoint the welcoming committee, and the doctor asked you to arrange for medical assistance to be waiting. Besides, Manchester has always been the final destination of flight WF254."

"You've thought of everything, haven't you?"

"I hope so. It never hurts to pamper to the people you've used, and if they are treated right in the end, it can make a difference to the way they view things. And it's important you and your crew don't think of us as being all bad. Our futures depend on it."

"You know, of course, that we can identify you."

"Yes, but there must be a lot of people who would fit our descriptions. England is a big place and you've no idea which part of the country to look."

"Maybe not, but perhaps one day we might even bump into each other again. I can also have a fair guess at tracking you down. You've obviously been trained, you and the Irishman. Which branch of the Military are you in? And the doctor, which hospital does she work in, or is she a GP? Maybe it wouldn't be as difficult as you think."

"That's up to you, Captain, but do you really want to do that? Do you want to see us behind bars?"

"I'm sure none of you would like that."

"Then don't do it, Captain. Just don't do it!"

"I hope I never see you again," he said laughing.

"Thank you, Captain Proctor. I hope so too!" David replied remembering his promise to knock him down if ever they did meet again!

"I must go and change course if we're going to drop you off first."

David watched him return to the cockpit. Liam followed and used the radio to contact a friend, giving him their ETA.

"Cabin crew, prepare for landing" the voice spoke over the intercom, and the passengers were checked to make sure they were strapped in.

The plane landed smoothly, and taxied the full length of the runway. It turned round ready to take off.

"Doors to manual" the voice spoke again, and David, Liam, Amy, Pam and Jack went to the exit door at the front of the plane. Chrissie opened it and threw out the rope ladder Liam had already secured in place.

Liam went first, landing nimbly on the hard surface, and putting his weight on the bottom rung of the ladder. Amy and Pam were the next to leave. Jack threw the two briefcases and Powalski's case onto the runway, and helped David down the ladder before climbing down himself. The rope ladder was dropped onto the ground and the door secured.

They turned and waved to the pilot. He acknowledged them with a salute, and the engines roared as the plane picked up enough speed for take-off.

Simultaneously a small plane taxied towards them, its door already open, and they were soon aboard. The Cessna followed in the direction of flight WF254, keeping to the grass and taking off before the larger plane had reached maximum thrust.

Flight WF254 requested permission to land at Ringway Airport, Manchester and they were welcomed back to England. It was a smooth landing in spite of the fact the pilot had been flying for many hours.

He was disappointed to see that not only were the emergency services standing by, but vehicles containing armed personnel were waiting to surround the plane, their lights flashing and headlights blazing. Those passengers who had been looking out of the windows looked worried and started to panic. They were not impressed with their welcome to the United Kingdom!

Armed guards boarded the plane first, their weapons pointing menacingly at the passengers, and their chests enlarged with bullet-proof vests. They wanted to know who were the hijackers so they could be taken off the plane before the passengers and crew.

It was only then that Captain Proctor announced they had already left the plane and were no longer on board. The only passenger who had boarded the plane in Chicago was Mr. Wainwright, and he was in no fit state to answer any of their questions. He was still unconscious and must be taken to hospital immediately.

Assuming the crew was still under threat, they started a thorough search of the plane until they were convinced the hijackers were definitely not there, and, disappointed to be baulked of their prey, stepped aside to let the medical team on board. Even so, they stayed where they were, machine guns ready, in case the hijackers were disguised as refugees and trying to escape that way.

Those passengers who were in need of hospitalisation were taken away by ambulance and everyone else, crew and passengers alike, was escorted to a private lounge, where they were told to wait.

Paula Smith came running up to them and threw her arms round Chrissie. She thought she might never see her again, and it was wonderful to know they were all safely back. She had already been interviewed by the police, and understood someone from the board of WFI was en route to Manchester.

The original passengers had arrived at their destination many hours late, and in hindsight she could laugh at some of the things they had said, but she didn't want to repeat the experience ever again! Over two hundred people, all wanting to complain to her at once, was not the best way of spending a morning, and she would have welcomed the support of another crew member. The only thing that had given her some relief was from the two couples that had been upgraded to first class. When they were told they could leave the airport and continue their journey, they had found Paula, and thanked her for looking after them so well. They said how much they had enjoyed the experience, and they would always fly with Wright Flights International in future!

Captain Proctor was the first member of the crew to be interviewed by the police and a representative from WFI. He told them clearly and precisely what had happened, and patiently answered their questions.

He thought it best not to mention that Zac was smuggling something on the flight. He was thankful O'Grady had taken Zac's case with him, as he didn't feel up to explaining that his first officer had admitted taking goods out of the USA. After all, it had nothing to do with him.

He told them that, when they had landed at Osijek, the hijackers had told everyone to remain on the plane, and had stressed they faced being shot if they left the protection of the aircraft. Captain Proctor had ordered his crew to remain on board away from the windows.

First Officer Powalski had deliberately disobeyed his orders, and as a consequence he had been killed. He had left the plane in the confusion caused by getting the refugees on board taking a gun one of the hijackers had dropped in his excitement. He must have run into some of the soldiers sent to find out what was happening to the plane.

Two of the hijackers had risked their own lives to go after him, but it was too late. When they found him he had had his throat slit. They had tried to recover his body, at no little danger to themselves, but the soldiers were running towards the plane, and they had to leave the body behind. One thing they were unable to explain was why Powalski had taken his case with him.

Malcolm Wainwright had also disobeyed orders, and he, too, had left the plane. The same two hijackers had risked their own lives a second time to save the chairman's son. As a consequence one of them had been injured, and if he hadn't received immediate attention, the captain said that he too would have died.

They spent a long time discussing how the hijackers had left the plane before it landed in Manchester. The authorities were not pleased that they had got away, and every effort must be made to find them. They thought it irresponsible of Captain Proctor to let them go, and told him he should have ignored their demands, and brought them back to Manchester. Captain Proctor pointed out that he did not have much say in the matter. He was not prepared to risk the lives of those on board by standing up to the hijackers at the last minute. A search of the airport in the south of England proved useless. They had an eyewitness to what went on, but his account hardly varied from those of the people on board WF254.

The plane was already being searched for forensic evidence, and everyone would have to have their fingerprints taken before they would be allowed to leave. It would only be a matter of time before the hijackers were caught.

By the time the crew had been interrogated the authorities knew every detail of the flight. It was then that they turned their attention to the refugees.

The officers' wife talked quietly, her children sitting silently next to her. She had harrowing tales to tell of the refugees passing through the town of Brod, and how her husband had insisted on getting his family out of the country. Her story was echoed by the others, and soon the interrogators had a picture of what life was like in Bosnia, and the gratitude of everyone who had managed to escape.

Nedzad and Mahmutovic told of how friends were being made to fight each other, just because they had different ancestors, and what would happen to them if they refused to fight. Janni had already been taken to hospital, and they were told they could visit him as soon as they were allowed to leave the airport.

The children were silent and confused. Those with mothers were the lucky ones, and the rest huddled together in small groups, brothers and sisters determined not to be separated. Experts from welfare were called in, and soon they were divided into small groups.

When everyone had finished their initial interview, Captain Proctor insisted they be allowed to go to the hotel where rooms were waiting for them. They were all in need of a hot bath, a good meal and a long sleep.

The first thing Chrissie did on entering her room was to ring Fiona to let her know they were safely back. Half an hour later she was knocking on the door.

It was a tearful reunion, and Chrissie introduced Fiona to her future stepfather. They spent a long time talking about the hijack, and by putting their feelings into words, they were able to confront the horrors and to concentrate on the fact they were safe.

Fiona told her mother the reason she had remained in England for the summer vacation was to spend more time with her new boyfriend. They were on the same course, and had fallen in love at first sight. If everything went well, she too would be getting married, so she could understand exactly how Chrissie and Frank felt, and she was in favour of an early wedding.

Frank and Chrissie lay in each others arms that night, and Chrissie felt more secure than she had since the death of her husband. The fact that their lives had been threatened had given them a different perspective on life. They now knew the value of life and love. Life was for living, and they intended to live every moment of it together.

— CHAPTER 16 —

The Cessna landed at a small airport where a car was waiting to take them home. Liam drove into the farmyard as Grandpa opened the door. Every time he had heard a vehicle he had feared the worst, both longing and dreading a knock on the door, dreading to learn of their fate, yet longing to see them again. Liam was the first to step into the kitchen.

"Well now, and that's not a very good welcome for the return of the adventurers," he said, "and himself with his arm in a sling!" he continued, trying to ease the way for David.

Granny was the first to move, pushing past Liam to gather both Amy and Pam into her arms. She laughed and sobbed at the same time and turned from one to the other, hugging and kissing each of them in turn.

Amy looked at Grandpa and was shocked at the expression on his face.

"Don't you ever do anything like that again lass," he shouted, gently shaking her shoulders and looking deep into her eyes. "How dare you put us through such agony. Have you any idea what we've been through these last few days?"

"I'm sorry, Grandpa," Amy replied, tears starting to run down her cheeks. "I had to help Pam, and couldn't think of any other way."

"You could have asked me." Grandpa was upset they hadn't even considered him. "And as for you, young man," Grandpa said turning to David, "you should know better than to involve your sister. And how dare you take my shotgun! You of all people should know the consequences of firearm misuse. It's the most irresponsible thing I've ever known you to do!"

"But it was me, Grandpa," Amy admitted, "David didn't know anything about it. I took it to London, but it's safe in Liam's office. We didn't need it after all. I'm sorry. Please forgive me."

Amy put her arms round the old man, and buried her face in his neck. Grandpa's hands were shaking as he led his granddaughter to the settee and sat down beside her. It took all her efforts to calm him down.

Jack wanted to know if his parents were aware of what had happened. Granny told him what they had discussed, but they had been cautious in putting their fears into words. Even though his parents might guess, they would probably dismiss it as being preposterous. Jack decided it would be better if they didn't know anything about it. He would say he had been staying with friends.

Granny and Grandpa kept asking questions until they had a pretty good idea of what had happened. They wanted to know why, when they had such a large plane, they hadn't brought more refugees back. The answer to that was simple. They had not known before hand what size the plane would be, and it had taken them long enough to board the refugees at Osijek. If there had been any more people David thought they would all have been caught. The soldiers were moving in and once they had surrounded the plane there was no way they could have got away.

They had not known that before they left, of course, but in hindsight they were grateful there were not more people waiting.

There was nothing any of them could say to stop Pam in her determination to return to Sarajevo. That was the only way she could think of to stop their identities being made known. Her passport said she was still in Bosnia, and if she could get back there, and leave through the proper channels, then no one would find out that she was the doctor on the plane. She felt it would be only a matter of days, once it was known that she had returned to the UK, for the authorities to realise that she had been involved in the hijack of flight WF254, and through her they could easily find the others.

So it was agreed that Pam would return to London with Liam. He would go and see Old Josh again, and make the necessary arrangements for travel documents for Pam to return to her colleagues. It would have to be an overland journey this time, but there was no reason why she should not be back at the State Hospital within a few days.

David would use his false passport to return to New York and Holly, and would soon be back with all his papers in order. Liam would have to return to the London office and be content with his lot until another opportunity to break away from his mundane existence came his way, and he promised to take care of Grandpa's shotgun until it could be restored to its rightful owner.

The press was able to put together their version of the facts. They were clamouring to speak to the crew at Manchester, and WFI had a hard time trying to keep them quiet. Eventually someone issued a statement, stating what had happened, and how the plane had returned to the UK with a number of refugees on board. They were now being looked after in the Manchester area.

They confirmed one member of the crew had been killed but not by the hijackers. He had left the plane and been shot by someone on the ground. One of the hijackers had been seriously injured trying to rescue Malcolm Wainwright, who was so badly hurt that they were concerned for his life. He was in hospital and would not be available for questioning for some time. Even though the hijackers had already left the plane before it landed in Manchester, the police were hopeful of finding them very soon. There were enough eyewitness accounts to make an early arrest likely.

The press was sorry not to be able to identify the hijackers. When they discovered that the first officer had been killed after deliberately going against their instructions, their imagination and enthusiasm soon turned the hijackers into heroes. Two of the hijackers had risked their own lives to find out what had happened to him. They had discovered his body, and tried to take it back to the plane, risking suffering the same fate if the soldiers had caught them. Unfortunately, the soldiers were getting so close that they had to leave his body on the ground, and make for the shelter of the plane.

They wrote about all the good things that had come out of the mission, and dismissed the use of firearms as an undesirable necessity. After all, they had neither killed nor maimed anyone. All the passengers were safe, and their luggage returned with the plane, only those items used by the refugees during the flight had been confiscated.

In fact, they had done everything they could to prevent anyone from getting hurt, and the death of the first officer was due entirely to the fact that he had disobeyed orders, and left the plane when specifically told not to. As regards Mr. Wainwright junior, he, too, had ignored their instructions, resulting in a near-fatal injury that would leave him partially disabled for the rest of his life. Also, if two of the hijackers had not risked their own lives in order to rescue him, he too, would have died.

They made a great fuss about the rescue, emphasising the injuries and risks Liam and David had taken, and pretty soon the press had convinced the rest of the country that what they had done was not only good, but brave as well.

All that remained now was to see what Wright Flights International would do.

Richard Wainwright arrived in Manchester on the first available flight from Chicago. He went straight to the hospital to see Malcolm and was relieved to learn that he would live, but was disappointed to hear he would probably never regain the full use of his arm. Richard would get the best American doctors to look at his son, and he felt confident they would be able to do a lot more than their English colleagues. Malcolm was still very weak, but the treatment he had received on the plane had undoubtedly saved his life.

Malcolm and Richard spoke frankly to one another as they had not done before, and Malcolm found his father so understanding that he told him all about the incident with his teacher, how Mr. Askew had been tripped up deliberately, and broken his neck. Malcolm had never expected him to die, and the only thought in his head had been to stop him from talking. He still regretted that night and told his father how sorry he was, and about the nightmares he had suffered ever since.

He explained that one of the hijackers had been at the same school, and somehow got a tape recording of what happened. He said Mr. Askew's voice could be clearly heard threatening them with expulsion for their actions, and the boy's subsequent conversation after he had been tripped down the stairs.

It was a good time to make a clean breast of everything, so Malcolm told his father how Jack had blackmailed him into buying an expensive car in return for the tape. It had never crossed his mind that Jack would have taken more than one copy. It had been a shock when he had demanded his co-operation in the hijack, and Malcolm thought Jack would blackmail him for the rest of his life.

Richard was appalled his son had suffered so much, and said if the hijackers produce the tape recording of what had happened, then Malcolm would be able to give their identities to the police. He had enough information to put them in prison if they ever tried to blackmail him again, and he convinced his son they wouldn't mention the incident again.

Malcolm told him everything he knew about Jack – his full name, where he lived, his interests, hobbies and friends. In fact, anything that would make it easy for him to be identified. Richard would set his people on looking for him as soon as he left the hospital and it would only be a matter of a few days, if not hours, before he would be traced.

Malcolm knew his father would stand by him, and with his influence and money, no harm would come to him. Richard assured him Jack would not contact him again and swore to have him killed if he ever went near his son again.

Having cleared up that point, father and son spent time together, going over the events of the last few days. Malcolm could vaguely remember leaving the plane to see what the others were doing, but he had drunk so much it was all fuzzy and unreal. He could remember being picked up, and feeling a sharp pain in his neck. He could not remember anything after that.

It was all very awful, and he didn't want to think about it any more. He felt safe in the hospital, and just wanted to be left alone to get better.

Richard Wainwright issued orders his son was to be kept quiet, and no members of the press be allowed to interview him.

The chairman of WFI talked to Captain Proctor, and learned how Malcolm had behaved on the flight, and how he had left the plane when specifically told not to. Frank emphasised how two of the hijackers had risked their own lives to save him, even though another of them had tried to persuade them to leave him in Osijek. He begged the chairman to be lenient with them.

At first Richard dismissed this request, thinking Captain Proctor was under considerable strain after his ordeal. But after having spoken to the rest of the crew, he began to realise that Malcolm had played a larger part in the incident than he had imagined and he did not want to let anyone know why Malcolm had been blackmailed.

There had been enough deaths over this business already. He had been genuinely upset when told how Mary McDowell had been murdered. His attempts at getting Callahan arrested for murder had come to nothing, so he had left instructions he was to be informed immediately the police had found out who had killed her. He had learned enough from his son to know that her death was totally unconnected with the hijacking, yet homicide still believed there was a connection. If that were so, then he would have to get his lawyers busy to prove that WFI had no obligation to her family.

He had written proof that Zac Powalski had been foolish enough to disobey orders, and his death was a direct result of his own actions.

Richard knew his lawyers would be able to prove WFI were not responsible for his death either, and they would not have to pay out a large sum to his next of kin.

He felt that he, personally, had come out of this situation better than he could have hoped. There was no getting away from the fact Malcolm would appear foolish for allowing himself to the blackmailed into getting the hijackers on board, but the fact that he had been injured just might be in his favour. People were always more lenient with someone who had been hurt. But whatever the outcome, he was prepared to shrug it off, and to laugh with his competitors. That would rankle with some of them, and if Richard appeared not to be upset, then it would take a lot of the enjoyment out of the situation for his rivals, and he hoped the whole incident would soon be forgotten.

On the other hand, a number of people had been saved, and members of the press, and consequently the majority of the public, were starting to look upon the hijackers as heroes. This in itself would reflect on WFI, and with a bit of strategic planning, could be used to his advantage. Maybe, just maybe, the situation was not as black as it appeared. WFI's reputation must be maintained at all costs, and passengers encouraged to continue flying with them. He would have to get his team of top executives working on that straight away. Above all they must keep the media fully informed of all they were doing. He could not afford to upset such a powerful body of people and he knew just who and where to offer sweeteners.

After careful consideration he came to a decision. He contacted the BBC and asked to be interviewed. He spoke frankly about the outcome of the hijack, the injuries sustained by his son, and how grateful he was Malcolm had not been left behind at Osijek.

He had personally spoken to the refugees and their plight had touched his heart. He could not see any good coming out of destroying the people who had made their rescue possible. It was a fact that WFI was a commercial company, but they also had a heart and he was a little hurt the hijackers had not approached him direct and asked him to supply a plane for their use. He had prepared a statement, and would be grateful if he could read it.

"Wright Flights International has decided it will not bring charges against the people who carried out the hijack of flight WF254, although no doubt criminal proceedings will be brought by the Aviation Authorities.

"As Chairman of the Board I want to make it quite clear that WFI will not tolerate any activity that will jeopardize the safety of our passengers, and anyone trying to do so in the future will be arrested and punished. Only on this one occasion will we be lenient with the people who physically carried out the rescue, but under no circumstances will WFI be sympathetic to any other cause."

Before the authorities could take the hijackers to court they had to know the identity of those involved. However, there had been so many people on board that very few fingerprints were retrieved, none of which matched any known criminal. The descriptions given by the crew and passengers were remarkably vague, and the photofit pictures compiled from them bore little resemblance to each other.

The police felt that an early arrest was unlikely, and after assessing all the evidence, decided that they would keep the case open but not waste valuable resources in pursuing it.

Amy was delighted when Jack offered to take her to London to collect Grandpa's shotgun. Liam was busy catching up on the paperwork when they arrived, and could only spare them a few minutes. Jack handed his keys to Amy and told her to put the shotgun in the boot of the car.

When she left the office, he confronted Liam, explaining how he would tell the police how they had got into the States illegally and Liam's part in the hijack. He would say Liam and David had forced him to go with them because of his connection with Malcolm Wainwright. He demanded a large sum of money for his silence.

Before Jack had time to jump out of the way, Liam had leapt out of his chair, and had both hands round his neck, forcing him back against the wall. Jack could hardly breathe and thought he was going to lose consciousness.

Liam spoke through clenched teeth, telling Jack he would kill him if he ever tried to get money out of any of them. The look on his face frightened Jack, and he was thankful to hear Amy coming up the stairs. They were still staring at each other when she entered the room, but denied that there was anything wrong.

Amy kissed Liam when they left, and Jack laughed and said he would be in touch again.

———◆———

Jack left Amy in the West End and arranged to meet her later. His next stop was at a certain shop in Soho. The old man came through from the back kitchen and either did not recognise Jack, or did not choose to.

He tried to let Old Josh know he had been there before, but the old man seemed not to know what he was talking about. Old Josh had his own way of dealing with trouble-makers, and Jack found it impossible to speak to him. He began to wonder if he had gone to the right place and was on the point of leaving when Old Josh said he would kill Jack if he ever saw him again.

Things were not going well for Jack and for the first time he felt out of his depth. These were professionals he was dealing with, and he was not sure what to do next. He decided he would wait for a few months before trying again.

———◆———

Much to her disappointment, Amy saw little of Jack in the ensuing days. He was pleasant enough when they met, but she had expected to be seen about the village with him, and wanted her friends to know she was going out with him.

When she asked him about it, he told her she was far too young and he did not want to go out with anyone who was not prepared to give a chap a good time. He had always wanted to join the mile-high club, and she had spoilt that for him, even though he had come to her aid when she needed him. He couldn't understand why she would not do what he wanted after he had risked so much for her. He was upset by her attitude, and did not mean to be let down by her again. Amy said she was sorry if she had let him down, and assured him she would not do so again. She was grateful he had helped her and would do anything he wanted.

Later Amy told David about her disappointment, and he said she should forget about Jack. He had a bad reputation and wasn't the sort of person he wanted his sister to go out with. He didn't understand why Jack had been so willing to help in the first place, until he received a call from Liam explaining how Jack had tried to blackmail him. David was furious.

He knew Malcolm had been blackmailed into submitting to their demands, and they could not have managed without his co-operation, but that Jack would try and blackmail them had never entered his head. He was not entirely surprised when Jack stopped him in the village a day or two later and said he had written a full statement of how they had succeeded in hijacking the plane and terrifying the passengers. He had written how Liam had used his position in the freight business in Shannon and how they had obtained illegal arms from a place in Soho. He said David was a ruthless thug who would not hesitate to kill anyone who opposed his will.

He threatened to send a copy of the statement to the police if David did not give him a large sum of money.

David pointed out that Jack had been a party to taking Grandpa's shotgun, which proved he was not as innocent as he was making out, but Jack said it had been Amy's idea and she alone was responsible. He would see to it that she took all the blame. David wanted to know why, if he was there against his will, he had returned to the motel after leaving Malcolm's apartment, instead of going to the police? That alone was evidence of his involvement, and if he tried to blackmail any of them again, he would kill him!

Amy contacted the hospital in Manchester, and learned that Malcolm was due to be discharged and would soon return to the States. She wanted to see how he was getting on, and asked Jack to go with her when she went to visit him. Jack thought it would be amusing to see Malcolm again, so agreed to drive her there, and hoped that they would spend a cosy evening together back at his place.

"Where's the tape?" Malcolm demanded as soon as he saw Jack. "I want to see it destroyed, even though you can't use it against me any more."

"It's here," Jack replied. "Do you want me to destroy it?"

"No I don't. I'll do it myself after I've heard it. I want to make sure it's the right one, and not a substitute."

He snatched the tape out of Jack's hand, and put it in his Walkman.

"Do I have your word there isn't another copy?" he demanded.

"Well no," Jack replied. "I may have some more copies in case I need to implicate Martin, but I can't use it against you any more. It's served its purpose and is useless so far as you are concerned. You've got my word on that!"

"I don't believe you. I thought I'd got rid of you before when I gave you the car. See what good that did for me."

"You gave him his car?" Amy said, shocked at what she was hearing and looking suspiciously at Jack. "I thought you won it in a competition."

"That's what he likes to tell everyone," Malcolm said. "He promised me he would destroy the tape if I gave him the car. And I believed him. He's nothing more than a thief. If I wasn't so ill, I'd get someone to kill him."

"Don't make a habit of that, Malcolm – first Mr. Askew and then me!" Jack said, trying not to laugh. "You're turning into a bloodthirsty thug, but you know I really don't have a hold on you any more."

"I don't know why you're laughing. It's not in the least funny. I hate you. Go away. I never want to see you again."

"That sentiment is reciprocated, but before we go, just remember your father has decided not to lay charges against us, and no good will come from you telling anyone who we are. I may not be able to use the tape again, but if I ever learn that you've told anyone who we are, then you'll be hearing from me, and you'll not like what I do to you."

"Are you threatening to beat me up again? Will you enjoy it as much as you did in Chicago? There's nothing you like better than to hurt people."

A look of annoyance crossed Jack's face.

"If you keep quiet, then there's no reason for any of us to contact you again," he said sweetly. "Do you understand that, Malcolm?"

"Yes," he muttered, "but go away."

"He meant it when he said he'd given you the car, didn't he?" Amy asked quietly as they walked back to the hospital car park.

"Of course, sweetheart. You couldn't expect me to miss an opportunity like that."

"But it was a terrible thing to do!"

"Oh grow up, Amy. This is the real world, not some make-believe place where everyone is nice all the time. You've got to take advantage of people where you can. It doesn't hurt to use anyone."

"Is that what you really believe?"

"Of course. Didn't we do that to get your cousin home?"

"That was different."

"Why? I can't see any difference."

"But it was different, nevertheless. We didn't ruin anyone's life for our own personal gain. What we did was to help the refugees."

"What about the co-pilot? He died and his family must be hurt."

"But that was his fault for leaving the plane. We couldn't prevent that."

"You can twist things round to suit your own ends. But forget about scruples. If you want to get on, you have to trample over people and as long as you're still going up, it doesn't matter how many people you hurt in the process."

"Does that include friends and family?"

"Anyone. I always look out for number one! If I don't, who will?"

"I can't imagine anyone wanting to look out for you until you change your attitude." Amy spoke quietly with a great deal of sadness in her voice.

"Hark at little miss innocent! You've been pleased enough to let your friends know we're going out together."

"That was before I got to know you. I don't want to have anything to do with you now."

Jack stormed off, got in his car and drove away at great speed, leaving Amy standing alone in the hospital car park.

She had a lot to think about on the train journey home. She remembered all the warnings she had been given about Jack, and was inclined to believe them! But now she was free of him, and even his betrayal had not the power to stop her from feeling good.

They had done it! They had actually hijacked a plane and flown it into a virtual war zone! Pam and her group of refugees had been brought back to England. Everything had worked out, and it was something they would remember for the rest of their lives!

— EPILOGUE —

The troubles in Bosnia worsened after they had got Pam out of the country, and within weeks David was back there, this time officially with his unit. He managed to visit the hospital in Sarajevo, and made discreet enquiries about Kajic. They said he had helped some refugees to escape, and as no one had heard from him since, it was assumed he had also left the country.

It saddened him to learn Kajic had not returned to his home, and had to assume he was just another statistic; another person who had disappeared without trace.

On his next leave, David took Pam and Amy on a shopping trip to Manchester. They were walking through the town when someone shouted to them, and they turned round to see Pam's brother Matthew. He was walking towards them holding hands with a pretty young redhead.

Matthew said he was particularly pleased to see them, as he wanted them to meet his fiancé. He had asked her to marry him, and they were in town looking at rings at that very moment! They certainly looked well together, and David shook his hand and gave the girl a kiss. He was struck by the softness of her cheek, and the perfume she was wearing brought back an elusive yet familiar memory. He closed his eyes in an effort to bring the uncomfortable feeling back into focus. Where had he met her before?

"Come and meet my Mom and her new husband," Fiona said, in an American accent.

They turned to look at the couple walking towards them, and the smile froze on their faces.

Chrissie and Frank Proctor were walking towards them, hand in hand.

Amy was the first to move. She took hold of her brothers' arm, and tried to steer him away. Frank took a step forward, and, remembering his promise made on the plane, hit out at David with a left hook. David was taken completely off guard, and went crashing to the floor.

They seemed to stay like that for a long time, until Frank stretched out his hand to help him up. David took it and looked him straight in the eyes. There was a lot of anger, and a relief of the emotions that had built up over the time of the hijack.

They were beginning to attract attention as people stopped to see what was going on. They were still clasping hands, as the humour of the situation dawned on them both.

How right Frank had been when he said that one-day they would meet again! And now Chrissies' daughter was going to marry Pam's brother, which meant they would be related!

In hindsight, David was pleased they had first met in Manchester, and not at the wedding!

A few weeks later, Jack Palmer was killed. They never did find out what caused his car to crash and burst into flames.

Lightning Source UK Ltd.
Milton Keynes UK
UKOW05f0341150314

228193UK00008B/111/P

9 781909 824072